THE DESTRUCTION OF EVIDENCE

Katherine John

Published by Accent Press 2010

Copyright © 2010 Katherine John

ISBN 9781906373832

The right of Katherine John to be identified
as the author of this work has been
asserted by her in accordance with the
Copyright, Designs and Patents Act 1988

All rights reserved. No part of this book may be
reproduced, stored in a retrieval system or transmitted in
any form or by any means, electronic, electrostatic,
magnetic tape, mechanical, photocopying, recording or
otherwise without prior written permission from the
publisher: Accent Press, The Old School, Upper High
Street, Bedlinog, Mid Glamorgan, CF46 6RY

Printed and bound in the UK

Cover design by Red Dot Design

Other titles in the
Inspector Trevor Joseph Series

Without Trace
9781905170265
£6.99

Midnight Murders
9781905170272
£6.99

Murder of a Dead Man
9781905170289
£6.99

Black Daffodil
9781906125004
£6.99

A Well-Deserved Murder
9781906125141
£6.99

CHAPTER ONE

12.30 a.m.

The July night was warm, the sky bright, with a full moon surrounded by a bevy of stars. The watcher crept in the shadow of the long wall that bordered the lane at the back of Main Street. The houses were terraced, Georgian, five-storey, and in excellent repair. The Mid-Wales town was a by-word for wealth, courtesy of the nouveau riche who were prepared to pay high prices to enjoy the architecture and scenery. The only locals who could afford to reside there were those who'd inherited money and property, and the underclass who'd been pushed out of the centre into the housing association estates on the outskirts.

The watcher knew there'd be room to park in the yard behind the Pitchers' house but too many windows overlooked the lane and the yard. If challenged, what explanation could be given for parking a car on private property at that time in the morning? Especially when logic insisted there were no grounds for suspicion.

But logic hadn't prevented jealousy consuming like a cancer. Was the betrayal a figment of an over-active imagination as they'd both laughingly – mockingly – insisted when confronted. Or was their denial a lie?

Questions seethed, poisonous and unresolved. Were the signals real? Were the glances exchanged in the bar innocent? Or sly, meaningful looks secret lovers arrogantly assumed no one else could interpret.

Was this expedition a fool's errand? Was there an innocent explanation for absence, or was there a clandestine assignation?

Careful to remain close to the wall, the watcher stepped into the Pitcher yard. Alun Pitcher's van was parked a few feet away. Next to it was Alan's wife, Gillian's, Mercedes and the two BMW sports cars that belonged to their eldest sons. Given the hour, it was reasonable to assume that four of the family were at home. The youngest son's car was absent, but he often stayed at his girlfriend's house. Would this be an exception? Would he return and …

If Michael Pitcher returned it would be in his car. The noise of the engine would act as an alert. There'd be time to hide.

The cellar had an up-and-over garage door, a standard door alongside it and two windows with frosted glass; frosted presumably so no prying, and possibly thieving, eyes could look inside. It was common knowledge that Alun stored the more valuable antiques in his cellar, not in his warehouse. The watcher also knew that Alun's carpenter son James occasionally worked late there, restoring damaged pieces.

The cellar was in darkness. No lights burned. The watcher ducked into a stone shed on the opposite side of the yard to the house. The building was crumbling, semi-derelict. The wooden doors had either fallen off or had been removed because they were in danger of doing so. Their splintered remains leaned against the old stone walls inside. In places the roof was open to the sky. As the watcher's eyes grew accustomed to the darkness, the outlines of wooden crates loomed.

They were stacked in the centre of the building next to an open chest that held gardening tools. The black shapes of a hoe, a rake and a spade stood sharp and distinct in the grey gloom.

The watcher reached for the hoe. The handle was cold, metal and, judging by its smooth surface, free from rust. Why were the tools here? The yard was paved; there wasn't even a planter, let alone a flower bed.

The rank, foul stench of urine and faeces, mixed with something even more unpleasant, emanated from the back corners. A derelict building in the centre of town would be a magnet for rats – and vagrants.

The watcher wondered why Alun Pitcher hadn't renovated the place. It was large enough to accommodate a garage, warehouse or workshop. Space was at a premium in the town centre. So why leave a building like this to rot in his back yard when, even if he didn't want it, he could so easily have rented it out?

Did Alun have plans he hadn't yet implemented? The warehouse he owned and used to hold his auctions on the outskirts of town was massive …

The watcher smiled. It was idiotic. To be standing in this stinking shed after midnight, pontificating on, of all things, Alun Pitcher's business affairs. How *they* would mock again if they could see …

A sound alerted the watcher. A footfall on a metal stair. Someone was climbing the fire escape that ran from the yard to the attic at the side of the Pitcher's house. Landings connected the fire escape to wrought iron balconies that spanned the width of the house on

3

the second and third floors. Both balconies could also be accessed from French doors to the house and both had sets of wrought-iron garden furniture. The staircase ended at attic level on a small platform that held two chairs and a table. Behind them was a door.

The watcher moved forward and saw a figure in front of the attic door. The figure stepped inside. The door closed.

An acrid tide of bile rose into the watcher's mouth. The figure had been little more than a silhouette; a dark shadow in a world of shadows. Dressed in black, a black baker's cap pulled low over the face, the watcher recognised it from the swaggering, confident walk and slim build.

Pain akin to knife wounds pierced; twisting, turning, tearing into a scream for revenge.

Lee Pitcher opened his eyes to see moonlight flooding in from the doorway. Someone had opened the outside door. Several friends had keys to the entrance to his room from the fire escape but only one had received an invitation to call that night.

'I thought you were never coming.'

'It's getting difficult. I can only stay until six.'

'I can't set the alarm. James and my parents are light sleepers.'

'The alarm on my phone is set to vibrate, I'll slip it under the pillow.'

Lee turned back the bedclothes and made room for his visitor. Clothes rustled as they were removed and dropped to the floor. Weight depressed the mattress and an icy leg moved against Lee's warm back.

'You're bloody freezing.'

'It's warm out there, but not on the bike.'

'You could have put a sweater on.'

'I was looking forward to you warming me.'

'Keep the noise down.'

'There was no light in James's bedroom window. The kitchen window's open. I heard the television.'

'My father falls asleep in front of it. Michael's out with Alison. They won't be back tonight.'

Cold lips sought warm ones. Freezing hands ran over the contours of a muscle-honed body.

Within minutes the only sounds in the attic were gasps of breath and murmurs of pleasure. Lee hoped, if any of his family overheard, they would assume he was having pleasant dreams.

The watcher remained, frozen in anger. An owl flew low, swooping behind the house. A fox ventured close to the bins outside the cellar door. The whine of a motor bike struck loud and discordant in the town centre.

Oblivious to the beauty of the night – to everything except escalating, volcanic rage the watcher was suddenly aware that silence had turned to buzzing. Loud, menacing, it filled the watcher's head.

Reacting without thought or plan, the watcher crossed the yard and put a foot on the fire escape. It took a long time to climb five floors. Perspiration streaming, the watcher finally faced the door. It was closed. The watcher depressed the handle expecting it to be locked. It wasn't. It opened inwards. Metal grated against stone when the hoe caught the lintel. The watcher had forgotten the hoe.

The scraping woke the two curled together in the bed. They sat up, alarmed. The duvet fell back and their naked bodies gleamed pale, silvered by the moonlight that poured through the loft lights.

For what could have been a second – a minute – infinity – the three of them stared silently at one another. Afterwards the watcher wondered how long they would have remained there, if Lee hadn't smiled.

The watcher saw it as gloating triumph. Lee opened his mouth as though about to speak. All the constraints that had been imposed on the watcher by family, education and civilization shattered in a red hazed instant.

The tip of the hoe caught Lee's forehead, slicing his face open from crown to chin, cutting through his nose, severing his lips, exposing bone, teeth and gristle.

Lee's lover was wide-eyed, open-mouthed, mesmerized by the blood that spurted from the wound. It sprayed bed, linen, wall and floor, gleaming dark and sticky in the moonlight. Lee's scream died to a soft moan; a gurgling resounded from his throat. The watcher lifted the hoe and struck again. The point caught Lee sideways across his eyes. A sickening crunch of breaking bones accompanied by the squelch of soft tissue filled the room. Lee's eye sockets caved in.

'Stop … Please …' Lee's lover wanted to shout but the words were hoarse, barely audible.

Crazed by grief, savage with passion, the watcher rained blow after blow after blow.

What was left of Lee slithered, slippery with

6

blood, sideways out of the bed. His body went into spasm when he hit the floor but the watcher could still see Lee's triumphant smile, although his head was smashed to a bloody pulp.

'Enough!' Lee's lover closed a hand over the watcher's; holding the hoe fast, before wrenching it free.

Sanity returned when the watcher saw Lee's broken remains. 'You – you made me do it. You made me … I love you … you betrayed me …'

The moon shone down, illuminating Lee's shattered skull and torso. Bloodied smears of bone fragments, hair and skin were spread over the wooden floor. Had that jellied mass been a living breathing human?

The sound of feet running up the stairs. The door handle was depressed from the outside. The lock held for an instant. But only an instant. The door burst inwards.

'Lee? You all right? I heard a cry …'

James switched on the light. Saw the two people in the room. The smashed and broken body on the floor. The blood.

'What …'

It was the last sound he made. Lee's lover leapt from the bed and brought the hoe down on James's head. There was a crack. A thud. James fell to the floor. Unlike Lee there was little blood. Just one groan. Then silence. The lover hit James three times again, before kicking his body aside and closing the door.

The watcher sank on the bed. 'What have we done?'

Naked, disorientated, the lover took command because the watcher couldn't. 'Pull yourself together.'

The whisper echoed around the room to the accompaniment of footsteps downstairs.

'James? Lee? Is everything all right up there?' A man's voice.

'Lee? James?' A woman called anxiously.

Lee's lover gripped the hoe. 'I can't deal with both of them.'

'I can't …'

'You just did. We can't risk screams that could be heard outside.'

'I can't …'

A footfall on the stairs.

Lee's lover handed over the hoe and went to the door. A Victorian bronze of the Dying Gaul stood on a side table. It was heavy. 'I'll wait for Alun to come in here. You run past him and deal with Gillian. Be quick. Don't give her time to cry for help.'

The watcher hesitated.

'You want to go to gaol?'

The watcher didn't move.

'You been inside a gaol?'

'I can't …'

'You have to. We have to.' Lee's lover watched the door handle, waiting for it to move.

Destroy the evidence.

Many criminals had tried to do that and failed. But they weren't criminals. They hadn't meant to kill anyone. They didn't deserve to be punished. But they'd need help. Professional help. Forensic technicians were clever these days.

There was someone. Someone with the knowledge. Someone they could trust. All they had to do was ask. Not phone. A call could be traced … one of them would have to go …

The door opened. Alun stepped in. The bronze crashed down.

Footsteps running down the stairs. Gillian Pitcher cried out once. Just once. Then silence.

Dress. Fetch help. Do what had to be done. Then home. They would be able to carry on as if nothing had happened – wouldn't they?

They'd expected anger from the cleaner. Cold commands were worse.

'There's no time for tears. There's too much to be done. Don't switch on the light. I can see all I want.'

'We'll never clean this. There's our DNA, the blood, the bodies …'

'Fire, bleach and water. We have to bleach and wash first, then burn the house and the bodies. Did you beat them all?'

'They're dead.' The watcher's voice was flat, devoid of expression.

'Is one intact?'

'I don't understand.' A note of hysteria crept into the watcher's voice.

'If one body is unmarked we'll hang it. Then we have murders and suicide. It can happen when one member of a family goes berserk. If they all have wounds the investigating officers will look for a murderer.'

'They all have wounds,' the lover reiterated dully. Shock had set in.

'You're covered in blood,' the cleaner studied the watcher.

'I showered before I fetched you,' the lover protested.

'You wore gloves when you went down the fire escape?'

'No. But I didn't touch anything …'

'We can't take the risk that you didn't. Both of you; shower. Now. There's a box of rubber gloves on the desk next to the jewellery case and tools. Put them on as soon as you're clean; two pairs, one on top of the other. Dress in Lee's clothes, we'll burn yours. Cover yourselves completely. If you're going to leave fibres leave his. Then set to work.'

'Work?' The watcher's voice was robotic.

'The bodies have to be wrapped and burned to destroy all traces of your DNA. Everything you've touched will have to be burned.'

'The forensic teams will know we destroyed the evidence.'

'They will know the *murderer* destroyed the evidence. But if you do exactly as I say they won't discover the identity of the murderer.'

'There are magazines and newspapers …'

'No. We need something thick, slow burning, not news or magazine print that will flare up and die down quickly. Traces of DNA can survive a flash fire. Strip naked, both of you, put your clothes in a pile with all of Lee's clothes except what you'll wear after you've showered. Search the house for bleach, cooking oil, alcohol, pressurized canisters, perfumes … anything flammable. Heap everything flammable in one spot in every room. Furniture, linens, paintings … Wash every inch of the fire escape. There's a hose at the side of the house. Don't forget the gloves. '

'Lee used them when he handled precious metals …'

'No talk. Put them on. Shower, then work.'

'And you?'

'Give me your keys. I'll fetch clothes you can walk away in. We'll burn Lee's when you finish.'

The watcher couldn't stop looking at the three bodies on the floor. 'Do we have to burn them?'

'Broadmoor is not a holiday camp,' the cleaner reminded them.

The warning brought silence.

'When you've finished piling everything flammable and soaking it in anything that will burn – shower again then wait for me here.'

'You can't leave us …'

'Dawn will break in three hours. By then we'll have to be long gone. Move!'

The watcher and the lover went into the shower.

The cleaner heard snoring emanating from the archway of the Angel. The drunk had vomited and soiled himself. There was a glint of metal at his neck.

The cleaner stooped down and tore off the chain that hung outside the T-shirt. Larry Jones was even better than suicide and murder. No one would believe a Garth Estate Jones innocent of a crime. The more heinous the better.

If they succeeded in destroying all the evidence this could be the last piece of an open and shut case.

Larry Jones deserved to rot in gaol. Everyone

knew that he hadn't been nailed for everything he'd done. Would it matter if he served time for something he hadn't?

CHAPTER TWO

12.00 Midnight

The July night was warm, the sky bright, with a full moon surrounded by a bevy of stars – and Ken Lloyd was plotting an escape to enjoy it.

Some men complained because their wives left them. He wished his would. His absence from her, for more than a few minutes, led to a full-blown tantrum that could last for days. She resented every second he spent away from her, whether it was a half-hour visit to his barber, a stroll with his beloved dog, Mars, a swift half in the pub, a solitary fishing expedition or – what she considered his ultimate abandonment – the odd day's work he put in at his friend Alan Pitcher's auction house.

It was worse when she insisted on accompanying him. She talked nonsense to everyone they met, stranger or friend and, if they met no one, she nagged him. Her life was boring because *he* was boring. *He* had no conversation worth listening to; the weather was too wet – too warm – too cold; the river bank too muddy; the walks where he exercised Mars were damp.

Ken had hoped for a quiet life in retirement. Happy in his own company or chatting to his friends and neighbours down the pub, he had chosen his hobbies to suit himself. When his attempts to interest Phyllis in some activity – any activity – that would give him a couple of hours peace came to nothing, he resorted to creeping out of the house when she was asleep.

After the first nail-biting occasion it had proved surprisingly easy. Since retirement he'd taken to opening a bottle of wine with their evening meal. By topping up his glass with water and allowing Phyllis to drink the lion's share, it wasn't difficult to persuade her to go to bed before him while he cleared their supper dishes. That left him free to sneak out with Mars and his fishing gear.

As usual, he waited half an hour before tip-toeing up to check Phyllis was asleep. He closed the bedroom door, ran lightly down the stairs and admired the night sky through the kitchen window while waiting for the kettle to boil.

He made four rounds of cheese and tomato sandwiches, filled his flask with coffee and stole into the utility room. A single thump of the tail was all the greeting he received from Mars. He commanded the dog to silence. He didn't have to whisper twice. The dog was more frightened of Phyllis than he was.

Mars waited patiently while he went down the cellar to fetch his rod and equipment. Phyllis's terror of spiders, damp and dirt kept her away from what he had made his domain. It was his "space" where he stored everything she complained about. The fishing tackle she insisted "stank". The car parts he scrounged as "spares" to keep his aged Astra on the road, because she wouldn't allow Mars to ride in their new Volvo. The waste paper and magazines he brought home from the auction house to turn into "bricks" in a machine he'd bought from a catalogue. She was happy enough to burn them in the drawing room but resented the time he spent making them.

Phyllis was right about one thing. The cellar did

need tidying. Stacks of old papers towered waist high, blocking the walkway from front to back, making it difficult for him to get at his rods. Unwittingly, he'd brought home enough to keep the fire going for the next two winters.

When he'd gathered everything he needed, he returned upstairs, clipped on the dog's lead, walked down the passage, closed the front door softly behind him and stepped outside. He had lived in the centre of town all his life and loved the place with a passion that transcended anything he felt for a living being. For him, walking along the streets bordered by classical Georgian houses was akin to a religious experience.

He checked his watch in the light of a street lamp. Midnight. Tim Pryce, the landlord of the Angel Inn across the road, was ejecting a drunk who was refusing to go quietly.

'Go back to whoever served you enough to get into that state. You'll get nothing from me,' Tim declared in a strong Scottish accent.

'I knowsh my rightsh …'

'Bugger off home.'

'I hashn't got a home. No onesh lovesh mesh …' The drunk swayed and squinted at Tim. 'Yoush tooksh my money, you bastarshd …'

'Not me. I haven't taken a penny piece from you. Now go home before I call the coppers.'

'Thatsh righsh, call the bloddysh coppersh, yoush …' the drunk's slurring protests came to an abrupt end. He slumped to the pavement.

Ken called out, 'Need a hand, Tim?'

Tim crouched down and examined the

troublemaker. 'No thanks, Ken. The idiot hasn't hurt himself, worse luck. It's a fine night. I'll prop him up in the yard so he doesn't throw up and choke to death.'

Built a century before the Georgian planners had moved into the fine old county town, the Angel had started life as a coaching inn. It still possessed a yard accessed by an arch alongside the main building, although the stables that had walled in two sides had long been converted into accommodation.

Ken crossed the road and looked down on at the figure lying in the gutter. 'I might have known. One of the Garth estate Joneses.'

'Larry, the oldest of Annie's boys and the worst of the lot. Only released from prison this morning, according to Pam and Alice.'

'Then we can take it as gospel,' Ken commented. Pamela George and Alice James were Tim's barmaids. Nothing happened in the town they didn't know about, and always before anyone else.

Tim hooked his hands beneath Larry's armpits and heaved. 'He's a dead weight.'

'Drunks are. Let me help.' Ken commanded Mars to "stay", and set down his kit and rod. He picked up Larry's feet. On the count of three, he and Tim hauled the unconscious figure into the shelter of the archway. They dropped Larry none too gently on the cobbles but Tim was careful to prop him upright, leaning him against a downpipe.

'What was Larry in for?' Before retirement Ken had been a meter reader. There wasn't a house in the town he hadn't been into, or a man, woman or child he didn't recognise on sight, or a family he didn't know by reputation.

'Does it matter?' Tim rose to his feet and stretched his back. 'Stealing cars, breaking and entering, assault, GBH, drug dealing, possession, take your pick, he's done the lot but Llewellyn and the other magistrates never send him down for long. Not that it would do much good if they did. From what I've heard gaols are like bloody holiday camps these days. TVs, DVD players, game machines in the cells, hot meals delivered three times a day by warders and nicely decorated common rooms for socialising. I'd give the scumbags bloody socialising if I had my way. Lawbreakers should be sent down to hard labour and solitary confinement on bread and water. To hell with "socialising" with old lags who can't wait to teach young cons old tricks.'

'From the look of this particular Jones he's not up to causing any more trouble tonight.' Ken picked up Mars's lead.

'Out to catch trout?' The whole town knew about Ken's problems with his wife. The nights he struck lucky were difficult to explain to Phyllis. If his catch was large, she refused to believe his cover story that he'd left the house only an hour or two before dawn.

'If they're biting,' Ken qualified.

'You know which way to throw the spare ones.'

'Join the queue.'

'Behind Alun Pitcher?'

Alun's house was next door but one to the Angel. Tim knew Ken worked the odd day for Alun in his auction rooms, he also knew Alun paid Ken handsomely for his time "cash in hand". Ken returned the favour by giving Alun the pick of his catch. But as the fishing rights Ken used were in the joint possession of the Angel and Alun's house, Tim felt he was due more of Ken's catch than Ken sent his way.

Ken refused to rise to Tim's bait. 'Alun does like his trout and sewin.'

The Pitcher's front door slammed shut. Alun's youngest son, Michael and his girlfriend, Alison Griffiths, were climbing into the sports car he'd parked in front of his father's house. A sash window opened on the floor above them. Alun leaned out.

'You've forgotten the keys to the warehouse, Mike. You promised to open up tomorrow, remember?'

'I remember. The van's due in at eight to pick up the Welsh dressers for London.' Michael left his car and caught the keys his father threw down to him.

'Eight, sharp,' Alun emphasised. 'The driver has other pick-ups.'

'I'll be there.'

'Make sure you are. Night Alison, Ken, Tim.' Alun waved then closed the window.

Michael returned to his car and drove off slowly. He drew to a halt outside the pub. 'Don't forget dad if you catch more than you can eat, Ken. He won't forgive you if you do,' Michael joked.

'You two are off out late,' Tim observed.

'We promised Alison's mam and dad we'd sleep at the lodge until they get back,' Michael explained.

'Someone said there'd been a spate of burglaries out that way in the isolated houses.' Tim heard a noise in the yard behind him. He turned to see his staff leaving by the pub's kitchen door.

18

'The lodge won't be isolated when they finish converting Bryn Manor into flats. Problem is Evans the builder is employing all sorts. Cash in hand always attracts troublemakers.' Michael repeated one of his father's favourite maxims without considering that it was exactly what his father did whenever he needed help with his business.

'Your mam and dad rented George Williams's flat in Rome again?' Ken asked Alison.

'George knew what he was doing when he offered it to them for Easter week two years ago. Now you can't keep Mam away from the eternal city,' Alison replied. 'She says she's attracted by the art and the sights but she always takes an empty suitcase "in case" she sees something worth buying. Last time they went, it cost Dad a fortune in excess baggage.'

'Darts night tomorrow, Ken. The team needs you,' Michael reminded him.

'I'll try to be there.'

'Don't try. Be there. Must go or the burglars will get to the lodge before we have a chance to put the lights on and scare them away. Night, Tim, Ken.' Michael hit the accelerator and drove off.

'Nice couple. Heard they've put in an offer for the old Rectory.' Tim was fishing for information and Ken knew it.

'You know this town for rumours,' he replied.

'I do, but everyone's waiting for Michael and Alison to name the day.'

'The boy's only twenty-one.'

'Old enough to have spent the last six years chasing after Alison.'

'Looks like he's caught her to me.' Ken moved

back as Pam edged her car out of the pub yard, past Larry's unconscious figure under the archway and across the dip in the pavement. She wound down the window.

'We've cleared and cleaned everything except the "Women in Business" dinner table. You're going to need a crowbar to remove them from the premises, Tim.'

'I'll set my daughter on them.'

'Judy's the worst of the lot, Tim,' Pam declared. 'We gave them four fresh bottles of wine before we totalled their bill. It's paid. The bar's locked, the takings bagged and in the safe but not counted.'

'Thanks, girls. And, thanks for working on your night off, Pam. I'm grateful,' Tim assured her.

'I had nothing better to do.'

'She'd forgotten it was singles night at the Castle Hotel,' Alice teased.

'I've just dumped one husband in the divorce courts, I'm not out to get myself saddled with another ...'

'See you tomorrow, Pam,' Tim cut her short before she embarked on her favourite subject. The cruelties and sins of her ex.

'I'll be here but don't expect me to be bright-eyed and bushy-tailed.' She gave a theatrical yawn.

'I'll be enjoying a lie-in,' Alice crowed.

'Rub my nose in your day off, why don't you?' Pam turned right into the one-way system. The moment she left, a police car pulled in and blocked the entrance to the yard. Two constables climbed out.

'Dai, Paula,' Tim nodded. 'What's brought you out of your cosy station and away from your cups of tea at this time of night?'

'Guess?' Paula questioned.

'Complaint from May Williams about shouting outside the pub?' Tim looked across the road at the first floor windows of the house next door to Ken's. The blinds twitched marginally wider. He stretched out his hand and wiggled his fingers in a parody of a "hello". The blinds immediately snapped shut.

'Bloody woman has nothing better to do than sit in her window day and all night watching the street. If a dog barks she's on the phone to the station to report animal abuse.' Dai walked under the archway and nudged Larry's leg with his foot. 'Dead to the world,' he pronounced sourly.

'He staggered in as I was closing. Started performing when I wouldn't serve him so I showed him the door.'

'Where'd he been to get in this state?'

'I have no idea,' Tim retorted. 'But there are one or two landlords in this town who are happy to keep serving as long as the customers keep paying, no matter what condition they're in.'

'Don't we know it,' Dai grumbled. 'You knock him out, Tim?'

'The fresh air did for him. You're welcome to take him home.'

'And risk him throwing up in the car, not likely. I'm off duty as of five minutes ago and I've no intention of putting in overtime to clean up a drunk's mess.' Dai turned to Ken. 'Off fishing?'

'Skateboarding.'

'Nothing like Welsh wit,' Dai quipped. 'Got any pies or pasties left, Tim?'

21

'Not sure. Want to come in and take a look?'

'Don't mind if I do,' Dai answered. 'Paula, fancy a pie and a pint?'

'No thanks,' she refused. 'If I don't crawl into bed in the next ten minutes I'll be joining Larry there, under the arch.'

'Want to take the car?'

'If that's your way of asking me to return it to the station because you want to drink more than the limit …'

Dai interrupted. 'As you're so tired I thought I was doing you a favour offering it to you.'

'All right, you've twisted my arm. I'll drive it back to the station.' She opened the car door.

'Pick me up at four tomorrow?' Dai asked.

'On condition you do the paperwork on May's call,' she negotiated.

'You know how to screw a hard-working copper.'

'You taught me. Well, hello there, important businesswomen.' Paula greeted a crowd of women who were leaving the pub by the front door. 'If only the clean-living townsfolk could see you high-society matrons now.'

'No jokes please, Paula, my head's already beginning to hurt,' Anna Harding one of the town's GPs pleaded.

'If any of you are going my way, I can offer you a lift.' Paula climbed into the driving seat of the squad car.

'I'll take you up on that,' Judy Howell went to the front passenger door of the squad car.

'What to the police station? You could walk it in the time it'll take you to climb in,' Police Inspector

Carol March laughed.

'I'm whacked. Bye, most adored father and thank you for doing us proud.'

'Sure you won' stay the night, Judy? I've a spare room.'

'Positive, but thank you for the kind invitation, Father,' she slurred.

Dai closed the door on her and Paula drove off.

'Night, Tim, lovely meal, see you soon,' Carol waved and set off briskly up the street to the taxi office. Anna and two others followed her.

'Great evening …'

'Bye, Tim, Ken, Dai …'

The three men watched the remainder of the women stagger on their four inch heels to the end of the road where they separated into groups at the crossroads.

'And they say men can drink. I just hope none of that lot end up like our friend on the pavement here.' Dai nodded at Larry.

'It's good to see women out enjoying themselves,' Ken said feelingly. He gathered his bag and rod. 'Hope the rest of your night is quieter, Tim, Paula, Dai.'

'Catch enough to keep a couple back for me.' Tim entered the pub and Dai followed.

Ken turned left at the end of the street and walked over the old stone bridge that crossed the river below the town. He unclipped Mars's lead as he stepped on to the path that ran alongside the riverbank. The collie raced ahead. Ken walked on, smiling at the sound of the women's laughter echoing from the town.

His "spot" was a clearing in a copse of trees, a fifteen-minute walk from the bridge. When he reached it he unpacked his gear, lowered his net into the water, and weighed the handle down with stones.

Mars continued to sniff around the long grass. Ken knew the dog wouldn't wander out of sight. He completed his set-up ritual by packing his pipe with tobacco. Phyllis thought he had given up smoking ten years ago. He hadn't disillusioned her.

After lighting his pipe, he cast his line into the centre of the river, sat on his portable stool, drew a deep breath of fresh, night air and looked up at the back of the buildings bordering Main Street, half a mile in front of, and above, him. Shadowy lights shone from behind the blinds and curtains of the upper stories of the Georgian town-houses.

A car engine roared in the distance and he heard the faint but unmistakable sound of a siren. An ambulance? Or the officers who'd relieved Paula and Dai answering a call? Had the burglars who were targeting the houses in the countryside around the town finally been caught?

He reached for a cheese sandwich and bit into it, savouring the lashings of French mustard he'd used instead of butter. He dribbled crumbs down his sweater. Phyllis would have scolded him for making a mess had she been watching. That knowledge made his sandwich taste all the better.

He lived for the spring, summer and autumn nights he spent on the river. He was free to enjoy the silence, to think of nothing and everything and, throughout it all, he was conscious of the line in the water. Any moment there could be a tug – and who knew what he might land. Trout, tench, bream, sewin … salmon.

He finished his sandwich and continued to sit, as still as the bronze statue in the town square, waiting for a bite.

The hours ticked past. The net he'd lowered into the water grew heavy with wriggling catch. Four trout and a salmon. Two trout for Tim, who'd slip him a bottle of brandy in return and two for Alun. He enjoyed helping out at the auction room. Being on hand at house clearances had netted him some good bargains, particularly in fishing tackle and flies.

Hoping to tempt one more unwary salmon, he changed his fly and cast his line out again.

CHAPTER THREE

2.55 a.m.
Ken knew something was wrong when Mars charged up and knocked over his flask. He looked up and caught a flash of light in the attic window of one of the houses above him. Too bright to be an electric bulb, the flare moved, dancing a vivid red, blue and orange. It was a full minute before he realised the blaze was in the top floor of Alun Pitcher's house.

He'd helped shift furniture for Alun and knew the layout of the house. The cellar was for storage, the next floor up, which opened on ground level on Main Street, housed the Pitcher Auction Rooms' suite of offices. The family lived on the third and fourth floors. But Alun's eldest son, Lee, a goldsmith, had converted the old servants' quarters in the attic into a studio apartment for himself with kitchen, bedroom and workshop areas and shower room. Had Lee been working late and grown careless with a soldering iron?

A second light suddenly burst into flame two floors below the attic, in the kitchen James had recently re-fitted. Seconds later, a window exploded. The air was still. Even from half a mile away Ken could hear the roar of flames. A dark shape emerged from the attic and clung to the fire escape at the side of the house before beginning its descent.

'Thank God.' Ken pulled his mobile phone from his pocket and dialled 999.

Twenty-five minutes later, hampered by his rod,

tackle and a plastic bag of wet fish, and by Mars pulling on his lead, Ken lurched into Main Street. The closer he drew to the Pitchers' house, the thicker the smoke. Black, blinding, dry and acrid, it clogged his nose, throat and lungs and stung his eyes. When Mars hung back and stood his ground, he physically dragged him.

Ken blinked hard, rubbed his eyes and made out the outline of a fire tender parked in front of the Pitchers' house. The firemen had attached hoses to the hydrants and were thrusting the nozzles through the smoke billowing from the axed front door.

When his eyes became accustomed to the searing atmosphere, Ken saw three parked police cars. Two blocked off either end of Main Street, the third blocked Church Street, a narrow thoroughfare that opened opposite the Pitchers' house and led around the side of the Anglican church.

Tim Pryce, the local police sergeant, Frank Howell, and Dr Edwards who lived in the manor at the end of Main Street, were standing behind the police car barricading the bridge end of the street. Two constables were shepherding a crowd of residents, including his wife, Phyllis, in her familiar green and red dressing gown, past the police car that blocked the entrance to Church Street. Ken ducked out of his wife's sight.

'The vicar's opened the church hall, his wife's serving tea and biscuits,' Frank Howell informed Ken mechanically before turning to look at him. 'Sorry, Ken. Didn't recognise you there.'

'Not surprising in this smoke.' Tim clamped his hand over his mouth.

'Are the Pitchers all right?' Ken asked urgently.

'None have come out that I've seen, and I've been here since the first tender arrived and went around the back of the house,' Dr Edwards volunteered.

'They didn't come out the back way. Frank and I reached there just after the blaze started,' Tim answered. 'The paramedics are kicking their heels, waiting on the firemen.' Tim pointed to an ambulance parked behind the police car at the opposite end of the street, close to the entrance to the lane that ran at the back of the terrace.

'I saw someone leave the attic by the fire escape.' Ken coughed when smoke hit his lungs.

'There are trained paramedics among the firemen. No doubt they'll be seeing to whoever it was around the back.' Tim looked at Frank. 'You said my call was the second emergency services received. Was the first from the Pitchers?'

'Fisherman down by the river.'

'You?' Tim asked Ken, who was watching the ambulance parked behind the tender in the hope of catching sight of Alun or his family.

'I saw flames in the attic then the kitchen just before the kitchen windows blew.'

'Kitchen window, that settles it. Three boys in the house, it's a chip-pan fire,' Frank affirmed.

'There were flames in the attic before the kitchen,' Ken reminded him.

'The fire in the attic could have spread upwards from the kitchen and you just happened to see it first,' Frank suggested.

Ken wanted to dismiss Frank's idea but living with Phyllis had given him a reluctance to argue,

28

even when he was certain he was right.

'There are two boys in the house, not three. Michael's spending the night with Alison in her parents' place. Ken and I spoke to them as they left,' Tim informed him.

'I'd better let the firemen know. I told them five people were inside. They'll keep sending people in until all the family are accounted for.' Frank walked over to the senior officers who were directing operations from the front of the building. He spoke to them for a few minutes and one of them accompanied him when he returned.

'Frank said one of you saw someone on the fire escape?' The fireman pulled off his helmet and wiped his forehead with the back of his arm but as he was wearing protective clothing all he succeeded in doing was smearing black smuts over his face.

'I did,' Ken confirmed.

'When was this?'

'When I phoned the emergency services. Half an hour or so ago.'

The fireman checked his watch. 'Thirty three minutes ago according to the switchboard. I just contacted the boys at the back of the building. There was no one in the yard when they arrived and no one's come out since they've been there.'

'Are you sure?' Ken was stunned.

'The first thing we check is the location of residents who could be trapped in the building. The boys on this street are still trying to reach the first floor but it's hopeless, fire's spread down from the floor above at the back of the building and the stairs are ablaze. The cellar's blazing too and flames are coming up through the floorboards to the ground floor.'

'The fire escape …' Ken began.

'Is off limits. It's red-hot.'

'Could whoever I saw have fallen from it?'

'If he'd landed in the yard we would have found him, or her. Do you know where the Pitchers sleep?' the officer asked.

'Alun and Gillian's bedroom is on the second floor from this level, third from the back of the house,' Ken answered.

'Front or back windows?' the fireman pressed.

'Alun and his wife sleep at the front. Left-hand window, one of the boys is in the room to the right, another has the two rooms at the back, but I don't know which son sleeps where, other than the eldest. Lee Pitcher has a room in the attic.'

The fireman ran back shouting orders. A few minutes later a hydraulic platform was raised level with the second floor windows.

'Alun's sensible,' Frank murmured. 'Once he realised the house was on fire and the stairs impassable, he would have led Gillian and the boys up to the attic.'

'It was on fire,' Ken reminded him.

'You only saw fire at the back of the building. The front is filled with smoke but it's not blazing. There are skylights in the attic, aren't there? The Pitchers are probably sitting on the roof right now wondering why it's taking the firemen so long to reach them,' Tim's voice was sharp

'The firemen at the back of the house should have seen the person I saw … unless …' Ken faltered. He

30

recalled the force of the explosion that had shattered the kitchen window. The fire escape was at the side of the house but it was within blast distance of the windows and the fireman had said it was "red hot". Had another window blown out when he'd been walking back to town? Had the force thrown whoever he'd seen off the escape and a rush of air somehow sucked him back into the flames? He shuddered at the thought.

Another fireman approached them. 'You have evacuated the pub, Tim? All of your rented rooms and self-catering cottages?'

'Been evacuated along with the whole street,' Frank confirmed for the landlord. 'The only bugger we couldn't move is May Williams. She's sitting above us in her window now, enjoying her grandstand view.'

'She should be moved …'

'She's an invalid and a cantankerous one. You want to move her, you try.' Frank folded his arms across his chest.

'I spoke to one of the senior fire officers. He agreed the wind's blowing away from this side of the street. Frank and his fellow police officers are monitoring the situation. If there's a threat to Mrs Williams's house we'll try again to move her,' Dr Edwards interposed.

'You don't think the fire's going to spread to the pub, do you?' Tim asked, suddenly concerned when a shower of sparks rocketed high into the night sky. 'The accountant's office is in between …'

'All depends on what combustible materials are in the buildings. The wall the accountant's shares with

31

the Pitchers' is hotter than hell. We got the keys from the manager and the boys have been in to check. I'll get someone up on the roof of the accountant's to check the Pitchers' roof in case they made it up there.'

'See, I told you that's what Alun would do.' Tim seized on the conjecture.

'Alun wouldn't go up there if the fire escape was all right …'

'But it's not, is it?' Tim interrupted Ken.

'Now. It was when I first saw the fire.' Sure of his facts Ken was more insistent than he had been earlier.

'No one could stand on the escape at the moment without full protective gear, that's for sure.' The fireman returned to his colleagues.

Ken watched the firemen on the platform adjust their breathing apparatus before axing their way through the window into Alun and Gillian's bedroom.

Frank moved between Tim and Ken. 'There's nothing you two can do here, so how about setting up a rest centre in your pub kitchen for the fire officers, Tim? It's time some of them took a break and your kitchen is at the furthest point from the accountant's before crossing the yard, so it should be safe enough.'

'If you want me to.' Tim was clearly reluctant to leave the scene. 'You'll let me know …'

'The minute I have any news on the Pitchers,' Frank promised.

'Do you want to come with me, Ken, or do you want to look in on Phyllis in the church hall?' Tim asked drily.

'I'll come with you.' Ken tugged on Mars's lead.

'Remember to serve coffee not beer, Tim.' Frank

shouted after them. 'The men are on duty.'

'Once a copper always a copper.'

'You should know,' Frank called back.

Tim eyed the dripping, bulging plastic bag Ken was carrying. 'You struck lucky?'

'A few trout. Your lodger's left.'

'Lodger?' Tim looked at him quizzically.

'Larry Jones,' Ken indicated the archway where they'd dumped him. The only sign that anyone had been there was a pool of vomit and another of liquid.

'No doubt those are his calling cards, filthy beggar.'

A fireman shouted. A blood curdling cry that cut through the hot, smoke laden air. Ken froze before running back in time to see one officer drag another out of Alun's bedroom window and on to the hydraulic platform. Tearing their masks from their faces, both officers leaned forward and retched.

Superintendent Regina "Reggie" Moore stepped out of her car, locked it, dropped her keys into the pocket of her lightweight coat and walked briskly towards Frank Howell. He waited for her in front of the safety barriers that had been erected around the burning house.

'Update me, Sergeant Howell?'

Frank knew better than to give Superintendent Moore anything other than a factual reply. But he cautiously incorporated an element of doubt. 'Too early to pinpoint cause, but arson can't be ruled out, Super.'

'It can't?' She raised one finely plucked eyebrow.

A senior officer joined them. 'Superintendent

Moore.'

'Chief Fire Officer Thomas.'

Frank knew that his Super and Huw Thomas were friends who moved in the same circles but no one would have guessed from the formal approach they adopted on the rare occasions their professional lives crossed.

'We've found one body, Superintendent, and, in accordance with the directives for deaths in suspicious circumstances left it in situ. I've called the pathologist but fires are still burning in the cellar, attic and kitchen areas of the building. Even when they're brought under control – and that could take some time – the shell will be too unstable to admit anyone intent on carrying out an investigative search without securing and shoring.' Huw Thomas led Regina out of earshot of Frank Howell and the rest of the officers.

She looked enquiringly at him.

'Two officers saw a corpse on the floor in the doorway of one of the bedrooms. Burned, but not so badly burned they couldn't see the skull had been shattered.'

'Are you telling me it was murder?'

'The room was full of smoke. But the only fires in the room were in a heap of furniture that had been piled at the side of the bed and on the corpse.'

'The body had been set alight?'

'All I have are the descriptions given by the officers who went in. You'll need to send for forensic teams.'

'I'll get Frank on to it right away.'

'You can use our investigative officers as well.

But no one will be able to go in until the fire is out and the building has cooled enough for us to secure it. A rough estimate is twenty-four to thirty-six hours.'

'Can't you do better than that?'

'I thought you'd know better than to ask that question.'

'Any survivors?'

'None we've seen. Officers have checked every room they can access. But that's not many at present.'

'How many were inside the building when it went up?'

'As you know, Alun and Gillian Pitcher and their three sons live there. But so far we've only found one corpse. Tim Pryce and Ken Lloyd saw the youngest son, Michael leave the house with his fiancée, Alison, around midnight. They said they intended to spend the night at Bryn Lodge. So we're presuming four adults.'

'Where was the seat of the fire?'

'Ken Lloyd …'

'The retired meter reader?' Reggie interrupted.

'That's him. He telephoned the emergency services on his mobile from the river bank. And, before you ask, he has a fishing licence.'

'I don't have to ask. I've met his wife. If I was married to her I'd spend my nights out of the house.' Reggie showed a rare flash of humour.

'He saw flames in the attic and moments later a fire in the kitchen that was fierce enough to blow out a window.'

'Two seats to the fire,' she mused. 'Then it's arson.'

'Not officially. Not yet,' the chief warned.

Frank Howell had called in every police officer, irrespective of whether they were on duty to help with the fire, but he hadn't managed to raise all of them. Dai Smith who'd been on duty until midnight and Grant Williams who'd taken a week's leave weren't answering their mobiles or house phones. Erecting barriers, waking and shepherding the Pitchers' neighbours to safety, closing Main Street and setting up traffic diversions had kept the remainder busy so he'd done what any enterprising Welsh officer would do in his place. Enlisted the help of a respectable local.

He telephoned a consultant surgeon who lived in a Victorian rectory a mile from Bryn Lodge, told him about the fire and asked him to drive Michael into town without giving him any reason beyond a fire in his parents' house.

Unsurprisingly, Alison accompanied them. When they arrived, Frank took them to the ambulance. As the paramedics were waiting there in case they were needed, it was hardly private but from the way Michael blanched on seeing his home; Frank decided the boy might need their professional services.

Huw Thomas and the Super climbed into the back of the ambulance with Michael, Alison and Henry Clarke, the ENT consultant who had driven them in.

Michael took one look at their grave expressions and feared the worst. 'Mam, Dad, my brothers ...'

Reggie glanced from Huw to Henry Clarke. Neither of them appeared to be prepared to speak, so she took control of the conversation.

'... Are they all right?' Michael began to tremble.

'We need to know how many people were in the house, Michael.' She spoke gently.

He stared at her.

'Were both your parents and your two brothers at home when you left the house?' she pressed.

Alison answered. 'Mr and Mrs Pitcher were watching television in the drawing room …'

'Which is where in the house?' Huw interrupted.

'On the first floor at the front of the house.'

'What were they watching?'

'What bloody difference does that make?' Michael snapped.

'It might make a difference if we know the length of the programme, Michael,' Huw answered quietly.

'The news. They always watch the midnight news before going to bed.'

'And your brothers?' Regina asked.

'Lee went up to his room after dinner.'

'Which was when?' Reggie took a notebook from her pocket.

'Around nine, maybe half past. I'm not sure of the exact time.'

'And Lee's room is in the attic?' Huw sat forward on the edge of the bench seat.

'He has a workshop up there as well as his bedroom. He's a goldsmith. He's working on an order for an antique shop in Hatton Garden. Restoring an Edwardian emerald and diamond collar, bracelet and earrings.'

'Was it unusual for him to go up to his room early?' Regina questioned.

'Not when he's working on something he's interested in. He loses all sense of time. I've known

37

him to work around the clock.'

'Was your other brother in the house?'

'James was in the kitchen pouring drinks. He and Dad often have a beer before bed. Mam has a G & T.' Michael's eyes were dark, anguished. 'The fire – when did it break out?'

'A witness saw flames in the attic and kitchen at around three o'clock,' Huw answered.

Michael glanced instinctively at his wrist but he'd dressed in a hurry and forgotten his watch.

'It's half past four,' Huw told him.

'And you only told me now,' he protested bitterly.

'No one knew where you were until our officers spoke to Tim Pryce. We assumed you were in the house …' Huw faltered when he realised what he was saying.

'You haven't found any of them have you?' There was a heartfelt plea in Michael's question. Huw Thomas thought of his men and what they'd seen in the bedroom.

He hated himself for taking away the boy's last scrap of hope. 'I'm sorry; we haven't found anyone alive, Michael.' He wanted to add "not yet" but he couldn't bring himself to utter the platitude.

CHAPTER FOUR

Larry Jones was vaguely aware of noise and confusion. People were shouting. The ground beneath him shaking. Were his cellmates Bimmo and Piggy fighting again … couldn't they let him sleep … what was that droning … the engine of a plane?

Was he on a plane? Going to Malaga or Majorca? He'd been to both. Booze; girls up for unlimited bonking; and a nightlife to make your eyes water. He couldn't wait. He opened his eyes, tried to move his head and cried out when shooting pains sliced through his skull.

There was no plane, only lights burning somewhere ahead in a stinking smoke-filled gloom and a disgusting metallic taste in his mouth. Then he remembered. He'd come home … only no one had been in the house. He'd gone for a drink … met a mate … more mates … more drinks … a meal … gone into town … where was he?

It was so dark he couldn't make out anything. And the place stank. Worse than the raw sewage that had spilled on to the beach when he'd been swimming in Spain.

His head hurt as if he'd been hit by a hammer. Had he? Had he been hammered? He had no memory of a fight. He cast his mind back before his last stay in prison and remembered … this was a hangover. He tried to sit up and realised he was lying in something soft. Soft and reeking. He made a supreme effort to get on his knees, fell back, crouched and gagged.

He retched so violently he lost control of his

bladder and bowels. He failed to stop the spasms, even when there was nothing left inside to come up.

A torch shone down from ahead of and above the murk that enveloped him. A voice snapped.

'Your name?'

He wanted to shout "Piss off" but between heaving and vomiting failed to get out a word.

The light drew closer. 'Your name? What you doing here?'

He remained crouching only just managing to shake his head.

The light wavered. The man who'd spoken shouted, 'Call a police officer, the Chief and get Tim Pryce. He knows everyone in town. If he's local Tim will know him.'

Larry wanted to yell, "That's right, call the bloody police. Larry Jones has had a few jars so lock him up again, why don't you." But he couldn't stop his stomach from cramping to rid itself of beer that was no longer there.

Huw Thomas made an excuse. He needed to leave the ambulance because he could no longer face the anguish on Michael Pitcher's face. Reggie went with him. They both started coughing when smoke hit their lungs. A fireman ran clumsily up the lane towards them, weighed down by full kit.

'Sir, ma'am.' He stood, fighting for breath in front of them. 'An officer found a man in a building at the back of the Pitcher's yard. We sent for Tim Pryce. He recognised him as Larry Jones. One of the Garth Estate Joneses. Tim threw him out of the Angel around midnight. He said Larry was so drunk then he couldn't even stand. But he's coming round now.'

'Was this Larry Jones in the building in the yard when you arrived?' Huw demanded.

'No one noticed him, sir.' The fireman admitted.

'Are you telling me that none of you thought to check the buildings in the Pitcher's yard before now?' Huw demanded.

'We were busy fighting the fire, sir.'

'You trying to be funny, officer?'

'No, sir.' The young man was smoke and smut stained and, from the defeated look in his eyes, exhausted. Huw recognised him as a new recruit and dropped his hectoring tone.

'Sergeant Howell?' Reggie called.

Frank Howell left the officers who were manning the barricade at the bridge end of Main Street and ran to Reggie.

'A Larry Jones has been found in an outbuilding at the back of the Pitcher house. Do you know him?'

'Yes, Super. He's a bad lot. Do you think …'

'I don't think, Sergeant,' she cut in brusquely. 'I work with facts, not thoughts. I want two officers in sterile clothes and a forensic team sent to the Pitcher yard A.S.A.P. And, I want everything done by the book. That means bagging this Larry Jones's hands and feet and covering his clothes to prevent cross contamination before we move him out. After he's been taken to the station I want every inch of the outbuilding examined and everything found there tagged and bagged. As soon as Larry Jones is in the station, I want his clothes removed and sent to the lab. And, I want a full body search conducted and filmed. By the book, Sergeant Howell,' she reiterated.

'I want no margin left for complaints or errors of judgement on this one. Nothing that can get a potential criminal case thrown out of court. Understood?'

'Yes, Super.'

Reggie led the way down the lane that skirted the end of the terrace and cut behind the houses. As they approached the Pitcher yard, the smoke grew denser, making it difficult to see and breathe. Through the smoke Reggie made out the tall, thin figure of Tim Pryce, standing next to balding, stocky Dr Edwards. Half a dozen suited firemen and three uniformed constables were also in the yard.

One of the firemen was standing at the open entrance to a dilapidated stone building. When Reggie and Huw joined him he shone a torch inside on a man who was squatting on the dirt floor.

'Don't step any further,' Reggie warned everyone. 'I've sent for a forensic team.' She looked down at the man. She could smell his lavatory stench from eight feet away. 'Are you Larry Jones?'

'That's for me to know and you to find out,' he cackled between heaving in great gulps of air.

'That's Superintendent Moore you're talking to, Larry Jones. So mind your manners.' Frank moved alongside the superintendent but was careful not to step past her. 'Forensic team are on their way, ma'am.'

'Thank you, Sergeant.' She continued to study the man on the floor. 'What do you know about this man, Sergeant Howell?'

'He was sentenced to six years for aggravated burglary, rape and GBH last May. He was remanded in custody before his case came up, but I wasn't expecting him to be out this soon.'

'Anything before that?'

'His record's thicker than yellow pages.'

'Check it thoroughly when you get back to the station.' Reggie didn't have to tell Frank for what. The torchlight illuminated smuts on Larry's hands, face and clothes. His shoes were scorched. He stank of smoke. His appearance suggested that he'd been closer to the fire than he now was.

Frank looked at Larry. 'On your feet, boy.'

'You can't bloody well tell me what to do. You …'

Knowing there was no way he could touch him before forensic arrived, Frank resorted to his most authoritative prison warder voice. 'Get up you lazy sod. Now!'

The trick worked. Larry Jones scrambled to his feet.

Three white suited and capped officers carrying forensic kits approached. They pulled on overshoes before stepping into the building.

'Bag his hands and feet. Once you've done that, remove the contents of his pockets,' Regina ordered.

'And watch where you're treading, he stinks,' Frank added superfluously.

Two officers moved gingerly forward and bagged Larry's hands and feet in clear plastic before turning their attention to the contents of Larry's pockets. They removed items one at a time with their gloved hands, sealing each in turn in a clear plastic bag before handing them to the third officer who stacked the bags in a plastic box.

Reggie addressed the officer who was stacking the bags. 'Step back here and hand me a pair of gloves please.'

He moved, handed her a pair and she snapped them on.

'Sergeant Howell, fetch a torch and shine it on this box for me, will you?'

Frank Howell did as she asked. She flicked through the bags, selected one and removed it from the box.

Huw peered at it.

'What does it look like to you?' Reggie asked.

Even the covering of plastic could not dim the glittering stones.

Huw recalled Michael's description of the pieces his brother Lee had been working on. 'Emerald and diamonds set in gold?'

Regina turned to Larry and held up the bag so the light of the torch shone on it. He began to shake.

'Where did you get this?'

'I don't know. I swear I've never seen it before ...'

'Itemise the rest of the contents of Mr Jones's pockets,' she ordered the officer holding the tray.

He flicked through the bags. 'Matches, cigarettes, lighter, cash ... a lot of cash. Notes folded in a gold clip ...'

'I loaned people money before I went inside. I got paid back today,' Larry protested defensively.

'In emeralds, gold and diamonds and well as cash?' Regina suggested derisively.

'I swear I don't know nuffin ...'

'Save your breath, Mr Jones. Sergeant, you know

what to do. I'll see you back at the station.'

'Congratulations, Reggie, you've got your man,' Huw complimented her.

'Have I, Huw?'

'He's a known thug with a record. He had the jewellery Michael Pitcher described in his possession. He had matches, a lighter, cash …'

'Don't you think it's just a little too pat?' she asked.

'You think he was framed?' Huw asked.

'I don't know, Huw. All I know are my limitations. If you'll excuse me I have to return to the station, wake up some people and set a murder investigation in motion.'

Reggie sat in her office and looked across her desk at Inspector Carol March. 'As soon as forensics has finished with him, I want you to conduct the interview.'

'You're the senior officer, ma'am.'

'Whether you're a natural or if it's down to your degree in psychology, you're the best interviewer we have. I've asked Sergeant Howell to set up the video camera. He'll sit in with you. I don't have to warn you …'

'No threats, no pressure, nothing physical and by the book,' Carol recited.

'That's why I want you to question Larry Jones and not one of the male officers.'

'Thank you for your faith in me, ma'am.'

Reggie sat back in her chair and watched Carol leave the room. She knew the other officers at the station called Carol March "Snow Queen" after the cold, dispassionate icicle-firing character in the Hans Anderson story.

But this was one instance when emotion could hamper an investigation. Too many officers and people in the town had known and liked the Pitchers. And with one of the family dead, probably murdered and, three more missing in the fire, the last thing she, as a newly appointed Superintendent, could afford to do was attract media criticism of her handling of the case.

The only officer she trusted to operate by the book was Carol March. She crossed her fingers in the hope that her Inspector would live up to her nickname and fire her icicles in the direction to bring in a clean, swift result.

'I can't remember nuffin. And that's the God's honest truth. No matter what you do to me you can't make me tell you things I don't know. And I don't know nuffin …' Larry Jones was gabbling. His mud-brown eyes rounded in fear. Nervous, he bungled a theatrical sign of the cross.

'I haven't asked you a question yet, Larry.' Carol took the vacant chair next to Frank's and faced Larry and a fresh-faced boy she recognised as a trainee solicitor from the local practice. Judy Howell usually acted as duty solicitor but given the amount of wine she'd drunk at the "Women in Business" dinner Carol guessed she'd been happy to delegate the privilege to a younger colleague.

Carol March pressed the record button, recited the date, place and names of everyone present, gave

Laurence Jones a formal caution notifying him of his rights, looked up at the clock and noted the time as 7.55 a.m.

'Before you start, I can't remember nuffin.' Larry stuck his thumb in his mouth.

'Does that mean you can't remember anything about your life before you were found in the building at the back of the Pitchers' house at four forty this morning, Mr Jones? Or you can't remember anything about yesterday and the early hours of this morning?' Carol remained impassive.

'Can't 'member yesterday,' he mumbled.

'Do you recall how you got that scratch on the side of your neck?'

'No. Did you lot do it?'

'Are you accusing an officer of injuring you?'

The solicitor whispered in Larry's ear.

Larry mumbled. 'No.'

'Let's start at the beginning, shall we?' Carol's voice hardened as she clipped her words. 'What is the first thing you remember doing yesterday morning?'

'Waking up in my cell with Piggy …'

'Piggy?'

'Piggy and Bimmo Jones, my cellmates. The screws think it's funny to shove all the Joneses together so when they call "Jones" everyone answers. So we give ourselves nicknames.'

'Yours?'

'Rambo.'

If Carol was sceptical, she hid it. 'What did you do after you woke up?'

'Had breakfast then they let me out of the lock-up.'

'You mean prison?'

'That's what I said, lock-up, innit. I picked up a travel warrant and my personal effects from the screws in the office, walked to the bus stop and took the bus to Bridgend. I changed buses there and took one for here.'

'So you, woke in prison?'

'That's what I said, innit.'

'Which prison?'

'Parc – not that it's like a bloody Parc …'

'You travelled here. What did you do when you arrived in the town?'

'Went home, didn't I?' he snapped. 'It's where I told the screws I'd be. The address I had to give the bastards …'

'Language,' Carol reprimanded.

'They knew I was coming. They should have been there, but they wasn't.'

'Who are "they"?'

'Family,' he mumbled.

'You were expecting them to meet you?'

'Not meet me in town, stupid …'

'You can stop playing the hard man, Larry. I'm not impressed,' Carol cut in flatly.

'Can't blame me …'

'Oh, but I do. Everyone has to take responsibility for what comes out of their mouths. Why didn't you expect anyone from your family to meet you in town?'

'Because they wouldn't have known what time my bus got in.' Larry tried to look subdued but Carol read sly defiance in his eyes. 'I thought they'd be home – waiting. I phoned Mam last week to let her know the day I was coming out. Paid for the telephone card with my last couple of bob. She said she'd be there. But there was no answer at the house and it was locked. Sharon Thomas …'

'Who's Sharon Thomas?' Carol interrupted.

'The bitch next door to Mam. She told me Mam had gone to Carmarthen for the day. Hadn't even left me a bloody key so I could let myself in. I wasn't going to hang about where I wasn't welcome so I went to the pub.'

'What time was that?'

'Dunno.'

'You must have some idea.'

Larry shrugged.

'What time did your bus get in from Bridgend?'

'Midday.'

'How long did it take you to walk home?'

'Didn't walk. Got my discharge grant, so I was flush. Got a taxi.'

'How long did it take to drive?'

Reggie was watching and listening in through the viewing window. For once Frank was silent, although he was clenching and unclenching his fists under cover of the table. If Carol's patience was wearing thin it wasn't showing.

'Twenty minutes or so.'

'And you stayed outside your house, how long?' Carol knew she had the advantage and she wasn't about to relinquish it.

'Five … ten minutes. What does it matter? I wasn't clocking myself in and out. I had enough of that in the nick.' Larry's voice rose precariously.

'How did you get from your mother's house to the

pub?'

'Walked.'

'How long did it take you to reach town?'

'Didn't go to town. Went to the Bush and had a couple of jars. They have a snooker table and a darts board …'

Carol didn't allow Larry Jones to digress. 'What time did you leave there?'

'Dunno. I met a mate. We went to the caff.'

'Name of this mate of yours?' Carol took a notebook and pencil from her pocket.

'He's a good mate. I don't want to get him into trouble.'

'Name?' Carol wasn't to be dissuaded.

'Mushy Lewis,' Larry mumbled.

'What cafe did you and this Mushy Lewis visit?' Carol asked.

Larry sat back in his chair. 'Just a caff.'

'It has to have a name.'

'I don't know it. It's on the Carmarthen road out of town. Does all-day breakfasts.'

'Pete's Fry Up?' Carol ventured.

'All I've ever heard it called is the caff.'

'How did you get there?'

'Mushy's bike. I rode on the back.'

'What time did you and Mushy get to the cafe?'

'Dunno.'

'This is getting monotonous, Larry. What time did you leave the Bush?' Carol demanded.

'When we were hungry.'

'Four – five – six o'clock?' Carol ventured.

'Maybe sixish.'

'What did you eat in the cafe?'

'I dunno. Our usual.'

'What's your usual?'

'Can't 'member.'

'You haven't a good memory, have you?' Carol snapped.

'Told you before we started I can't 'member nuffin.'

Carol leaned across the table. 'I suggest you start trying, Larry. Where did you and this Mushy Lewis go after you left the cafe?'

'Dunno. To a pub I suppose.'

'Which pub?'

'Dunno. Maybe lots of pubs.'

'Did you and Mushy Lewis stay together?'

'Couldn't have. He wasn't with me when you found me, was he?' he challenged.

'Where does Mushy Lewis live?'

Larry turned to the solicitor. 'I don't have to answer that, do I?'

'No you don't. But you heard the officer's caution same as me, Larry.' He sounded half asleep. 'You don't have to answer any questions, but if you refuse it could go against you in a court of law.'

'You can't put me in no court … I done nuffin …'

'Do you remember being in the Angel?' Carol broke in.

'Tim Pryce's Angel?'

'If there's another pub called the Angel in town, I don't know it, do you?' Carol gazed coolly at Larry.

'No. Was I there?' Larry Jones's nervousness escalated into fear.

'You don't remember being there?'

'No.'

51

'You arrived drunk and demanded to be served.'

'Who says so?' Larry demanded truculently.

'Several eye-witnesses.'

'Eye-witnesses! You mean bloody lying Tim Pryce and his lying barmaids. Stuck-up bitches, they don't like me. . . '

'They're not the only ones who saw you there, Larry. Do you remember asking Tim to serve you?'

'No, but he wouldn't have. He banned me.'

'So why go there when you know he isn't going to serve you?' Carol questioned.

'Told you, I can't remember nuffin about yesterday.'

'For someone who said he couldn't remember anything, I think you've done very well, Larry.'

'I don't remember being in the Angel. And that's gospel.'

'You don't remember Tim Pryce asking you to leave?'

'Nope.'

'You don't remember him escorting you to the door?'

'Nope. But he wouldn't "escort me". He'd kick me out into the street. That's how the bastard behaves.'

'We have witnesses who say that you were drunk.'

'There you are then,' Larry snapped triumphantly. 'If I was drunk, I wouldn't 'member, would I?'

'You walked out of the pub on your own two feet.'

'I can't 'member doing that.'

'What can you remember between the time you left the Angel and waking up in the building in the

Pitcher's yard.'

'I keep telling you, I can't remember going into the bloody Angel.'

'Do you remember waking up in the building at the back of the Pitcher house?'

Larry nodded.

'You remember being searched.'

'Robbed more like. I want my things and my money back. I know what you lot are like for thieving ...'

'Larry, making accusations against the police won't help you,' the solicitor warned.

Carol sat back in her chair and stared at Larry for what seemed like a very long time, although the clock in the interview room only ticked off two minutes. Finally, she reached down besides her chair and lifted a cardboard box on to the table. She opened the lid and removed a clear plastic bag. The gold, emeralds and diamonds glimmered through the plastic sheath.

Carol's voice rang loud and clear. 'What do you know about these?'

'Nuffin.' Larry's voice dropped to a whisper.

'You've seen them before?'

'Only when the bloody copper ...'

Carol rapped her pencil on the table. 'You mean the officer ...'

Larry's voice dropped to a barely audible whisper. 'When the officer showed them to me.'

'Where did he find them?'

'Dunno.'

'Did he, or did he not remove them from your pocket?'

'He said he did. But that's what the coppers do

round here, innit, they drop stuff in your pockets so they can stitch you up.'

'Are you accusing a police officer of planting evidence on your person, Mr Jones?' There was frost in Carol's voice.

'He said them jewels was in my pocket. I didn't put them there.'

'Yours were the only fingerprints on the bag.'

'I never touched it …'

'Would you like to make a formal complaint against the officer who arrested you Mr Jones?'

Larry shook his head. 'I feel sick. I …' He retched and turned, emptying the contents of his stomach on to the floor.

Carol had the last word. 'Interview with Mr Laurence Jones terminated at 8.46 a.m.'

CHAPTER FIVE

'No! No! Absolutely not! I will *not* go back to Wales,' Peter Collins declared vehemently.

'The sheep have missed you.'

'If that's your idea of a joke, Dan …'

'Inspector Evans, to you, Sergeant Collins, this is a formal meeting,' Superintendent Bill Mulcahy admonished Peter.

'Damn you, Joseph, you brought this on us,' Peter Collins turned on his long-time friend and colleague, Inspector Trevor Joseph. 'You know I hate the bloody place. There's nothing there …'

'The countryside's pretty. I miss it,' Dan interrupted. He spoke slowly, as always, in the Welsh lilt he hadn't lost in fifteen years of exile in England. It was never easy to gauge Dan's mood. But Trevor saw his colleague's mouth twitch. Dan was amused by Peter's anger and determined to milk it for all it was worth.

'You brought this on yourself as much as Trevor,' Bill insisted. 'If you two hadn't done such a good job of solving the Llan case, this …' Bill consulted the e-mail printout in his hand. 'Superintendent Reggie Moore wouldn't have heard of you. He appealed to upstairs for your help as soon as the forensic team made their preliminary report. Said he didn't have any officers experienced enough to tackle a high-profile case of this complexity and his entire force admired you for the professionalism you exhibited while working in difficult circumstances the last time you were in Wales.'

'Of course the circumstances were difficult; we were in the middle of nowhere surrounded by bloody Neanderthals who wanted to lynch us.'

Bill allowed Peter's swearing to go unchallenged. 'Naturally, upstairs were only too delighted to acknowledge your superior talents and comply with Superintendent Moore's request.'

'I am not flattered and more than happy to go on record as giving Trevor all the credit for Llan. He is the senior officer. Inspector to my mere sergeant.'

'Humility doesn't become you, Collins,' Bill snapped.

'I take it we have no choice in the matter?' Trevor enquired.

'None,' Bill answered shortly. 'The locals are out of their depth and upstairs are forecasting flak from the media until the case is wrapped. Multiple murders of an entire family are rare and this is a particularly nasty one. Everyone wants a quick, clean, open and transparent investigation and an iron-clad, unshakeable conviction.'

'I've said it before, Joseph, and I'll say it again. Shovelling other people's shit is all you get for being good at your job.' Peter only resorted to using Trevor's surname when he was angry.

'What do we know about the case, sir?' Trevor bowed to the inevitable.

'Not much more than the reports on television and in the press. A witness spotted a fire in the family home around three o'clock in the morning four days ago. Firemen arrived at the scene and eventually managed to bring the fire under control. The first forensic teams went into the building around midday on the second day. It took that long for the building to cool and be made safe. The teams found the corpses of four adults. They were still in situ this morning, pending further tests, but the pathologist is hoping to move them later today or early tomorrow. Initial reports suggest they were killed before the fire took hold. It's probable the fire or fires were set to destroy evidence. One person was taken into custody at the scene and is helping the local police with their enquiries. The names of the victims are being withheld until relatives have been informed.' Bill left his chair.

'The media statement is "arson and murder". Did the Superintendent say how they died?' Trevor enquired.

'All he says in his e-mail is he'll brief you in full when you get there.'

'Why not e-mail us everything he has now?' Peter growled.

'Security.'

'Security!' Peter exclaimed. 'It's a bloody multiple murder. Given the gossip machine in small towns – particularly Welsh ones – that means that right this minute every resident within ten miles of the victims' house knows more than the locals.'

'Possibly, possibly not.' Bill commented airily. 'The superintendent will meet you at the police station at two o'clock. Addresses of station and crime scene are on the e-mail.' Bill handed Trevor his copy.

'I've never heard of locals crying for help before an investigation gets underway,' Peter continued to grumble. 'The bodies can't be cold yet ... no pun intended. In my book that makes it a local affair.'

'Didn't you hear me say that Superintendent Moore has admitted the locals are out of their depth?' Bill questioned tersely.

'Out of their depth,' Peter mocked. 'I bet you fifty pounds to a penny it's a political case. The locals know more than they're letting on and don't want to upset any big cheeses in the town with criminal tendencies so they've called in the fall guys to take the heat. And we've drawn the short straw.'

'And on what inside information have you based this opinion?' Bill demanded.

'Instinct and a nose for trouble,' Peter replied.

'Ah, the scientific approach,' Dan teased.

'You're ordering us to walk into a lion's den and I don't like it.' Peter refused to see any humour in the situation.

'Keep your warped opinions and sense of humour to yourself, don't provoke any lions or upset any locals, and do your job, Sergeant Collins. That's an order.' Bill opened the door of Trevor's office.

'Any idea how long this secondment is likely to take, sir?' Trevor asked.

'Too long to suit Peter.' Bill almost smiled. 'Best pack a fortnight's clothes. If you have to stay longer you may strike lucky and find a laundrette or laundry in the town. It'll take you about five hours to drive there. Dump the open case files you're working on, into someone else's in-tray.'

'And if we need help when we're there?' Trevor persisted.

Bill eyed Trevor, 'Use the locals. If you run into trouble with them contact me and I'll see what I can do.' He closed the door behind him.

'Ah-ha, see, Bill knows the locals are trouble and we won't be able to use them.' Peter kicked his chair in annoyance when he rose to his feet. He went to the window, sat on the sill and continued to glower at Trevor and Dan.

'Good luck with coping with Peter, Trevor. If you need help with him, don't call me.'

'Very funny,' Peter made a face at Dan's back as he left.

Trevor returned to his desk and sifted through the files he was working on, stacking the ones he could pass on to one side.

'Damn it!' Peter exploded. 'This couldn't have come at a worse time, Daisy's pregnant …'

'Four months; and if you're worrying about her getting enough rest she'll have more peace and quiet without you around to bother her.'

'Rubbish! I do all the housework.' Peter countered.

'Not according to Daisy.'

'Working the hours she does, she doesn't know the half of what I do. Just takes it for granted.'

Trevor glanced at his watch. 'Seven. Can you clear your in tray by half past?'

'As if it's not bad enough having to come in at six in the morning …'

'Can you, or can't you?' Trevor cut in.

'If I must,' Peter muttered mutinously.

'It'll take us about half an hour to get home and pack. We'll leave as close to eight as we can make it, to give ourselves extra traffic time in case we need it. I'll drive.'

'The hell you will. I'm about to become a father.

59

We'll take my car and that's not up for discussion.'

Trevor didn't waste his breath protesting. He and Peter had joined the force together. Their friendship went back more years than he cared to remember. He had long since learned that the only way to deal with his friend when he was in one of his moods was to leave him alone until he snapped out of it.

Trevor carried the last half a dozen files he hadn't managed to pass on into Bill's office.

Bill looked up as he tapped on the open door. 'You leaving now?'

'Home to pack, then we'll be on our way.'

Bill beckoned him in. 'Close the door and take a seat, there's a few things you need to know.'

'Not Peter?'

'I'd prefer to forgo the delight of speaking to Peter direct and delegate his briefings to you.'

Trevor suppressed a smile. He was one of the few people who knew the Peter Collins, behind the confrontational mask. 'Peter's bark is worse than his bite.'

'I discovered that years ago, but I'd still prefer not to listen to the noise he makes.' Bill sat back in his chair. 'I've just had upstairs on the phone. The case is complex, the town's full of rumours.'

'As Peter said, small towns are always rife with rumour.'

'These are spreading like wildfire. Some people believe the local force is involved.'

'In the murders?' Trevor looked up in surprise.

'Murders and or cover-up. Initial reports suggest the killer or killers have done a first-class job of destroying all the forensic evidence, which means a certain amount of professional know-how.'

'Everyone who watches TV crime shows these days knows about forensic evidence and how to destroy it,' Trevor commented.

'A suspect was formally charged with arson half an hour ago.'

'Then we're not needed.'

'According to upstairs you'll be needed more than you were before he was charged. Reggie Moore's holding off on a murder charge. I suggest you take a good look at the evidence for arson when you get there.' He faced Trevor. 'You're thorough, Trevor, but a word of caution. Be doubly certain of the facts on this one. The last thing upstairs, Superintendent Moore, the locals or you and Collins need, is a balls-up.'

'We'll do our best.' Trevor opened the door.

'I know you will. It's Collins I'm not too sure about,' Bill added loudly for Peter's benefit when he caught sight of him in the corridor.

'Sorry, my love, but it can't be helped.' Trevor opened a drawer, lifted out a dozen pairs of boxer shorts and tossed them into the open case on the bed.

'It's what you get for being good at your job.' Lyn set their six month old son down on the pillows and refolded Trevor's underwear neatly in the case.

'Shovelling shit,' Trevor murmured.

'Babies present.' Lyn reprimanded him.

'I'll be more careful when Marty starts talking.'

'He's learning and you're anything but careful,' she said. 'It'll be all the harder to keep your conversations clean if you don't start watching what you say now.'

'Blame Peter. He complained that shovelling other people's … ordure … was our reward for being good at our job.'

Lyn laughed. 'He's probably right. Bet he's pissed off at having to leave Daisy. They're going through an unusually good patch at the moment.'

'Now who's swearing?' Trevor dropped a stack of freshly laundered shirts into his case and picked up his son who immediately started pulling his hair and nose. 'You'll look after Mummy while I'm away, won't you, Marty?'

'Of course he will.' Lyn went into the en suite and filled a toilet bag with soap, toothpaste, Trevor's cologne and after shave.

'Most coppers' wives play hell with them when they have to work away.'

'I'm not most coppers' wives.' She took Marty from him and handed him the toilet bag.

'Thank heavens.' He packed the bag on top of his socks, casual trousers and sweaters, closed the case, zipped it and hugged her. 'Love you.'

'Love you too. I'll invite Daisy in for a curry tonight. We might even open a bottle of wine.'

'Daisy can't drink.'

'I know.' Her smile broadened. 'But don't worry I won't have more than two glasses. Not when you're not here to see to Marty.'

'I'll phone you when I know what's happening.' He lifted the case from the bed. 'How do you fancy a trip to Wales? We'll probably be working all hours but there might be a holiday cottage there that I can rent for a week or two.'

'If we can see you for an hour or two in the evening it might be fun exploring a new place.'

'It's the nights I'm thinking about.'

'I know. But Marty might not settle in a strange place and if he doesn't, you won't be in a fit state to work.' Lyn handed him his suit carrier. 'Don't forget this.'

'It's at least a five-hour drive with breaks …'

'I can drive for five hours,' she interrupted.

'It won't be easy for you with Marty to look after. But if I get a day off I could come down and get you.'

'I can drive myself and Marty, thank you very much.'

He sat on the bed and pulled her and Marty on his lap. Then kissed her, long and lovingly. The doorbell rang.

'That's Peter.'

'You will drive carefully, won't you?'

'I'm not driving.' Trevor took his case and suit carrier and ran down the stairs. He opened the front door, handed them to Peter and picked up his laptop and briefcase.

'Drive carefully, Peter,' Lyn shouted down. 'That's my husband you're chauffeuring.'

'No more than thirty miles an hour all the way,' Peter called back.

'That a promise?'

Peter looked up the stairs and grinned at her. 'Would I lie to you and my godson?'

'No more than thirty miles an hour, my backside.' Trevor gripped the handle on the passenger door when Peter pressed his foot down on the accelerator. The speedometer hit eighty. Peter overtook a tractor and only just managed to avoid an oncoming milk tanker.

'We've been doing five miles an hour behind that tractor.'

'It was ten and you can drop back to thirty now,' Trevor ordered.

'Can I now?' Peter compromised and the accelerator hovered between forty and fifty.

Trevor tried to distract him. 'Did you manage to get through to Daisy before you left?'

'She was incommunicado in theatre.' Peter's partner was a surgeon in the burns unit of the local hospital. 'I left a voicemail and told her I'll phone her later, when I get a chance.'

'If you don't get an answer this evening, try our house. Lyn said she was going to invite Daisy in for a curry.'

'Know something? I wasn't happy when Daisy told me she'd bought a house a couple of doors from yours, but it's working well.'

'Because our wives can console one another when we're up to our neck in work?' Trevor asked.

'Because I can borrow your beer when I run short. Is this it?' Peter read the road sign on the outskirts of a town.

'It is.' Trevor checked his watch. 'Quarter past one.'

'Made it in five hours five minutes, despite the tractors and herds of cows blocking the road.'

'One herd and I'd rather arrive in one piece than break records.' Trevor relaxed his hold on the door handle. 'You drive like an idiot. I don't mind you killing yourself, but please, don't take me with you.'

'I gained enough time for us to have a pub lunch, didn't I?' Peter slowed when they entered Main Street.

Trevor looked out of the window. 'This is it.'

'"This is it what"?' Peter dropped to crawling speed.

'The crime scene. Number eight.' Trevor studied the smoke-damaged blackened facade. The pavement in front of the house was sealed off with scene-of-crime tape. The windows had been boarded over and two men were replacing the front door under the watchful eye of a uniformed constable. An enormous mound of flowers rose outside the police tape, from ground level to the tops of the windows.

'Work can wait until we're due to meet the Great Welsh Chief,' Peter said. 'I'm starving.'

'When are you not?'

Peter ignored the question. 'There's an interesting old pub two doors down with a food sign, and a parking space in front of it. The gods are smiling on us. Ready to pick up some gossip?'

'Be careful what you say,' Trevor warned after Peter parked the car.

'It's me, you're talking to.'

'That's why I'm concerned.'

'Moan, moan, nothing but moans.' Peter climbed out of the car, locked it and followed Trevor into the cramped hallway of the pub. Both had to duck their heads below the lintel when they walked through the doorway into the main bar. They were greeted by stares and absolute silence.

Ignoring the people watching them, Trevor glanced around the bar. It was long, wide and low-ceilinged with small, deep-set windows that overlooked an old stone wall at the back. An alcove set into the right-hand side opened into a dining room with tables set with silverware, napkins and glasses. The walls had been stripped back to the original grey stone, the floor was flagged but there were none of the fake antiques or olde worlde ornaments Trevor had come to expect in renovated coaching inns. Just simple pinewood tables and chairs, and Victorian and Edwardian photographs on the walls. Closer inspection of the photographs revealed them to be all of weddings with the happy couples emerging from what appeared to be the same church porch.

'Can I help you?' An attractive blue-eyed, dark-haired barmaid in a black mini-skirt and low-cut, strappy red top moved along the bar and flashed her breasts and a smile at Peter. Trevor reflected that although his colleague was living with Daisy, it hadn't stopped women from homing in on him.

'You certainly can,' Peter returned her smile with an empty one. 'What you serving that's tasty?'

'Menu's on the blackboard. I recommend the roast lamb with spinach, carrots and sweet potatoes.' She licked her lips.

Peter read the board. 'The lamb is tempting but we're in a hurry. How quickly can you serve up burger, chips, onion rings and a diet coke?'

'Ten minutes.'

'That's me sorted.'

'Nice to see you eating healthily away from Daisy's influence,' Trevor quipped.

'Daisy likes well-built men of substance, not skinny runts like you.'

'I'll have a ham salad sandwich and diet coke, please.' Trevor had put on weight since he'd married Lyn because she insisted he eat regular meals. But it was no more than four or five pounds and, although he and Peter were roughly the same height, at a few inches above six feet, he was three stone lighter.

'Where are you sitting?' the barmaid asked.

Trevor looked around. The bar was crowded. There were a few elderly and middle-aged couples, whom he assumed were local, but the majority of the customers were hard faced men and women he recognised as journalists.

'The vultures have gathered at the feast,' Peter murmured.

'This will do fine.' Hoping none of them would recognise him or Peter, Trevor pulled a stool up to the bar and sat down.

The barmaid poured their drinks and served them. 'I'll get your order to the kitchen.' She walked past a man who stopped her. He spoke to her and she shook her head.

'Someone's asking questions about us,' Peter said.

'Can you blame him given the location of this pub? That's if he's the landlord,' Trevor replied.

'You, gentlemen, all right?' The dark-haired, sardonic-featured man walked down the length of the bar and confronted Peter and Trevor.

'Been seen to, thanks,' Peter replied. 'You the landlord?'

'I am.' The fact that he didn't introduce himself wasn't lost on either Peter or Trevor.

'Efficient barmaid you have there,' Peter complimented him.

'She is.'

'You always this busy at lunchtime?' Peter sipped his drink.

'Not always,' he replied evasively.

'So these people are tourists?' Peter suggested.

'If you're bloody journalists …'

'We're not journalists,' Trevor interrupted softly.

'I haven't met one yet who wasn't a liar, especially about what they do for a living.' The landlord stared belligerently at Trevor.

'We're not journalists,' Trevor repeated.

The landlord had been about to embark on a rant and wasn't to be dissuaded. 'Bloody gutter press turning tragedy into entertainment for the idiot masses. Asking insensitive questions and not listening to answers. Making up lies about decent folk. Alun Pitcher and his family were good, honest, hard-working people. Ready to do anyone a favour. Never did any soul any harm, then some maniac comes along and murders all of them …'

'Michael wasn't murdered.' The barmaid returned and set Trevor's sandwich in front him. 'Sorry, sir, your burger's going to take another five minutes,' she apologised to Peter.

'Thanks, I'd prefer it cooked to raw.'

'Why are you here if you're not journalists?' the landlord asked bluntly.

'Business meeting,' Trevor cut his sandwich into smaller pieces.

'One of the family survived?' Peter reminded the barmaid.

'What's it to you whether or not one of the Pitchers is alive?' The landlord glared at Peter.

'Nothing. I just heard the headlines on the car radio,' he said conversationally. 'I thought they said the entire family had been killed.'

'As I said, bloody gutter press, never get their facts right.'

'So did one of the family survive or not?' Peter pressed.

When neither the landlord nor barmaid answered Peter's question, Trevor said, 'I take it you've a few reporters in town.'

'Look over your shoulder,' the landlord raged. 'We're bloody inundated. Some of the buggers tried to book in here. I might have to serve them food, but I don't have to give the bastards house room.'

A man walked up to the bar with an empty pint glass and handed it to the barmaid. 'We can hear you all over the bar, Tim. Give it a rest. Now the coppers have caught the one who did it, there's nothing more to be said before the funeral. Afterwards, the Pitchers can rest in peace and the town get back to normal.'

'Normal! Normal!' the landlord repeated in a strained voice. 'This town will never get back to what it was before this happened, George, and you know it.'

'I hate the swine who killed Alun and his family as much as the next man. If we had capital punishment in this country I'd be the first to volunteer to slip the noose round his neck ...'

'Talk. That's all you've ever been good at, George.' Tim took George's glass from the barmaid. 'Customer's burger should be ready,' he snarled.

'I'll look in the kitchen.' She scurried off.

'You can have your pint, George. And, you,' he glowered at Peter, 'can have your bloody burger. And that's it. This is a pub not a bloody gossip shop. I'll have no more talk about the Pitchers in here. They were good friends of mine. All of them.'

Trevor picked up his plate and glass and climbed off his stool. 'Table's free over there.' He pointed to the back corner of the bar.

Peter followed. 'But are the natives around it any friendlier?'

CHAPTER SIX

'Take no notice of Tim,' the barmaid set Peter's meal, cutlery and napkin in front of him. 'He was a close friend of Alun Pitcher but I think he's forgotten we all were. The Pitchers were nice people. It's not bloody fair. No one should have to die that way. Horribly murdered in their own home.' She bit her lip and brushed a tear from her eye.

'I'll second that, love.' Peter sprinkled salt on his chips.

'Nothing like this has ever happened in this town before.'

'It doesn't happen often in the country, love.' Peter forked chips to his mouth.

'I couldn't believe it when I saw it on the TV news. And not just the local news. It made headlines on the national. When I walk round town, I keep looking over my shoulder. I know everyone says they've caught him but I can't help wondering if he's the right one. If he isn't, there's a murderer walking free and who knows who he'll kill next …'

'Have the police said who they've arrested?' Peter feigned innocence.

She lowered her voice to a theatrical whisper. 'Not officially but everyone knows it's one of the thugs from the Garth Estate, Larry Jones. He was released from prison the morning before the fire and he came in here that night, drunk as a skunk. Couldn't even stand up straight. Tim took him outside and he passed out cold on the pavement. But,' she glanced over her shoulder to make sure no one was close enough to overhear. 'People are saying more than one person was involved.'

'Why would they say that?' Trevor finished his sandwich and handed her his plate.

'Alun Pitcher was over fifty but he was a strong man and so were his sons. I was in school with the middle one James. I knew him well. He was a really nice boy.' She wiped her eyes again and looked towards the bar. When she was sure that the landlord was nowhere in sight, she leaned even further over their table.

Peter eyed her cleavage and wondered if her top was about to burst its seams beneath the weight of her breasts. If she was wearing a bra, he couldn't see it.

'No one believes one man on his own could kill a strong man, his two sons and his wife, especially when he was falling down drunk only a couple of hours before. Wouldn't the others have come running and put up a fight as soon as he attacked one of them?'

'Depends whether they were already dead or not. There was a fire wasn't there?' Peter bit into his burger.

'They're saying none of them died in that fire. They were all dead before it started. And, another thing. Alan Pitcher was an antique dealer. He did house clearances and stored some of the more valuable things in his cellar. The last house he cleared was full of ...'

'Pam!'

'Got to go.' She picked up Trevor's empty plate and glass and scurried off.

'Another five seconds and I would have had an

eyeful of boob. But they were silicone,' Peter said disparagingly. 'I prefer the real thing.' He pushed the last onion ring into his mouth and wiped his lips on his napkin. 'Do I have time to go to the little boys' room before our meeting?'

'If you don't stop to talk to anyone.' Trevor reached into his trouser pocket. 'I take it this is on me?'

'Senior officer's prerogative to buy the junior officer lunch.'

'Guess who's going to get stuck with the dinner bill,' Trevor threatened.

'Expenses. If she comes back and you find out whose house Alan Pitcher cleared of what, let me know.' Peter left the table.

By the time Trevor and Peter left the pub the workmen had finished replacing the door on number eight. The gleaming UVPC glared white, bright and shiny in stark contrast to the smoke-damaged walls on which little of the original cream paint could be seen. The same uniformed constable they had seen earlier was still standing outside.

They climbed into Peter's car, Trevor entered the police station's postcode into the SatNav and they followed a torturous one-way route to a large, detached four-storey Victorian building that dominated the square in the centre of town. It bore the legend, POLICE STATION 1874 pressed in concrete over the entrance.

'Car park at the back by the look of it,' Trevor said.

'Think it's safe to leave the car here?' Peter eyed a boy who was ostentatiously smoking a spliff in full view of the station's windows.

'As safe as anywhere in town.'

'You're probably right.' Peter parked the car, locked it and they entered the building. An officer in a neatly pressed, new uniform that marked him as a rookie stood behind a high desk that faced the front door in the tiled reception area.

Peter approached the desk. 'Where's the cameras?'

The rookie looked at him in bewilderment. 'Sir?'

'The last time I saw a station like this was in a film about Jack the Ripper. Is this the set?'

'They're building a new station, sir,' the rookie informed Peter brightly. 'It will be finished in six months.'

'With electric lights and indoor plumbing?'

Trevor ignored Peter and showed the constable his warrant card. 'Inspector Joseph and Sergeant Collins to see Superintendent Moore.'

The rookie snapped to attention. 'She's expecting you, sir. You'll find her in her office. Straight down the passage, it's the one on your left.'

'"She", Peter repeated sotto voce. 'I thought the name was Reggie. But then, I should have known it would be a woman screaming for help.'

Trevor pretended he hadn't heard him. 'Thank you, constable.'

'Sweet, sir, Tony Sweet, sir. This is the biggest case we've had in the town. The forensic teams have been working flat out since the fire service stabilised the house; a full team from this force, and complements from outside. The Home Office pathologist started work ...'

74

'Thank you constable. I am up to the task of updating these officers on the situation.' A woman stood in the corridor behind the desk. She was suited up in protective clothing and her hair was covered by a sterile bonnet. The lines around her eyes and mouth suggested middle age. She eyed Trevor. 'You are Inspector Joseph?'

'Inspector Trevor Joseph and Sergeant Peter Collins, ma'am.'

'My office is this way.' She walked down the corridor and opened a door. 'No one is to disturb us, Constable Sweet. If anything urgent comes up, tell Inspector March to deal with it. If it's life-threatening, my mobile will be switched on. But, warn her it had better be life-threatening.'

'Yes, Super.'

'Can we call you Super too?' Peter asked.

Regina Moore gave him a withering look that might have had an effect if Peter had any respect for rank. 'Superintendent Moore will do, Sergeant Collins. Your reputation has preceded you.'

'I'm flattered.'

'You shouldn't be,' she informed him icily. 'What do you know about this case, Inspector Joseph?' She closed her office door.

'Beyond your e-mail asking for assistance and the press reports, nothing. I assume you're investigating an arson attack and the murder of four adult members of the same family?'

'The barmaid in the pub ...'

'Which pub?' Reggie interrupted Peter.

'The Angel, a couple of doors down from the crime scene,' Peter continued blithely. 'We arrived 'early so we stopped there for lunch.'

'The first rule of policing is to never listen to pub gossip, Sergeant Collins.'

'On the contrary, Superintendent Moore,' Peter demurred. 'I've found information gleaned that way can be invaluable, provided it's treated with caution.'

'The barmaid? Five six, short dark brown hair, grey eyes, well-endowed?'

'That's the one.' Peter was amused by the standard police description with the addition of "well-endowed". If he had been in his own station he would said something more descriptive and, less PC.

'What exactly did Pamela George tell you that you found valuable?'

'I'm at the "treating information with caution stage".' Peter's face was expressionless but Trevor knew his colleague's tongue was firmly in his cheek. 'The barmaid – you said her name was Pamela George?'

'I did,' Reggie confirmed.

'She said the victims were dead before the fire was started.'

'That's more of a hope for the Pitcher family, than a proven fact. The post-mortems haven't been carried out, so cause of death has yet to be established, Sergeant Collins.' Reggie stripped off the white bonnet, boiler suit and overshoes.

'I was told there was little forensic evidence,' Trevor commented.

'Try none. Nothing that links to the killer or killers. And absolutely nothing of use so far in the house. But the forensic teams and pathologist are still looking.'

Peter and Trevor waited for the Superintendent to sit behind her desk before taking two of the chairs set in front of it. Without protective clothing she looked younger. Trevor lowered her age from late forties to mid.

The laptop on the desk was connected to a photographic printer. A stack of files alongside bore a case number, the address of the crime scene and the logo of the local force. Superintendent Reggie Moore clearly wasn't an officer who wasted time.

Reggie picked up two files and handed one to Trevor and one to Peter. Trevor opened his file and saw a floor plan.

'The Pitcher house?'

Regina opened a third file and set the papers it contained in a neat pile in front of her. 'Scale floor plans of all five floors of the Pitcher house and photographs taken in the immediate aftermath of the fire. If Constable Sweet has filed the photocopies in order, you're looking at a plan of the cellar.'

'A large open area with a staircase that climbs above a double door and a single door. Toilet and wash-hand basin to the right at the bottom of the staircase. Doors open on to a yard.' Trevor checked.

'Both doors are fire damaged behind recognition but one was an up and over, not double door,' she corrected. 'The staircase on the front wall next to the entrances is on the back wall if you are viewing the house from Main Street – that's the street the pub is on,' she added. 'It leads up to a landing that opens on the ground floor. Alun Pitcher had an office suite there. Three rooms and a small conference room with a cloakroom and WC built directly above the one in the cellar. The cellar only covers about two-thirds of the floor area of the upper stories. A door leading out of the office suite connects with a hall on ground level at Main Street. As you walk in through the front door on Main Street you face a staircase that leads to the Pitchers' living quarters on the three floors above the office suite. To date we have no idea how the killer or killers entered the Pitcher's house. The emergency services were called by a witness who saw the fire and spotted a figure on the outside metal fire escape at attic level shortly after seeing the flames. The escape has no lock and can be accessed from ground level next to the cellar. Anyone entering the Pitcher's yard could have walked on to it.'

'Any sign of forced entry?' Trevor asked.

'None.'

'Are there gates to the yard?'

'No,' Reggie looked down at the plan. 'The entrance to the yard, which is wide enough to take an HGV vehicle, is off the lane that runs at the back of the terrace. The Pitchers used the yard to park their vehicles.'

'Trusting souls,' Peter commented.

'This is a quiet Welsh market town, Sergeant Collins. Everyone knows everyone else.'

'And everyone is totally honest?' Peter raised his eyebrows.

She disregarded his question. 'As you see from the sketch, the fire escape leads from ground level to attic. There are three balconies on the back of the house all accessed from landings on the fire escape and also from inside the Pitchers' private accommodation. The photographs of the cellar that were taken after the fire are behind the plan.'

Trevor and Peter turned the pages and flicked through the dozens of photographs detailing scenes of total devastation.

'It's impossible to determine anything from these,' Peter grumbled.

'Forensic are trying,' Reggie snapped. 'Alan Pitcher was an antique dealer. According to the people who worked for him he stored valuable items in the cellar awaiting auction.'

'Are you considering theft as a motive?' Peter asked.

'I wouldn't rule out any motive at this stage but as Inspector Joseph is here to assume responsibility, the motives are his to determine.'

'If it was theft, the thief or thieves would have needed a vehicle,' Trevor observed. 'And, please call me Trevor.'

'Only in private senior officer situations, Trevor. As for vehicles, I have officers out interviewing the neighbours. We're collating their reports as they come in but so far we have no sightings of any strange vehicles in the vicinity on the evening before or during the early hours of the day of the fire.'

'Any familiar vans?' Peter asked.

'One of Alan Pitcher's which hasn't moved since he parked it in his yard around six o'clock on the evening before the fire, according to the landlord of the Angel.'

'We've met him. Friendly fellow,' Peter said.

'Tim Pryce's private accommodation overlooks the Pitcher's yard. A catering van brought supplies to the pub around seven o'clock. It was their last call of the evening and the last witnessing of a vehicle in the lane. But, as I said, we have officers making door to door enquiries. If anyone did see anything out of the ordinary that evening, it will be reported. Alun and Gillian Pitcher and their sons were popular. They had a lot of friends in this town.'

'Any enemies?' Trevor checked.

'None known.'

'Isn't that odd for a businessman?' Peter queried.

'Not in this town. You won't find anyone who'll say a word against the Pitchers. Alun and Gillian worked tirelessly, fundraising for medical charities and the local hospice. They were also heavily involved in the community. Alun was a Freemason and chairman of the Rotary Club, Gillian was on the committee of the Amateur Dramatics Society and various Arts Clubs. Alun employed three people full-time in his business and up to a dozen part-time. Those are jobs this town can ill afford to lose. He attracted visitors from all over the country with his antique auctions. Well-heeled people who patronised the local hotels, B & Bs, pubs and restaurants. I've lived here two years and I've never heard anyone voice a complaint about Alun or the way he ran his business.'

'Did this saint work for personal gain, or altruistic reasons?' Peter asked.

'As far as I and most people in this town know, Alun Pitcher was an honest hard-working businessman,' Reggie shuffled the photographs of the cellar together and turned the page.

'He could have had secrets,' Peter persisted.

'If he did, I'm not aware of them.'

'They wouldn't be secrets if you knew about them,' Peter countered.

Trevor frowned at him before studying a street map of the town pinned to the wall above the superintendent's desk. He checked it against a photograph clipped to the back cover of the case file. It was a blown-up aerial shot of Main Street and the thoroughfares in the immediate vicinity. 'Is the lane at the back of the terrace busy?'

'No. It's too narrow to be a short-cut even at peak traffic times,' Reggie explained. 'There are passing places but for most of its length it's barely the width of one vehicle. In my experience it's only used by those who have reason to call at the back of one of the houses.'

'But delivery vans use it when they visit the pub. And the furniture in Alan Pitcher's cellar must have been brought in by van,' Trevor mused.

'Alan's van. The back lane isn't one-way or little known if that's what you're implying,' Reggie interposed. 'Everyone in town knows about it as well as tradesmen, builders, delivery van drivers, window cleaners – the list is endless.' Reggie turned to a plan of the ground floor of the Pitcher house. 'We've a lot to cover in this briefing. The next plan is of the office floor. Front door opens from the street into a small hallway. Directly opposite the front door, as you step inside, is the staircase that leads up to the Pitchers' family living quarters. The only door other than the front leads to an inside hall, office suite and staircase that connects down to the cellar. The first firemen on the scene went around the back because that's where the fires had been sighted.'

'Fires?' Trevor checked.

'The witness reported seeing flames in the attic windows and minutes later the kitchen, two floors below. The first tender to arrive went into the yard and the officers fought the fires at the back of the house. The officers in the second fire tender axed the front door so they could get their hoses inside the house. The ground floor was full of smoke that had come up from the cellar and down from the kitchen but nothing on that level was actually burning. The office door was locked with no signs of forced entry.'

'Can we move on to the crime scene?' Trevor set the photographs that had been taken of the cellar and office floor aside and turned to the plan of the floor above. Peter and Reggie followed suit.

'The Pitchers' kitchen is at the back of the house above the office suite, the drawing room at the front above the hall. There is a windowless cloakroom off the passage that connects the two rooms and staircases that lead down to the offices and up to the bedrooms. Both kitchen and drawing room run the full forty-feet width of the house. The balcony on that floor can be accessed from a door in the kitchen.'

'Large rooms,' Peter checked the measurements.

'The damage to the kitchen is comparable to that in the cellar,' Trevor studied the photographs of the burned-out room.

'We've had a few results in from the forensic teams. The thick layer of ash on the floor is principally wood ash from the kitchen units and table and chairs,' Regina revealed.

'And the black shiny pieces scattered among them?' Peter asked.

'The kitchen had recently been refitted by one of the Pitcher sons with granite worktops and a black slate floor. The granite and slate splintered in the heat of the fire. Early indications suggest cooking oil was splashed around, the sink filled with it and set alight. It's believed that's what caused the window above the sink to blow out after the fire was set. The explosion was heard by a fisherman by the river about half a mile away.'

'Is he the witness who called the emergency services?' Trevor asked.

'Yes.'

'His name?' Trevor took a biro from his shirt pocket.

'Ken Lloyd. You'll find it on the list of witness statements in the appendix to the file. We're lucky he called when he did. Even five minutes later the fire crews would have met a very different scene. Although the kitchen, cellar and attic have been wiped out, thanks to him, we've been able to make the building stable enough for our teams to work in.'

Trevor flicked through the pile of "scene of crime photographs". 'Depending on the quantity used, the oil could explain why the kitchen was gutted and the drawing room, staircase, cloakroom and passageway were relatively untouched apart from a few "spot fires" and smoke damage. What about the fire in the cellar? Have we any idea why that was so severe?'

'Ken Lloyd worked occasionally for Alun Pitcher. He told us Alun stored paint, paint thinner, stripper, stain and various chemicals he needed for his business down there. Most were flammable and, although we've no proof, it's possible they were splashed around like the cooking oil,' Reggie added.

'Where were the bodies found?' Trevor set the photographs of the first floor aside.

'The two sons and Alun Pitcher in the attic; Gillian Pitcher on the floor of the master bedroom. The door was open. Her feet were pointing to the landing, her head inside the room.'

Trevor set the floor plan of the bedrooms and attic on top of his file. 'The crosses are where the bodies were found?'

'Correct.' Reggie confirmed. 'AP is Alun Pitcher, GP Gillian. The eldest son who slept in the attic studio is LP – Lee Pitcher, the younger son JP – James Pitcher.'

'Four bedrooms, all en-suite, two at the front of the house, two at the back?'

'The last plan is that of the attic floor that the eldest Pitcher son, Lee, converted into an open-plan flat and workshop.'

Peter studied the photographs of the victims. 'I thought I'd seen it all.'

'Now perhaps you understand why I've asked for your assistance. Like every town we've had dealings with major crimes but our murders to date have usually been domestic. There've been burglaries in some of the larger houses on the outskirts of town; we've had drug- and alcohol-fuelled violence and minor misdemeanours such as car theft, but never before have we encountered murder on this scale.'

'Has the pathologist moved the bodies out of the house?' Trevor didn't look up from the photographs.

'No, and he won't carry out the post mortems until he does.'

'And the forensic teams haven't come up with any DNA or other tangible evidence?' Trevor checked.

'Not as yet, no.'

Peter asked the question he knew was uppermost in Trevor's mind as well as his own. 'Are there indications that the murderer or murderers had professional knowledge which assisted them with the destruction of evidence?'

Reggie looked him in the eye. 'Just how many rumours did you hear in the pub, Sergeant Collins?'

'Before Peter answers that question, I'd like you to explain exactly why you called us in so early in the investigation, Superintendent Moore.' Trevor finally set the photographs aside.

CHAPTER SEVEN

Reggie met Trevor's probing gaze. 'Would you believe I called you in because I could see from the outset that this was going to be a complicated case?'

'Why complicated?' Trevor demanded.

'No doubt you heard in the pub that we have someone in custody.'

'A Larry Jones, a thug from Garth Estate. A sink estate?' Peter suggested.

'That description would apply to the Garth Estate,' Reggie conceded.

'You've charged him with arson,' Trevor checked.

'We have.'

'Not murder?'

'No.'

'He was found at the scene?'

'He was,' Reggie concurred. 'And that was the first anomaly that alerted me. It seemed too much of a coincidence for the perpetrator to be found lingering in the vicinity of the crime. Especially, as he was seen comatose drunk only three and a half hours before. Apart from the things found on him ...'

'What things?' Trevor broke in.

Reggie frowned. 'If you don't mind I'll come to that later. I've given the forensic teams all the time they want to carry out their investigation because to date they haven't discovered a shred of physical evidence that places Larry Jones in the Pitcher house. Not a hair, fingerprint, or fragment of DNA. I am loath to hurry them and demand reports because haste can lead to sloppiness and we – you – Trevor, need to be sure of the facts.'

'Because of the number of South Wales Police Force cases that have resulted in overturned verdicts at a second trial?' Peter suggested bluntly.

'There have been miscarriages of justice,' Reggie acknowledged.

'More than in any other force in the country.' Peter had made a statement not asked a question.

'Are you suggesting there are corrupt officers on my force, Sergeant Collins?' Reggie enquired defensively.

'You deny the possibility?'

'It's every straight copper's nightmare,' Reggie conceded. 'The over-zealous colleagues who're so certain they've caught the villain they fabricate evidence to secure a conviction. I can't deny we've had some high-profile cases turn sour. The Cardiff three, the Swansea two, the murder of a Cardiff newsagent and the tampering with witness statements that led to the wrong man being convicted. Last year ten officers were suspended from the South Wales force, four for alleged offences of dishonesty, perjury and deception. As I've already explained, Alun Pitcher was a popular man. His family were well liked. I don't want questions raised about the way this case was handled by the locals because of the actions of an over-enthusiastic officer, especially as we've an ex-con in custody.'

'The right ex-con?' Trevor couldn't resist asking.

'Again, that's now your, not my, question to answer. Why do you think I asked for help? Every interview and piece of evidence on this case, not only needs to be seen to be carried out and collected by the book, but also objectively and professionally. When I asked for a capable and honest officer to head this investigation because I suspected my team to be out of their depth, yours was the first name mentioned. You have a reputation for being incorruptible, Trevor.'

'I told you,' Peter crowed. 'You get the lousiest jobs because you're good at cleaning up other people's messes.'

'This ex-con ...' Trevor began.

'Can we return to the photographs of the victims,' Reggie interrupted. 'What I can tell you is that all of them were beaten.'

'Weapon?' Trevor asked.

'Pathologist wouldn't commit himself other then to say that in three cases it was long, thin and cylindrical, possibly with a sharp edge or point at one end.'

'And the fourth?'

'A large heavy object.'

'So, we're looking for a raving nutcase or nutcases, possibly out of their, his or her tiny mind on drink or drugs, with the strength to wield blunt instruments,' Peter concluded.

'I'd hold back on the psychiatric angle unless you're talking socio or psychopath.' Trevor recalled the conversation he'd had with Bill. 'Would a disturbed person who'd bludgeoned four victims about the head have the presence of mind to set fires to destroy the evidence?'

'Again, that, Trevor, is your question to answer.' Reggie failed to keep the relief from her voice.

'If he, she or they weren't "mad, bad and

dangerous to know",' Peter quoted, 'He, she or they must have had a bloody good motive for doing what he, she or they did. Any ideas, Superintendent?'

'Apart from theft, none.'

Silence settled heavy in the atmosphere as they all studied the photographs of the corpses.

Trevor pushed one photograph in front of Reggie. 'This corpse isn't as badly burned as the others. It appears to be wrapped in something.'

'Brown paper tied with string before being set alight,' Reggie informed him. 'All four were treated the same way. Forensic said the murderer or murderers couldn't have come up with a better way to destroy evidence.'

'Poor buggers,' Peter said feelingly. 'If they were alive …'

Reggie interrupted him. 'It's useless to speculate. The pathologist won't commit one way or the other until he's had a chance to examine their lungs for smoke inhalation.'

'This suggests we're looking for a cool-headed killer,' Trevor said thoughtfully. 'It takes time and intelligence to wrap damaged or, hopefully for the victims' sake, dead bodies in paper and string and set fire to the paper to destroy all traces of the assailant's DNA. And, then to move on to set fires in the house, presumably with the intention of destroying evidence that could implicate the criminal. I use "criminal" loosely. Four healthy adult victims all brutally battered suggest more than one killer to me.'

'Look at the last photograph,' Reggie flicked to the final page of photographs.

Trevor recognised the fragments. 'Slivers of latex.

Proof gloves were worn?'

'Two slivers of more or less identical size found in the attic bathroom. The forensic team have suggested at least two sets were worn, one on top of the other. The bathroom in the attic didn't suffer as much as the studio. The door was closed and it protected the area from the worst effects of the fire. The fire service managed to douse the flames before they spread. The floor, walls and suite had been cleaned with bleach. There were pools of it on the floor and in the shower.'

'Bleach doesn't destroy all traces of blood,' Peter said soberly.

'No, it doesn't,' Trevor agreed. 'But it will dilute and destroy any traces of DNA. Given the victims' injuries, what do you think the chances are of the murderer sustaining wounds?'

'Impossible to say until we get the PM results,' Reggie said. 'As you see all the corpses have been burned. Alun and Gillian Pitcher's less than the other two but even if any of them fought back I doubt any traces of skin, blood or DNA will be found under their fingernails. Their hands have been reduced to ash and charred bone.'

'Forensic occasionally produce miracles,' Trevor said.

'Look at the positions of the victims. All are flat on their backs, their arms at their sides.' Peter studied the photographic evidence. 'No obvious sign of a struggle.'

'They were wrapped in brown paper and tied up,' Reggie reminded him.

'Given that no one in their right mind would allow

themselves to be parcelled without putting up a fight, I think they were either dead or unconscious before the fire was lit. What do you think?' Trevor turned to Reggie.

'It makes sense.'

'The killer could have been threatening to kill one of them unless the others complied. The men wouldn't have put up a fight if someone had a knife to the throat of the woman.' Peter continued to flick through the file.

'Do we know if anything valuable was taken?' Trevor asked.

'Jewellery identified as being taken from Lee Pitcher's attic was found in Larry Jones's pocket. His statement is in the appendix.'

'Valuable jewellery?' Trevor checked.

'Yes.'

'And you've only charged him with arson.'

'And breaking his parole. He was supposed to sleep at home.'

'You do have him in custody here?' Trevor sought confirmation.

'At the moment he's in the cells and he'll remain there until he's finished helping with our enquiries. Then he'll be returned to prison.'

Peter scanned the statement. 'Looks like you've a case against him for theft and arson given what you found on him.'

'Theft possibly. Arson would be circumstantial. We have possession of matches and we've had the forensic report on his clothes. The soot and smuts on them could be down to him being physically close to the fire in the yard. But as I said there's no physical evidence to place him in the house. As for anything being missing, we haven't taken the surviving member of the family back into the house and won't until after the bodies have been moved,' Reggie divulged.

'Was Larry Jones known to the Pitchers?' Trevor asked.

'They hardly moved in the same social circles. But Larry's family are notorious. They're known in town and to anyone who reads the crime reports in the local papers.'

Peter pulled a cigar from his pocket and proceeded to unwrap it.

'No smoking in this building,' Reggie warned him.

'He never lights them indoors,' Trevor assured her after giving Peter another warning look. 'I take it Larry is known to the local force.'

'He is,' Reggie agreed. 'You can look at his file but I can sum up by saying he's the product of a single mother who is herself a product of several generations of an extended dysfunctional matriarchal family who have produced vast numbers of children from different fathers. School recorded him as an illiterate truant. He has no legal employment record. Larry spent his teenage years in and out of youth custody. Since the age of eighteen he has served five prison terms. The last sentence was six years for aggravated burglary, rape and GBH. He spent some time in custody before the case came up but even so he served only ten months from the date of sentencing. He was released the morning before the fire in the Pitchers house.'

'Has he ever been convicted of arson?' Trevor asked.

'No.'

'Murder?'

'No. But he has been convicted of rape and GBH.' Reggie took another file from her desk and handed it to Trevor. 'Larry's record. I'll have copies made for you. Breaking and entering, robbery with violence, drug dealing, stealing cars, driving without tax, licence and insurance, aggravated burglary, drunk and disorderly, receiving stolen goods, threatening behaviour – as well as rape and GBH.'

Trevor scanned the list while Reggie updated him on the events on the night of the fire.

'A police patrol stopped at the scene a few minutes after Ken Lloyd and Tim Pryce had moved Larry into the archway.'

'Coincidence?' Trevor closed Larry's file.

'No. A resident had telephoned the station to report a disturbance in Main Street.'

'The resident been interviewed?'

'Probably.'

'You don't know?' Trevor returned Larry's file to her desk.

'If she hasn't we'll get round to it. Have you any idea of the number of people we've had to interview. Of the volume of work ...'

'Yes.' Trevor cut her short as he flicked through the witness statements. 'This Ken Lloyd who reported the fire at three o'clock, what was he doing out at that hour of the morning?'

'He's a fisherman and often visits the river at night. He has domestic problems,' Reggie explained briefly but Peter wasn't prepared to let it go.

'Adulterous or nagging wife?'

'Nagging,' Reggie replied tersely. 'He noticed Jones had left the archway when he returned to the street after reporting the fire. At four forty a m, when the fire was still burning in some areas of the Pitcher house, Larry Jones was discovered asleep in a derelict building in the Pitcher yard. I supervised the initial search. Exhibit A was found in Larry's pocket.' Reggie pushed a photograph across her desk. 'You have copies in your files.

Peter looked at it and whistled. 'Is it paste or the real McCoy?'

'Diamond and emerald, necklace, bracelet, ring, tiara and brooch. Lee Pitcher was a goldsmith and, according to his youngest brother Michael, was restoring the set for a Hatton Garden jeweller.'

'Fingerprints?' Trevor asked.

'Only Larry's on the bag.'

'On the jewellery?'

'None. The set had been washed possibly under pressure from a hose or shower head according to the expert who examined the pieces. He discovered moisture caught in the intricate gold setting. A few stones had been slightly loosened.'

Trevor stroked his chin. 'I can see why you called us in early in the investigation.'

'I thought you might. Shall we visit the crime scene?'

Ten minutes later they left the station and the square, turned into Main Street and headed down the lane that ran at the back of the houses. Trevor allowed

Reggie to walk ahead while he stood back and surveyed the width of the thoroughfare that was bordered for the most part by shoulder-height old stone walls.

'I wouldn't like to drive a HGV down here,' Peter commented.

'You haven't a licence,' Trevor reminded him.

'No doubt if I tried I'd be picked up. Until now the local coppers probably haven't had anything better to do than pull over motorists.'

Trevor looked back at Main Street. 'This lane may be known in the town, but Superintendent Moore's right. It's not a feasible short-cut.'

'Which means it's principally used by local residents.'

'Are you two coming?' Reggie called back.

'On our way.' Trevor started walking again.

'Do you think Larry Jones burgled the Pitcher house?' Peter asked.

'You don't?'

'The pieces found in his pocket are way out of a sink estate thug's league. Although I suppose he could have taken them on impulse if he saw them lying around. Even a thug knows gold can be melted down and stones prised from settings.'

'He's been convicted of burglary before.' Trevor stopped again and looked over the wall, down towards the river.

'So you think it was simply an opportunist burglary. He saw an open door or window and went in with the intention of thieving?'

'It's possible.'

'And the murders?' Peter asked.

'He was just out of gaol and undoubtedly reluctant to return there. If the Pitchers had disturbed him he could have lashed out.'

'And killed all four of them?' Peter was clearly sceptical.

'You want to play devil's advocate?'

'You have to admit, Reggie's right, it was a convenient find. Ex-con just released from prison sleeping in outbuilding of burning house with stolen jewellery in pocket.'

'He'd been released that morning. He could have met up with a professional thief, who was after something specific.' Trevor turned back to the lane. 'Alun Pitcher was an antique dealer.'

'Few professional thieves, outside of a couple of specialists, who steal to order for collectors, bother with antiques. They're easy to trace, which rules out auction rooms and difficult to dispose of to the legitimate trade. And, most home grown thieves I've come across would baulk at one murder let alone four. I suppose there are the Mafia and Eastern Europeans, although it beats me what they'd be doing in a quiet Welsh market town. On the other hand, the destruction of evidence has the hallmark of a professional.' Peter thrust his hands into his pockets.

'And it's better to think professional criminal gang, than consider the local force involved.'

'Agreed,' Peter concurred.

'And better still to keep an open mind,' Trevor advised.

'You're beginning to sound like Dan and Bill Mulcahy. Is it something that comes with promotion?'

'Stop winding people up and you might find out.'

'What and give up my hobby? Bloody Mary! I can smell the stench of the fire from here. Do you think that's what hell smells like?'

'Haven't you read your Bible lately?'

'I've been waiting for the graphic version with pictures to come out.'

'By all accounts the fires in hell are eternal and fed by brimstone.'

'What is brimstone?' Peter asked.

'Some think it's a reference to volcanic activity and sulphurous rocks.'

Peter smiled. 'Then that'll give the Larry Joneses of this world something to look forward to.'

Reggie was waiting for them in front of a twelve foot break in the wall manned by two uniformed officers. She effected the introductions. 'Inspector Trevor Joseph, Sergeant Frank Howell and Constable Jim Murphy. They've been informed that you are here to take charge of the investigation.'

'Sir.' They both acknowledged Trevor.

'And Sergeant Peter Collins,' Reggie added, downgrading Peter to an afterthought.

Peter nodded to the officers.

'This is the rear entrance to the Pitchers' yard.' Reggie walked through the gap. 'Has it been quiet, Sergeant Howell?'

'Apart from journalists sniffing round,' Frank replied. 'They keep trying to rent rooms in the pub and adjoining houses that overlook the yard. But they picked on the wrong neighbours. Tim Pryce and the accountants tipped us off and we sent them packing.'

'Carry on the good work, Sergeant.' Reggie preceded Trevor and Peter into an open area the size of a tennis court. The reek of fire was overpowering at close quarters.

Trevor looked around. 'Where did you find your suspect?'

'There.' Reggie turned and indicated the building. Trevor saw two suited figures inside sifting through debris. 'The family vehicles.' Reggie pointed to the left-hand side of the yard. 'The two BMW sports cars belonged to the eldest sons; the SLK coupe was Gillian Pitcher's, the Mercedes Sprinter van, Alun's.'

'Alun Pitcher drove the short straw,' Peter observed.

'His Bentley's in the garage.' Reggie pointed to a double garage in the bottom right-hand corner of the yard well away from the house and the fire. 'He only took it out on high days and holidays. Given the way he worked, there weren't many of those. His is the only car that hasn't been damaged by burning debris.'

'You've checked it?' Trevor noted the dusting of grey fingerprint powder on all the cars.

'Along with the other vehicles. No recent alien fingerprints were found on the inside or outside of any,' Reggie confirmed.

A mobile HQ unit was parked next to the cars, close to the boundary wall.

'The sports cars are tasty if you're into joy-riding,' Peter looked around. 'This yard is an open invitation. I'm surprised there isn't better security.'

'Most of the taking without consent …'

'We call it Twocking,' Peter smiled at Reggie. A smile she didn't reciprocate.

'As do the ones who indulge in the practice in this town, Sergeant. I prefer to call it by its rightful name, thieving. Ninety per cent of the cars that are taken are stolen from the town and supermarket car parks,' she continued. 'As for security, if you look up you will see that most of residents, commercial and private, in this street have CCTV.'

'So theft is a problem.' Trevor eyed the cameras that had been fixed at attic level.

'No.' Reggie was emphatic. 'This morning I checked the statistics on this lane. In the past five years the pub's been broken into twice. Tim Pryce has security connected to the station. On both occasions the culprits were found on the premises. One was down to youngsters, the oldest nineteen the youngest twelve. They were after alcohol. The second occasion a tramp smashed a window, climbed in, downed the best part of a bottle of brandy and fell asleep on the floor of the bar. The accountant's next door to the Pitchers was broken into last summer. Attending officers found the same tramp who'd broken into the pub a year earlier sleeping in the kitchen. He'd helped himself to tea and biscuits. The only other incident was on the evening of last year's summer festival. A crowd of drunks went on the rampage through the town, came down here and smashed a few windows. We made six arrests. The magistrate gave them a caution and ordered them to pay compensation.'

'This town is a real hotbed of crime,' Peter mocked. 'What do your coppers do for kicks on their shift? Knit or crochet?'

'That is the crime sheet for one lane running at the

back of Main Street, Sergeant Collins. We have our moments,' she retorted.

'If there haven't been any serious break-ins, why the security cameras and burglar alarms?' Trevor asked.

'Insurance company offered lower premiums for heightened security. Most of the residents took up the offer.'

Trevor noticed the remains of a camera fixed to the eaves of the Pitcher house. 'Was that connected to a recorder?'

'Yes, but it was switched off last night.'

Trevor raised his eyebrows.

'According to the youngest son, Michael, his father only switched it on when he heard a noise at night. As far as Michael could remember, that hasn't happened for the past couple of years.'

'Yet there's a fire escape that runs up to every floor at the back and connects with balconies in front of french windows.' Trevor continued to study the blackened smoke- and fire-damaged back of the house.

'All the doors and windows have high-security locks. We've checked,' Reggie informed him. 'Without a history of serious burglary in this area, you can't blame Alun for not being meticulous. Michael said his father only switched on the burglar alarm when the house was empty for more than a day. He couldn't even remember when that last happened as the sons haven't holidayed with the parents in years.'

'How old were they?' Peter asked.

'The oldest, Lee, twenty-five, James, twenty-three. The youngest Michael twenty-one.'

'How did Michael survive the fire?'

Reggie stared thoughtfully at Trevor. Until that moment she hadn't been sure how much attention he'd been paying to what she'd told him. 'He spent the night at his girlfriend's as he'd done every night that week. It's an isolated house, her parents are away and they'd promised to keep an eye on the place.'

'Then you do have burglars operating in the area?' Peter leaned against the wall.

'There has been a spate of them lately in the isolated houses on the outskirts of town but not in the town itself.'

'I'll need to interview Michael Pitcher,' Trevor said.

'Sergeant Howell sent for Michael after the fire broke out. The fire service wanted to know the location of the members of the family. When Michael was told that none of them had survived he collapsed. He's under sedation in the local hospital.'

'Then I'll have to wait until he's in a fit state,' Trevor walked towards the house. 'But for now I need to examine as much of the crime scene as the forensic teams will allow. You're using a generator?'

'It's noisy,' Reggie conceded. 'But the fire service ordered the electricity cut for safety reasons. I arranged for temporary lighting to be installed as soon as the building was declared safe so the forensic teams could start work. Do you want to go into the house?'

Trevor looked up at it. 'After we've checked if any new information's come into HQ.'

CHAPTER EIGHT

Peter opened the door of the mobile HQ. Reggie and Trevor walked in ahead of him. A constable was inputting information from a pile of statement forms on to a computer; another was printing photographs and placing them in files. They both stood when Reggie entered.

'This is Inspector Joseph and Sergeant Collins. They have been seconded to work on this enquiry. Inspector Joseph is the senior investigating officer. Inspector Joseph, Sergeant Collins, Constables Paula Rees and Damian Howell.'

Trevor nodded to both of them in response to their "sir".

'Any developments?' Trevor asked.

'Nothing new in the witness statements so far, sir,' Paula Rees answered in a Welsh lilt. 'Officers are still out door to door. As soon as the last sheets come in, I'll finalise the timeline. This is where it's at for now, sir.' She handed Trevor a file.

'Thank you.' Trevor turned to Damian. 'I take it those are the latest photographs of the crime scene.'

'I've been printing them off as and when forensic bring in the camera cards, sir. The last arrived twenty minutes ago.' Damian was even paler than Paula; strain was evident in the taut expressions around both their mouths and eyes.

'Are you all right, Constable?' Reggie asked Damian.

'Yes, Super.' He didn't sound convincing.

'You knew the Pitchers, didn't you?' Reggie

probed.

'Yes, Super.'

'How well?'

'I was in school with Lee. We are … were the same age. But I've set my personal feelings aside, Super,' he insisted.

'And you're coping?'

'Yes, ma'am.'

'And you, Paula? I heard you were close to James,' Reggie probed.

'I went out with him a couple of times when we were kids.'

Reggie gave Paula a look that suggested she was still a child. 'I'll arrange for you to be taken off the case, Constable.'

'If you take every officer who knew and liked the Pitchers off the case, Super, you'll have no team left,' Paula said quietly.

Trevor studied Damian Howell. His speech was slow and laboured, but so was Dan Evans's. It was a trait some Welshmen had. 'Did you know the rest of the Pitcher' family, Constable?'

'It was impossible not to know them in a town this size, sir.'

'You're right, Constable Rees,' Reggie allowed. 'I can't possibly take all the officers who knew the Pitchers off the case. But, if either of you find the inquiry difficult to cope with at any stage, come to me.'

'Yes, Super.'

Trevor saw Paula wipe a tear from her eye. He glanced at Peter and saw that he was also watching her and Damian Howell.

Peter picked up one of the photographs that pictured a pile of black dust. 'So this is the kind of town where everyone knows everyone else?'

'It is, sir,' Damian confirmed.

'What's the consensus on the Pitchers?' Peter was checking what Reggie had told them and she knew it.

'You won't find anyone who didn't like the family, sir. This is a tragedy not only for them but the town. Good jobs are hard to come by in this part of Wales. Alun Pitcher was an employer. His antique business and his sons' jewellery, carpentry and plastering businesses brought tourists and trade into the area,' Damian answered as if he were reading an autocue.

Reggie looked through the window at the house. 'Has anyone other than the forensic workers entered the house today, Constable Rees?'

'Only the fire investigators, Super.'

'We made sure they were suited up,' Damian added.

'Where are the suits?' Peter asked.

'In the inner office, sir.' Damian left his desk and opened the door behind him.

Peter followed Trevor through the door, picked out a sterile white boiler suit from a box and climbed into it. White paper hats, masks and overshoes were stacked in a second box. While Peter fished out two pairs of masks, overshoes and a couple of bonnets, Trevor pulled on a suit.

Reggie waited until they'd dressed before donning a fresh pair of overalls and tucking her hair beneath a bonnet. All three snapped on gloves. Carrying their overshoes they left the HQ and went to the cellar. The aluminium up and over door had buckled from the heat. The remains of the white UVPC door alongside it had been removed. Trevor looked through the gap and saw four people, anonymous in masks, bonnets and suits, sifting through the ashes on the floor. One of them looked up.

'Anything, Ted?' Reggie asked.

'Wood ash, traces of solvent and other flammable liquid, nothing unexpected. The staircase to the office suite collapsed an hour ago. The glass in this door was definitely smashed in from outside and we've found other, alien glass fragments mixed with traces of petrol.' Ted Gant rose stiffly to his feet and walked to the entrance to meet them.

'Fire bomb?' Reggie asked.

'Nothing sophisticated. I'm guessing petrol in a glass bottle with a paper fuse. I've sent fragments for analysis so we may know more later.' Ted arched his back and stretched his arms. 'I'm getting too old to crawl on my hands and knees.'

'Inspector Joseph, Sergeant Collins, Ted Gant, local forensics.'

'Pleased to meet you.' Trevor didn't waste time on preliminaries. 'Have you found any fingerprints?'

'None apart from the family's and Alun Pitcher's employees. Terri Langston – expert from a neighbouring county,' he explained for Trevor's benefit, 'is working in the kitchen. She may have something for you.'

'What about the floor above this?' Trevor asked.

'Fortunately we finished there before the stairs caved. The door to the office suite was locked before the room burned. We dusted what we could reach for

105

prints, the only ones we've found belonged to the Pitcher family and Alun Pitcher's employees. Same result from the dusting of what was left of the staircase between the ground floor and the family's private accommodation, although we did find smudges on the front door that was axed by the fire service and also smudges on the floor.'

'Someone in stockinged feet?' Trevor suggested.

'Possibly.'

'So the killer could have accessed the house from the front door or the fire escape?' Peter questioned.

'If it was the front door they were either expert lock pickers, had a key or the door was opened for them from the inside,' Ted pointed upwards. 'If you're heading for the kitchen, use the fire escape but don't step off the balcony. Terri's squared off the interior and they're going over the floor inch by inch. She'll have your heads on plates if you blow one speck of potential evidence from one square to another.'

'You've been up there,' Reggie guessed.

'Needed some fresh air. This place stinks. Not that the kitchen is any better.' Ted rubbed his shoulder. 'We went over the fire escape and balconies again this morning and found zilch.'

'Nothing?' Trevor said in surprise.

'Not one fingerprint, trapped hair, fragment of paper or scrap of forensic evidence on the railings or steps. The entire surface had been cleaned. There's a hose still connected to a tap at the side of the building. And before you ask, we've dusted it. No prints, just smudges.'

Peter walked over to the steps and ran his hands

over the rail. The fire escape, railings and balconies were black powder coated wrought iron, but the areas that had been close to the seat of the fire had burned rust red. 'Given the size of the staircase and balconies that must have taken an hour or two.'

'Less if there was more than one person doing it,' Ted said.

Trevor glimpsed movement in the yard adjoining the Pitchers. He looked at Reggie. She'd seen it and called to an officer standing guard at the entrance.

'Constable Murphy, see that the adjoining yards are kept clear will you?'

He nodded and when he moved Trevor saw that he was even paler than Damian and Paula.

'He knew the Pitchers as well?'

'Jim Murphy is the same age as Constable Rees, they would have both gone to the local comprehensive. This is affecting the whole town, and badly,' she answered briefly.

Trevor turned back to Ted. 'Have all the entrances to the building been checked?'

'Yes, and there's no indication of forced entry on any of the floors. Of course, there's the kitchen window that blew out …'

'You need a build up of hot air pressure to blow out a window. It wouldn't have exploded if the glass was already broken,' Peter said drily.

'Sorry, not thinking straight. Not enough sleep,' Ted apologized.

'Occupational hazard, mate,' Peter pulled on his overshoes and started to walk slowly up the fire escape, looking around as he climbed.

'So, someone let the killer into the house,' Reggie

said thoughtfully.

'Or a door was left open, or the killer had a key.' Trevor looked up at the balconies. 'I agree with Mr Gant. The cleaning of the fire escape and balconies suggests the outside staircase as our killer or killers' entry and exit point. But, on which floor did he she or they enter the building?'

'Terri might be able to help you there.' Ted turned back to the cellar.

'Good work, Ted,' Reggie shouted after him.

'Patronising bugger,' he called back.

'I mean it.'

'So do I,' he retorted.

Peter, Trevor and Reggie stood side by side, their backs to the balcony rail facing the remains of the scorched and shattered French doors, gazing into what had been the Pitchers' kitchen. The area had been given greater importance than the cellar as six suited workers were sifting through and examining the ash on the floor. One of them looked up at Reggie.

'I'm good at my job, Reggie, but I'm not a miracle worker. If you want results, give us the time we need to examine the scene.'

'I'm not chasing, Terri …'

'That's a first,' Terri broke in sceptically.

'I'm showing Inspector Trevor Joseph and Sergeant Peter Collins the layout of the house. Inspector Joseph is taking over the investigation.'

Terri sat back on her haunches.

'Good luck, Inspector. I've never seen a crime scene as clean as this.'

'So I gather after talking to Mr Gant.'

Spotlights shone into the room from makeshift tripods illuminating total destruction. The entire area was coated in thick black dust and ashes. Wooden cabinets had been reduced to charcoal. Granite worktops had crashed down and splintered adding to the cinder strewn rubble. Metal taps, sink, stove and everyday utensils had been twisted by the heat of the fire into macabre and fantastic skeletal shapes.

'Looking at this it's amazing the rest of the house is more or less intact.' Peter studied the scene with a professional eye.

'The sink was filled with cooking oil and set alight. The fire investigator told me it would have shattered the window above it within minutes. More oil was sprinkled around the room. But the solid oak door to the passage was closed and the fire service arrived within fifteen minutes of the call being made. It would have been a different story if the door had been left open. The first officers on the scene concentrated on containing the three major seats of fire. Here, in the attic and the cellar. They succeeded. There's localised burn damage from the individual fires in the rooms and extensive smoke damage throughout the house. But the officers did well. From a forensic point of view we were fortunate to have areas left to work in – not that we've found anything of note yet.'

'Not so fortunate for the family.' Peter said grimly.

'If they were already dead nothing could have helped them,' Terri brushed her gloved hands together to rid them of dust. 'As well as traces of cooking oil, we've found mixed ashes that suggest that here, as in the bedrooms and living room, combustible items were heaped together and set alight.'

'Something significant?' Trevor asked one of the women who slipped a piece of shrivelled plastic into an evidence bag.

'It's worth checking for fingerprints, but don't hold out hope. We haven't found any prints so far except the ones that should be here.'

'There were three main seats to the fire, here, the attic and the cellar,' Trevor said thoughtfully.

'Yes,' Reggie concurred.

'The fisherman – Ken Lloyd – who alerted the emergency services saw the attic fire first, then this one?'

'Correct.'

'He didn't see the one in the cellar.'

'He didn't report seeing it,' Reggie informed him.

'This figure he saw on the fire escape, he saw it after he saw the flames in the attic and kitchen?'

'He made a statement to that effect.'

'Could he have seen the fire in the cellar if it had burned the same time as the other two?'

'His view might have been obstructed by the wall in the lane.'

Unable to take out his notebook and pencil and risk contamination, Trevor looked to Peter.

'I'll add it to my mental list of things to be looked into,' Peter murmured.

'Is the Home Office pathologist still here?' Reggie asked.

'On one of the floors above,' Terri answered.

Trevor left the balcony for the staircase and began climbing.

'I can tell you one thing about the Pitchers,' Peter said as he stepped off the staircase and on to the balcony of the bedroom floor.

Trevor knew he was waiting to be asked. 'What?'

'They couldn't have suffered from vertigo.'

'Do you, Sergeant Collins?' Reggie was amused.

'Only in tall buildings with high ceilings built on the side of a cliff face.'

'I'd call it a steep hill rather than a cliff face,' Reggie passed him.

Peter took a deep breath to steady himself and kept his back to the spectacular view of the river that meandered through sheep-speckled fields on the valley floor.

Trevor turned and looked at the river. In one or two places it was little more than a shimmer of water in between trees. 'Do you know exactly where Ken Lloyd was fishing when he saw the fire?'

'No,' Reggie admitted.

'I thought he'd been interviewed?'

'He has but not exhaustively. I thought it more important to concentrate on the salient facts.' Reggie checked her watch. 'I and all my officers, senior and junior have been working flat out since this crime was reported.'

'I'm sure you have.' Trevor checked his gloves before trying the handle on the French door. It opened into a bedroom. 'Hello, anyone here?' he shouted.

'I know that voice.'

Trevor recognised the Irish brogue. 'Patrick?'

Patrick O'Kelly walked into the bedroom. 'You're a long way from home, Trevor Joseph.'

'I could say the same of you.'

'You investigating this mess?'

'It's his prize for being good at his job,' Peter looked around. 'The gorgeous Jen with you?'

'If you mean Dr Jennifer Adams, she is. Not that she'll be happy to know you're asking after her.' Patrick's eyes shone brilliant blue above his mask. 'I'm just about to give the order to move the bodies. Want to inspect them before they go?'

'I thought you were never going to ask. The real thing is always much better than photographs.' Peter walked further into the room – and away from the balcony.

'We're not likely to mess anything up?' Trevor examined his overshoes for signs of dirt.

'Unfortunately not,' Patrick said. 'I've never seen a crime scene this clean of outside contamination and neither have the forensic teams. There's plenty of blood, tissue, DNA and hair but only the victims'. Whoever did this should write a manual on how to destroy evidence. Follow me.'

Peter, Trevor and Reggie trooped behind him, through the bedroom on to a landing and into what had been the master bedroom.

Gillian and Alun Pitcher had possessed good taste. The floor was sanded wood, now blackened by soot. The original cream paint shone through the smoke stains on the walls. Gold still glinted in the brocade curtains. The remains of the damaged furniture was recognisable as eighteenth-century antique, but

Trevor expected no less from a dealer who would have had the pick of the pieces coming through his auction rooms.

The linen had been stripped from the four-poster bed. The frame was untouched. Fragments of brown paper and string adhered to the charred body lying on the floor beside the bed.

'Whoever did this made a few mistakes.' Patrick peeled back a fragment of paper. 'Gillian Pitcher's body was wrapped in brown paper and tied with string like the others, but then bedclothes were heaped over it. Given sufficient time we might have only found ashes and skeletal remains but when the first two firemen entered the room with extinguishers the body was smouldering. They pulled back the duvet and doused the fire before beating a retreat. They doused a little too vigorously for my liking. Less force would have given me more to work with. But apparently both went into shock at the sight of her injuries, so I have to forgive them.'

'How did she die?' Trevor asked.

'Not one hundred per cent sure. All four victims were beaten. You'll get my PM reports when I've completed them and no guesses beforehand. But I can tell you that this victim and one other had multiple fractures to their skulls, long bones and ribs. Another, four fractures to his skull.'

'Were they dead when they were beaten?'

'Loss of blood and marrow stains suggests that the injuries were inflicted during life.'

'They must have screamed,' Peter was mesmerized by Gillian Pitcher's broken, blackened corpse. Pale bones protruded through her scorched and seared skin. Her face was untouched by fire, but mashed to a bloody pulp.

'Her hyoid bone was broken.'

'She was strangled?' Trevor had worked on cases where the only evidence of murder was a broken hyoid bone. The single bone in the body not connected to any other, a fracture was usually a sign of strangulation.

'Pressure was applied to her neck. But more than that I can't say until I get her back to the mortuary for a full PM and examination of her lungs.'

'Weapon?'

'We found a metal hoe on the attic stairs that matched the pattern of injuries on three of the four victims' skulls and bodies.'

'Odd thing to keep in a house without a garden,' Peter commented.

'There was a set of garden tools with similar metal handles in the derelict building where we found Larry Jones,' Reggie chipped in, 'but no hoe.'

'What were the other tools?' Trevor asked.

'I'm not sure.'

'I'll check,' Peter volunteered. 'A hoe's an odd choice of weapon.'

'Not your usual axe or blunt instrument,' Patrick concurred.

Trevor recalled Reggie's briefing in the station. 'Three bodies were found in the top floor studio?'

'I'll take you to them.' Patrick returned to the landing and climbed the stairs.

Alun Pitcher was just inside the attic to the left of the door. He was on his back, his arms bound by his side, his body burned to a greater degree than his wife's. His head had been smashed in, his nose and the front of his skull shattered.

Patrick indicated the injuries. 'He was hit by a larger object than the hoe.'

'Any idea what?' Trevor asked.

'Dents on his skull match projections on a bronze sculpture found beside the bed. I've sent it to the lab for further examination.'

'The sculpture?'

'A bronze copy of the Roman Dying Gaul. You'll have to step past this one to reach the other two.' Patrick walked around the bed.

'I suppose this room's been checked and nothing found that shouldn't be here,' Trevor asked.

'I do like working with a copper who's on the ball. It saves repetition. Be careful, the fire wasn't as bad as the cellar and kitchen but the floorboards are weak beneath that pile of charred linen and books. And stay clear of the bathroom. Team's working in there.'

Patrick's assistant Jen, appeared in the doorway. 'Good to see you, Trevor. Did you have to bring Peter?'

'I'm his page boy,' Peter joked.

'We're not promising good news, but someone took a shower in here after Lee and James Pitcher were beaten. We found traces of the victims' blood around the plughole. Heavily diluted, smudged by gloves but there.'

'No alien DNA?' Trevor asked.

'Unfortunately not, but we do have this.' She held up a white plastic bucket.

'Looks at though it should be in the Tate modern.' Peter gazed down into it. 'Sink traps?' he questioned.

'Someone showered in the cubicle, before wiping the surfaces with neat bleach. From the smudges we know latex gloves were worn. Afterwards, the sink, shower and bath traps were unscrewed and plunged into a bleach mix in this bucket. We've sieved the contents and found a few slivers of latex. We also found latex around the pipes below the trap. The teams are searching the sewage pipes in the hope of finding a hair or fingernail, so far they've drawn a blank. I'm guessing you've a lot of leg work on this one.' Jenny gave Peter a bright artificial smile. 'It couldn't happen to a more deserving officer.'

CHAPTER NINE

The corpse that had not yet been formally identified as James Pitcher's, was lying on the floor of the attic studio between the bathroom door and the bed. It was on its back; jaws open, teeth wide apart in a final, silent scream; legs straight, arms at its side.

The phrase "lying to attention" sprang to Trevor's mind although he knew the position was down to the body being wrapped and tied before rigor had set in. But there was pathos about the rigidity, as though the victim had been desperately trying to straighten up to meet eternity.

Had he or the other victims been conscious when they'd been parcelled? Had they known their killer intended to burn them? Had the last emotion to register been terror?

Trevor stepped closer, crouched, and examined the charred pattern of twisted string, visible above the fine coating of ash that covered the blackened skeletal frame.

'Careful, it'll crumble if you touch it.' Patrick warned.

Trevor rose and moved away from the corpse.

'I've injected the string with glue, but it'll take a couple more doses to hold the ashes. We ran out of adhesive this morning after strengthening the one downstairs. I've sent for more but it's going to take care and skill to get all four corpses, to the mortuary without damaging them further. That's far enough,' Patrick snapped at Reggie when she stepped too close. 'I don't want currents of air blowing around.

You can never be sure what they'll carry. Jen?' He shouted to his assistant who'd returned to the bathroom. 'Chase up the glue?'

She stuck her head around the door. 'No point, Boss. They've been told we need it urgently. They'll bring it as quickly as they can.'

'Where's the last corpse?' Trevor asked.

'The other side of the bed. Watch where you step and move slowly.' Patrick ordered.

Trevor crept around the bed and stared down at the remains of the fourth member of the Pitcher family. Like the other two men, the corpse was little more than a collection of blackened charcoal bones in a scorched compote of tissue too badly burned to make out distinguishing marks. If Patrick hadn't told him the sex, he wouldn't have been able to distinguish it as a man. Not for the first time, he envied Patrick his objectivity. But then, he'd never met a pathologist who hadn't looked on human remains as anything more than a collection of inanimate objects.

Fuzzy charred remnants of hair clung to the splintered top and sides of the skull. Trevor averted his gaze from the shattered eye sockets that appeared to be staring blankly upwards. He tried to picture the man. Just over four days ago this carbon shell had been a healthy being. Happy – depressed – busy – indolent – it didn't matter. Like him – he'd been alive. Breathing, thinking, capable of feeling pleasure and pain.

A tidal wave of rage welled within him. Anger that four people had been robbed of their lives. No one had the right to steal the life of another …

'Seen all you want? Or would you rather continue philosophising?' Patrick's question shattered and scattered Trevor's thoughts.

The comment hit home. Philosophy had no place in a murder inquiry. 'For now. You doing the PMs today?'

'I'm a genius, not superman,' Patrick said drily. 'It'll take us the next couple of hours to stabilise these ready for moving. Plus, I've worked twenty-four of the last thirty-six hours so I'm creased. I need to be on the ball for a PM And four in succession will tax even my powers of concentration. I'll start first thing tomorrow. But I won't promise to finish one let alone two in a day. Especially that one ...'

'You know how it is ...'

'Too well,' Patrick complained. 'You want the results yesterday. Sorry, I'm human. The minute I've packed these off to the mortuary and supervised their arrival, I'm for a hot shower and, one, maybe two, very large malt whiskies. If I've any energy left after dinner I'll look through the scene of crime photographs. If anything strikes me I'll give you a ring.'

'Crime of passion springs to mind.'

Trevor turned. Peter was looking over his shoulder.

'Those fractures on the skull, ribcage and long bones aren't just down to the heat are they?' Peter asked Patrick.

'No. They're down to sharp blows with a metal hoe.' Patrick looked into the bathroom. 'Aren't you finished in there yet, Jen?'

'Almost.' She walked out and dropped a clear

plastic envelope into an evidence box. Two other boxes, both full, stood next to it.

'Something?' Trevor eyed the boxes.

'You know how it is.' She looked back into the bathroom. 'You can always find an item that warrants further analysis.'

'For instance?' Peter pressed.

'Fragments of soap, plastic bottles, nail scissors, hairbrush, could harbour a trace of DNA ...'

'Prints?' Trevor pressed.

'Nothing's showed so far. But there're other techniques we can try. Just don't get your hopes up.'

'That's what I love about scientists. At best things may be "possible". A "probable" is grounds for optimism and celebration. Nothing is ever hopeful or finite,' Peter grumbled.

'It's possible but not probable that you're human, Sergeant Collins.' Jen flicked through the rest of the contents of the box marked BATHROOM. 'A few hairs, but as they're the same colour as the ones in the hairbrush they're probably the victim's. I've bagged a comb, toiletries, toilet roll, razor, cologne, deodorant, moisturiser ... basically if it wasn't cemented to the floor, it's in here, but don't go expecting us to pull out any evidence from here that will stand up in a courtroom.'

'What did you find in the bedroom?' Trevor noticed a box marked ATTIC.

'Quite a bit given that some areas were smoked not burned. Tissues, clothes, used condoms – and before you ask, too burned to hold any DNA. Remains of wrapped condoms, alarm clock, mobile phone, oh and,' she waved a bag under Peter's nose.

'Your low-life, relatives, Sergeant Collins. Bed bugs.'

'Bed bugs! Didn't they die out in the last century?' Peter glanced around warily and Jen laughed.

'Tenacious little sods are making a comeback. Check your clothes carefully every time you travel on public transport. Best to strip off and shower before entering your house.'

'In the garden, so I can give my neighbours a thrill?' Peter suggested.

'Only if they want to look and I can't see many wanting to do that. But be warned, they're expert hitchhikers.'

'Are those alive?' Trevor asked.

'Smoked and roasted but given their superbug ability to survive all attempts to exterminate them, I wouldn't be surprised if we find a couple of live ones cowering in a secluded nook or cranny,' Jen slipped the bag back into the box.

Patrick looked at Trevor above his mask. 'I know what you're thinking.'

'Is it possible?'

'In theory.'

'Is this conversation private, or can anyone join in?' Peter demanded irritably.

An officer appeared at the top of the stairs and handed Patrick a box. 'Quick drying adhesive and sterile syringes.'

'Right, Jen, stop flirting with Peter and start working.' Patrick opened the box. 'Body bags?' he asked the officer.

'On their way. We haven't a bloody conveyor belt

to the mortuary out there.'

'Don't you *love* working in the sticks?' Patrick winked at Trevor.

'We'll leave you and your team to it,' Trevor replied diplomatically.

'Right minions, get to work and fast,' Patrick commanded. 'If you're staying at the pub we'll see you there tonight, Trevor.'

'If not, see you at the mortuary tomorrow.'

'Something, I'm so-o looking forward to,' Peter blew Jen a kiss. 'Are we staying at the pub?' he asked Reggie as they made their way down the stairs to the bedroom level.

'I asked Inspector March to find you somewhere that isn't booked for the next couple of months. There's a lot of holiday accommodation in this town. I thought you wouldn't want to move on every few days.'

'We're going to be here a couple of months!' Peter glared at Trevor.

'However long or short our stay we won't want the hassle of moving every couple of days.' Trevor stepped on to the fire escape from the bedroom balcony. 'You said Larry Jones was still in the station?' he asked Reggie.

'At present. He'll probably be moved to a secure unit after the hearing in the magistrates' court tomorrow.'

'Can I interview him?'

'We've interviewed him already,' Reggie said. 'You can watch the recording.'

Trevor took a few moments to look down at the river. 'I'll watch it. But I'd still like to talk to him myself.'

'I'll contact his solicitor to check she has no objection.'

Trevor started the long descent to the ground. Despite the tragedy he'd witnessed in the building he had to suppress a smile when he saw Peter staring resolutely at the handrail, not the panoramic view when he followed him down.

Trevor and Peter sat beside Reggie in the viewing room and watched the figure on screen. Larry Jones looked younger than Trevor'd expected from his police record. If he'd seen him in the street he would have put him in his late teens not the twenty-seven on his last charge sheet. He was whippet-thin, with broken teeth and a metallic rash of eyebrow, ear, nose, cheek, upper and lower lip piercings. His head was shaved; the crown tattooed with a swastika; his forehead with a dotted line and the legend "TEAR HERE". His police-issue blue paper boiler suit was stained with tea and tomato sauce, his face smudged with dirt. There were dark circles beneath his sunken eyes and he looked as though he hadn't slept in days.

'Baby thug dreaming of growing up into a hard case.' Peter kept his gaze fixed on the screen as he pushed a cigar into his mouth.

'His mother's twice his size, twice as ugly and has twice as many tattoos.' Frank Howell set a tray of tea and biscuits on Reggie's desk.

'Father?' Peter asked.

'God might know, doubt his mother does. There are eight Jones brothers and two sisters. To quote the Welsh vernacular, "all rough as a dog's ..."' Frank glanced at Reggie, '"rear end; tough as dried shit and twice as nasty."' He handed the mugs of tea around. Trevor noticed the sergeant served Reggie before him and Peter. A reminder that however the investigation ended, when it closed, he and Peter would return to their station, leaving Reggie to run her patch, recommend promotions and make or break careers.

He turned back to the screen and noticed Larry's hands clasped on the table in front of him. 'His nails and hands are clean. You allowed him to wash before questioning?'

Reggie hit the pause button on the machine. 'I told you, I had his hands and feet bagged. Forensic scraped his skin, finger and toe nails and took his shoes and socks. Samples were taken during a full body search. Afterwards we allowed him to shower.'

'If we hadn't he would have stunk out the interview room, sir,' Frank interposed.

Peter leaned towards the screen when the questioning began. The officer conducting the interview was attractive; slim, blonde with even features and soft grey eyes that occasionally hardened to steel.

After ten minutes Peter removed the cigar from his mouth. 'Your Inspector is good. Doesn't let the pressure up for a minute.'

'I'm sure Inspector March will be delighted to get a commendation from you, Sergeant Collins,' Reggie responded.

Trevor noticed Peter was watching the interviewing officer more closely than Larry Jones and wondered if Daisy's influence would ever curb his wandering eye.

They watched intently until Carol pronounced the interview at an end. The screen went blank and Reggie switched off the machine.

'Still want to interview Larry Jones, Inspector Joseph?'

'First I need to talk to the officer who found and arrested Larry Jones in the derelict building at the Pitcher house. I'd also like to talk to Inspector March about her thoughts on that interview.'

'Fire Officers discovered Larry Jones. Sergeant Howell,' Reggie indicated Frank, who was stacking their tea cups on a tray, 'was the first officer on the scene.'

'Coincidence?' Trevor asked him.

'A fireman alerted me that a man had been found. Constable Murphy and I responded.'

'I arrived a few minutes after Sergeant Howell and Constable Murphy, called in suited forensic officers, and oversaw the bagging and initial search of Larry Jones. I witnessed the officers remove the jewellery from the pocket of Larry Jones's jacket. And, as I told you earlier and you heard Inspector March say, the only prints found on the bag containing the jewellery were Larry Jones's.'

'Smudges?' Trevor checked.

'Yes,' Reggie conceded. 'The bag and the pieces had been handled by someone wearing gloves. But that someone could have been Lee Pitcher. Michael Pitcher said his brother was fanatical about cleanliness when it came to antique pieces. He always wore latex gloves lest the perspiration from his skin damage or stain delicate surfaces.'

'So the gloves were already in the house?'

125

'Michael said Lee always kept a box in his room.'

There was a knock at the door. It opened in response to Reggie's "Enter."

Carol March walked in. Peter looked up; she made no attempt to introduce herself.

'Thought you should see this right away, Super.' She handed Reggie a sheet of paper.

Reggie read it. 'When did this come in?'

'The hospital telephoned the news half an hour ago. When I saw the record of the call, I rang back and asked to speak to a doctor. Those are the notes I made on our conversation.'

Reggie turned to Trevor. 'You can forget about interviewing Michael Pitcher any time soon, Inspector Joseph. He was discharged from hospital at midday. His girlfriend drove him to her parents' house. While she was making lunch, he drank a bottle of vodka, swallowed a pack of paracetamol and jumped into the river behind the house. She dragged him out and called the paramedics. They pumped his stomach. He'll live, but he's been admitted to the local psychiatric hospital.'

'Don't tell me,' Peter mocked. 'Medical opinion is, "he's too unstable to be interviewed".'

'The boy's lost his entire family,' Frank snapped.

'Given his present place of abode, "convenient" is the word that springs to mind,' Peter countered.

'Michael Pitcher was at his girlfriend's, miles away from Main Street when the fire broke out.' Frank had softened his tone but Trevor saw anger in his eyes.

'How exactly do we know that?' Peter challenged.

Trevor flashed his colleague a warning look but

for reasons best known to himself Peter had chosen to needle Frank.

'I was the first police officer at the scene. The landlord of the Angel Hotel was already in the Pitcher's yard …'

'What time was that?' Trevor broke in.

'Three twelve.'

'Exactly?'

'Within a minute or two. I took the call myself from the emergency services at three minutes past three. I asked Jim Murphy who was in the station with me to contact officers both on and off duty and order them to Main Street. I ran to the Pitcher's yard because I'd been told the fire was at the back of the house. The fire tender arrived a couple of minutes after me. The officers ordered Tim Pryce and myself to Main Street for our own safety.'

'The fire was reported to the emergency services when?' Trevor looked from Frank to Reggie.

'The first call from the fisherman was logged by the emergency services at 3 a.m.,' Reggie answered. 'A second was made by Tim Pryce the landlord of the Angel at two minutes past three.'

'Was the fire visible from the Angel?' Trevor asked.

'The back of the building, yes. The Angel's yard adjoins the Pitchers'. The fire wasn't visible in Main Street when I arrived. I could smell burning when I left my car but there wasn't any smoke in the street, not then.' Frank divulged. 'Tim Pryce was in the Pitchers' yard watching the fire escape, hoping to see survivors. He said he'd been woken shortly after three o'clock by an explosion. He'd looked out of his

127

bedroom window and seen flames shooting from the second floor of the Pitchers' house.'

Trevor frowned. 'The Angel pub is next door but one to the Pitchers' house.'

'The back overlooks the Pitcher's yard. Alun Pitcher bought the accountant's yard from them twenty or more years ago because he needed more space to park his cars and vans.'

'Is Tim Pryce's bedroom at the back?'

'I presume it is, otherwise he wouldn't have seen the fire.'

Trevor ignored Peter who was trying to catch his eye. 'To return to Michael Pitcher. Who sent for him after the fire was reported?'

'I did,' Frank volunteered. 'Tim Pryce told me he'd seen Michael and Alison drive off around midnight. At that stage none of the services knew how many people were in the Pitchers' house or the location of the family bedrooms. It's a large house.'

'We noticed,' Peter chipped in, aware just how much he was irritating Frank.

'I telephoned a neighbour of Alison – that's Michael's girlfriend – and asked him to drive Michael into town. Henry Clarke – he's an ENT consultant, went over there, woke Michael and Alison and brought them in.'

'How far is it from Main Street to Michael's girlfriend's house?' Trevor asked.

'At night, on empty roads, no more than twenty minutes, twenty-five if you stick to the speed limit,' Carol said.

'Is the timeline finished?' Trevor asked.

'It's still being linked to witness statements,'

Carol told him, 'but I can get you one as far as it's been updated.'

'Thank you.'

Carol left the office. She returned a few minutes later with a sheaf of papers. She handed one to Trevor and one to Reggie.

'We have to share,' Peter complained.

'They're still being processed. I thought you would like the final version when it's ready.' Carol pulled up a chair and sat down.

'Why didn't you send a police car to pick up Michael Pitcher?' Trevor asked Frank.

'All available officers were clearing and securing Main Street,' he explained. 'We haven't huge resources like you in the city. We had neither officers nor car to spare.'

'You do like to improvise in the sticks,' Peter goaded.

'As I said Henry Clarke is a consultant …'

'And that makes him honest?' Peter faced Frank. 'Haven't you heard of Harold Shipman?'

Trevor interrupted. 'To return to Michael Pitcher. I take it he's intelligent and educated.'

'It's no secret that patients in a psychiatric hospital can't be interviewed without their doctor's consent and it's also common knowledge that it doesn't take much of an actor to fake mental illness,' Peter said.

Reggie finally allowed her anger to surface. 'Are you making an observation from personal experience, Sergeant Collins?'

'Professional experience, Superintendent Moore. Forgive my cynicism,' Peter didn't sound in the least apologetic. But when you've been in the job as long as I have, it's difficult to think the best of people – especially the recently bereaved who stand to gain from murder. I take it he is heir to the family's considerable estate and, no doubt, insurance policies?'

CHAPTER TEN

Trevor broke the silence. 'Do we know anything about Michael Pitcher's relationship with his parents?'

'They were close. The whole family were,' Carol March answered briefly.

'You knew the Pitchers?' Trevor waited for Carol's response. She was attractive, well groomed and, like her boss, projected a professional image. He sensed it would be difficult to get to know the woman behind the uniform.

'Everyone in the town does – did.' Outwardly Carol remained cool and composed, but Trevor sensed she was tense. Stress or grief?

'You knew them socially?' he asked.

'I keep telling you, practically everyone in this town knows everyone else,' Reggie reminded Trevor tersely.

'There's a difference between being aware of someone and knowing them socially,' Trevor replied.

'Mrs Pitcher and my mother were at school together,' Carol divulged. 'They are – were members of the local amateur dramatic group. Families and friends are expected to support the productions. I saw the boys around town as well as in the theatre. When I returned here about seven years ago, the first place I went to look for furniture was Alun Pitcher's auction rooms. I told James what I wanted. He tracked down some original Art Deco pieces and restored them for me at a reasonable price.'

'You haven't always lived here?' Trevor checked.

'I grew up here but left to pursue a career elsewhere. When my professional and personal life didn't develop the way I'd hoped. I returned and joined the force.'

'Were the Pitchers too close?' Peter questioned.

Frank bristled. 'What are you are insinuating, Sergeant Collins?'

'Don't you think it's odd? Three adult sons, all living at home. I couldn't wait to get away from my parents. Left home at seventeen …'

'No doubt your parents were glad to get shot of you,' Frank broke in.

Reggie gave Frank a warning look at the same time Trevor fired one Peter's way.

'The Pitchers' adapted their house to accommodate the family's needs. They all had private space,' Carol observed. 'When Lee converted the attic into a studio flat six years ago, they turned his old bedroom into a second lounge so the boys could entertain their friends away from their parents.'

'You went there?' Peter filched his cigars from his pocket.

'Occasionally,' she faced him coolly almost daring him to probe deeper.

Peter accepted the challenge. 'To visit which one of the Pitcher boys?'

'Generally as one of a group,' she answered tersely, clearly resenting the personal nature of Peter's questions. 'This town offers an excellent social life for those who chose to participate. There's something on almost every night of the week.'

'Like what?' Trevor asked.

'Concerts, amateur and professional theatre

productions; an art house cinema is attached to the professional theatre and we've a multiplex a few miles away. There are excellent restaurants in and around town. And that's without the clubs, the Rotary, WI, Arts society, Round Table, Charitable committees …'

'You sound like an advertisement for Wales. "For a good social life move west",' Peter mocked.

'I wouldn't live in rural Wales if I didn't believe the quality of life superior to that offered by most cities and towns in the UK, Sergeant Collins,' Carol answered.

'What can you tell me about Michael Pitcher?' Trevor asked Carol.

'He graduated in fine arts a couple of months ago. But he's been cleaning and repairing paintings for his father since he was in Tertiary College. When he went to Art College he asked some of the pub landlords and Dr Edwards if he could hang his paintings on their walls. As a result he established a lucrative sideline in portraits of people, pets, houses and local landscapes.'

'I know what you're thinking, Inspector Joseph. But I knew the Pitchers,' Frank interposed. 'Michael was devoted to his parents and brothers. He can't bear the thought of what's happened to them and that's the only reason he's had a breakdown. We've the right man in custody and we need look no further.'

'There'll be no conviction without evidence and aside from the jewellery found in Larry Jones's pockets which he could have stolen before the fire was set – or picked up outside the house after it had been discarded by a thief …'

'Or been planted on him,' Peter interrupted Trevor.

'Are you suggesting …'

'Not suggesting, just thinking out loud,' Peter parried Frank's glare.

Trevor glanced at his watch. 'As there's no chance of interviewing Michael Pitcher at present, can we discuss your interview with Larry Jones, Inspector March?'

'You've seen the recording?'

'Yes.'

Reggie broke the impasse between Frank and Peter. 'Sergeant, check on forensics' progress at the Pitcher house?'

'Yes, Super.' Resentful at being dismissed Frank picked up the tray of teacups and rattled and clunked his way out of the room.

Trevor waited until Frank closed the door. 'Have you had occasion to interview Larry Jones before yesterday, Inspector March?'

'Several times when I was a constable and again after my promotion to sergeant but I'd have to check the records to find out exactly how often.'

'Have you known him to lie?'

'Often and brazenly.'

'Did you believe him when he insisted he hadn't seen the emerald and diamond jewellery found in his pocket before it was shown to him?'

'No, but I accept it's possible he was so drunk he can't remember how he came to be in possession of it,' she said cautiously.

'Given your previous knowledge of the suspect do

134

you believe him capable of arson and murder?'

Carol hesitated. 'Given Larry Jones's previous convictions for GBH, most of which were down to consumption of alcohol or illegal substances, he's proved himself capable of mindless violence. If no one was around to check his behaviour, yes, I believe him capable of murder. He has no record of arson that I'm aware of.'

'So you think he did murder the Pitchers?'

'In my *opinion*,' Carol laid stress on the last word, 'he is capable of murder. But I have a few problems equating the murder of Pitchers with Larry's movements that night.'

'Such as?' Trevor sat back in his chair.'

'All four Pitchers were fit healthy people, especially the two sons and Alun. They were used to lifting and moving heavy furniture. James and Lee Pitcher exercised frequently at the gym. I've seen them there myself. The pathologist confirmed there are marks on all the victims that suggest they were beaten, if not to death, then severely before death. A person who is being assaulted cries out in pain or for help. The noise would have brought the other occupants of the house running to the scene. And, even if the one who was being attacked had been taken by surprise and was too badly injured to fight back, the other three would have had no problem overpowering Larry. Three against one are good odds. Especially if the one is drunk.'

'Three of the bodies were in the attic,' Trevor reminded her.

'The strongest three of the four. I don't believe Larry could have beaten two let alone three simultaneously. If he was beating one, surely the others would have overcome him. And, even without the cries, the sound of a single body – let alone three – falling to the floor would have alerted Gillian Pitcher who was almost certainly in the master bedroom on the floor below.'

'The bodies were trussed up,' Peter mused.

'You think they entered attic one at a time so he could tie them up individually and gag them so they couldn't alert the others?'

'We have to consider all possibilities.' Peter raised his eyes to Carol's. She looked away.

'A drunk would have difficulty moving around quietly.' Trevor played devil's advocate. 'Was Larry breathalysed?' Trevor asked Reggie.

'When we got him to the station,' Reggie answered. 'He had 90 micrograms of alcohol to 100 millilitres of breath.'

'So, basically he wasn't in any state to plan the perfect crime or tiptoe silently around the Pitcher house,' Peter contributed.

'Are you saying you don't think Larry Jones acted alone?' Trevor aimed his question at Carol but looked to Reggie.

'Do you think Larry Jones was the fall guy for an accomplice, Inspector Joseph?' Carol showed her training by answering his question with one of her own.

'You know the Pitchers, the town and Larry Jones. I don't, which is why I am interested in your opinion.'

'If it's opinions you want and not hard facts, I have a few more,' Carol added. 'The landlord of the

Angel, Tim Pryce and Ken Lloyd, the fisherman, stated that Larry Jones was comatose at midnight. If Larry did manage to break in and kill all four Pitchers, was he capable of exercising sufficient rational thought to cover his tracks only three hours later? And, did he have the knowledge needed to destroy all the physical evidence linking him to the crime? The one thing all the technicians working in the Pitcher house agree on; is that the perpetrator or perpetrators did a first-class job of scouring the crime scene. Take the sink traps. It would take a steady hand to unscrew those. Would a drunk have a steady hand?'

'That's a valid observation.' If Trevor had already thought of it, he gave no indication. 'Superintendent Moore?'

'I'll wait until all the forensic reports come in before venturing an opinion.' She read her watch. 'It's the tail end of a long day and I doubt tomorrow is going to be any shorter. I suggest we adjourn until first thing in the morning when hopefully we'll be in possession of some new evidence. Do you know if accommodation has been found for Trevor and Peter, Carol?'

'Yes. There's been a glut of cancellations in the town's hotels, guesthouses and holiday cottages.'

'I wonder why,' Peter stared at the ceiling.

'Tim Pryce said they could have one of the stable cottages in his yard for a month, or longer if needed.'

'We won't be needing it that long,' Peter commented acidly.

'They are reasonably comfortable,' Carol assured Trevor, 'with two en suite double bedrooms, kitchen and sitting room.'

'Fine, as long as we're not expected to do our own cooking as well as work on the case.' Peter left his chair.

'You can eat in the pub or Tim will send food in if you prefer.' Carol also rose to her feet. 'The pathologist and most of the people from the outside forensic teams are also staying at the Angel.'

'Great, we get to eat and sleep this case nights as well as days,' Peter said.

'You did say Larry Jones was still here?' Trevor checked with Reggie.

'In the cells, yes,' Reggie informed him.

'I'd be grateful if you'd ask his solicitor if I can talk to him either before or after he appears before the magistrate tomorrow.'

'Judy Howell is his solicitor. She'll want to be present,' Reggie warned.

'I assumed she would,' Trevor replied.

'Is this the cottage Goldilocks broke into or the one obsessive compulsive Snow White cleaned when the dwarves were busy mining? No, don't tell me, I've just hit my head on one of the damned beams, so it must have been the dwarves.' Peter dropped his bags and stretched out on the sofa in the living room.

Trevor looked around. 'We could do with a couple more inches clearance on the ceiling.'

'Short people the Welsh.' Peter rubbed his head.

Trevor went into the kitchen. 'At least this is full height. It's a fully fitted modern extension. Oven, microwave, fridge, freezer ...'

'If it's all the same to you, I'd prefer to live with

my love than set up home with you.' Peter interrupted.

'If we're here any length of time, the girls could come down and stay for a few days.'

'That wouldn't be a bad idea, if we were going to be here for any length of time.' Peter stretched his arms above his head and yawned.

'You've solved the case?' Trevor asked.

'I'm relying on you to do that.' Peter left the sofa, picked up his bags and headed up the stairs. 'Bloody swining bastard …'

'The ceiling on the stairs is low too,' Trevor called after him.

'Thank you very much for that information after I've discovered it.'

Trevor picked up his case and briefcase and followed Peter, but he was careful to duck. He found Peter staring through the open doors of both bedrooms.

'Have you ever seen so many Laura Ashley chintz frills out of a shop before?' Peter asked in disgust.

'You take the pink, I'll settle for blue.' Trevor walked past him into one of the rooms. He opened the door to the en suite bathroom. 'The good news is a power shower as well as bath.'

'With complimentary lavender- and rose-scented toiletries?' Peter suggested caustically.

Trevor examined the contents of a gingham-lined basket. 'Royal Jelly, actually and locally made aromatic pine candles.'

Peter leaned against the door. 'You can't seriously expect me to sleep in that room?'

'Why?'

'I'm allergic to pink roses.'

'The best way to deal with an allergy is to build immunity. Close the door, I'm about to phone, Lyn.'

Peter didn't attempt to move. 'Do you think Daisy will drive here and rescue me if I cry help?'

'No, she's a sensible lady. Give her my love and commiserations.'

'For having to live without me?' Peter suggested.

'For having to live with you.'

'You could have refused to bring me.'

'I need my official goader.'

'You accusing me …'

'As goader you have your uses. You've annoyed most of the locals already, and angry people make mistakes.'

Peter closed the door.

'A cottage, how lovely …'

'Don't get too excited, darling,' Trevor warned Lyn. 'I have a feeling this case is going be a difficult and time-consuming one.'

'So, even if we drive up you won't be able to spare Marty and me any time.'

'Give it a couple of days, and I'll be better able to gauge it. But if I put in for some leave, you could come up when we've wrapped the case. The countryside is pretty and the cottage comfortable, if not to Peter's taste.'

'What's wrong with it?'

'Low ceilings and girly furnishings.'

The sound of Lyn's laughter echoing down the line made Trevor even more homesick.

'Poor Peter.'

'Poor me, having to live with him. Is Daisy with you?'

'Coming round in an hour.'

'Have fun.'

'You too, darling. Marty and me miss and love you.'

'Me too.' Trevor ended the call, went into the bathroom, stripped off and stepped under the shower.

Half an hour later, he went downstairs. Peter had already foraged a bottle of malt and poured two measures.

'Saw Patrick and Jen when I picked this up in the pub. I said we'll eat with them in ten minutes.' Peter handed Trevor a glass.

'Since when do you volunteer for shop talk over dinner?'

'The way I see it, the sooner we get started the sooner we finish and go home.'

'How's Daisy?'

'Desolate at my absence.'

'Really?'

'Is she hell! She was waiting for a delivery of Indian takeaway when I called, preparing for a night of slushy weepy DVD's with your missus.'

'Nice to know they can survive without us.' Trevor sipped his whisky.

'You may think so, I don't.'

'If you don't mind, I'll stash this in the fridge until later.' Trevor carried his glass into the kitchen. 'I've eaten with Patrick before. It's not a good idea to drink beforehand.'

'Comes to something when the pathologists can

out-drink the coppers.' Peter emptied his glass in a single mouthful.

'I'll have the garlic mushrooms followed by the T-bone steak, rare. So rare the outside has just brushed against a hot frying pan,' Jen ordered. 'A vodka tonic to begin with and a bottle of Rioja with the food.'

'It's easy to see who you've been working with for the past year,' Trevor scanned the menu.

'You saying I don't give my staff time to read the menu, Trevor?' Patrick challenged. He barked his own order. 'Fricassee of liver in wine cream sauce with shiitake mushrooms.'

Trevor looked at the waitress and recognised her from that morning. He recalled the name Reggie had given her. 'Pamela George isn't it?'

'You've a good memory, or have you?' she added suspiciously. 'I don't remember telling you my name.'

'Beautiful girl like you, we made enquiries.' Peter eyed her breasts, shown off to full advantage in a blue silk top, even lower-cut than the red one she'd worn earlier.

'You're the coppers who are in one of the stable cottages, aren't you?'

'That's right, darling,' Peter winked at her. 'And mine's smoked salmon pate, with a T bone to follow with chips, and I don't want mine well done, I want it cremated.'

'I'll have the same.' Trevor closed the menu and set it aside.

'Pamela,' Tim Pryce bellowed at her through the open door as she scribbled on her notepad.

'It's all right, Tim. They're the coppers you've agreed to put up in one of the cottages.'

'That right?' Tim entered the dining room and walked over to the table. Patrick had chosen one in the corner of the room, well away from the passage and – as it was too early in the evening for most of the forensic technicians who had worked late and were still showering – private.

Trevor introduced himself and Peter. 'Inspector Trevor Joseph and Sergeant Peter Collins.'

'They brought police in to work on a local murder?' Tim managed to sound both incredulous and disgusted.

'These two officers are very experienced,' Patrick assured the landlord solemnly. 'In fact so experienced I have wondered if murderers follow them around to test their skills.'

Tim's face darkened. 'The Pitchers were close friends of mine …'

'No one meant any disrespect, sir. What happened to Mr and Mrs Pitcher and their sons is an appalling tragedy.' Trevor left the table and pulled out an empty chair. 'We can do with all the assistance we can get to apprehend whoever killed them. If you knew the Pitchers, you could help us with our enquiries. Please, join us?'

Mollified, Tim hesitated. 'Later perhaps. I've a bar to run.' He left them.

Pamela finished taking Trevor and Patrick's order and disappeared in the direction of the kitchens.

'Dinner rules,' Patrick sipped a whisky he'd brought into the room with him. 'No pre-guessing the outcomes of the PMs, no pre-emptive ideas, no shop

143

talk …'

'The last thing Trevor and I want is to be stuck here, in the Welsh sticks for weeks on end, so how about a few forensic facts? Is the house really as clean as everyone's telling us?' Peter asked.

'From what I've heard, the only fingerprints and DNA traces found so far, not that there's many, belong to family, and people who had reason to visit the house.'

'But we've found a couple more things that may interest you, Inspector Joseph, Sergeant Collins.' Ted Gant walked into the dining room with Terri Langstone in time to catch the tail end of the conversation. 'May we join you?'

'Please do.' Trevor rose and lifted a chair out from under the table for Terri.

Peter lifted his glass to Ted. 'Please, tell all.'

CHAPTER ELEVEN

'We found the remains of a battery wall clock in the cellar,' Terri sat opposite Patrick. 'Burned, but the face was comparatively intact. The hands had stopped at two fifty seven.'

'Which means? Peter demanded impatiently.

'The fire in the cellar was set around the same time as the one in the attic. Apart from the witness who saw it blazing just before three, a mechanical alarm clock was piled on top of a bonfire of books and clothes in the studio flat. It had stopped at two fifty three.' Jen sat back in her chair so Pamela could set her garlic mushrooms in front of her.

'What about the kitchen?' Trevor asked.

'The only time we have for that is when the flames were spotted by a witness at two fifty five. The fire was too intense for the granite worktops to survive, so there's little hope of finding anything left of a clock. That's if there was one besides the ones on the stove and microwave which have both disintegrated.' Jen speared a mushroom with her fork and dipped it into a pot of garlic sauce.

'Can you estimate the exact times the three fires were lit on the different floors?' Peter asked.

'Certainly, as soon as you buy us a reliable crystal ball that can look into the past,' Jen nibbled the mushroom.

'Point me to the shop,' Peter quipped.

'If all the fires were set alight by one person he must have been nimble to get them going so close to one another four storeys apart,' Patrick chipped in.

'Nimbler than a thug with the alcohol level of Larry's,' Peter observed.

'Thank you.' Trevor took his and Peter's smoked salmon pates from Pamela.

Ted waited until Pamela had served him, Patrick and Terri the seafood cocktails they'd ordered in the bar and left. 'There weren't three separate fires, there were nineteen, all started in different rooms and on different floors. The only floor that didn't have a fire lit on it was the ground floor that housed the office suite. All the damage between the attic and kitchen floor was caused by the fires below and above.'

'Was anything flammable thrown around the attic?' Trevor asked.

'No traces of flammable liquids just combustibles heaped together,' Jennifer replied. 'Clothing, books, cologne, after shave, deodorant cans … mechanical alarm clock …'

'It takes time to build bonfires. I take it the arsonist or arsonist used whatever was at hand,' Peter spread his pate on toast.

'Except in the cellar. There's no evidence to suggest heaping of combustibles,' Ted ferreted around in his seafood cocktail and extracted a king prawn. 'Only traces of petrol in glass bottles and Alun Pitcher's employees insist he didn't store any there. So we're back to the petrol bomb theory.'

'Patrick …'

'I warned you Trevor, no guesses. You want hard facts you can have them after I've done the PMs.'

'This isn't a PM question. The bodies were wrapped in brown paper and string before they were burned?'

146

'You saw them.' Patrick said impatiently.

'Was anything poured on them?'

Patrick nodded. 'Why do you think I've spent two days examining the bodies in situ?'

'To piss us off,' Peter suggested.

'Another remark like that, Sergeant, and I may leave them there for another week.'

'What was used?' Trevor ignored Peter and wished Patrick would.

'Alcohol.'

'A lot?'

'It's difficult to estimate but I'd say enough to get a fire going. Don't quote me but possibly a bottle of brandy on each,' Patrick answered.

'Were the Pitchers drinkers?' Trevor asked.

'We found the remains of a number of bottles in the kitchen. There was also a well stocked cocktail cabinet in the living room,' Terri answered. 'You'll get our reports in due course.'

'In the meantime we sit and twiddle our thumbs,' Peter complained.

'Have you been on a police course that taught you to do that clockwise as well as anti-clockwise?' Jen enquired in a patronising tone.

'Forget twiddling. We'll be too busy interviewing witnesses, and checking statements,' Trevor corrected Peter. 'Starting first thing tomorrow morning.'

'What I don't get,' Patrick contemplated a shrimp on the end of his fork, 'is no one has a bad word to say about any one of the Pitchers. Father, a well liked businessman, mother, a tireless charity worker, good looking young sons, bent on making their own way in the world.'

147

'Some people are good,' Jen murmured. 'It's just that we don't generally meet them in our line of work except as victims.'

'Another month and the boys wouldn't have been in the house,' Ted Gant said. 'The three of them had just closed on a deal to buy an old rectory. They intended to move in together and convert it into flats.'

'How do you know that?' Trevor asked.

'Local priest. He came round to pray for their souls. The Catholic church is at the end of the street next to the opening to the back lane.'

'Were the Pitchers Catholic?' Peter asked.

'Not that I'm aware of.' Ted finished the seafood in his cocktail and pushed the salad base away.

'Did you find out anything else from the priest?' Trevor asked Ted.

'No. He prayed for the Pitchers when I told him they were still in the house. That's when he told me that the boys were hoping to move out at the end of the month. He mentioned he'd frequently enjoyed Alun's hospitality and whisky and the Pitchers more or less kept open house and had a large circle of friends who called on them at all hours.'

'That coupled with the absence of an obvious break-in suggests they knew their killer,' Patrick commented.

'Which rules out the man in custody,' Ted said thoughtfully. 'If they knew anything about Larry Jones they wouldn't have allowed him into their house.'

Peter made room on the table when Pam entered with a tray of drinks 'As all Trevor and I've had from the locals since we've arrived is "everyone here

148

knows everyone else in the town" it stands to reason the Pitchers knew their killer unless he parachuted in. As to whether knowing everyone in town, is a good or bad thing, I defer to those with experience of a commune-style lifestyle. What do you say, Pam?'

'It depends on whether or not you have secrets or bad habits you want to hide.' Pam set bottles of wine on the table and pints of beer in front of Trevor, Patrick and Peter, adding a whisky chaser to Patrick's place setting.

'I'll give you a hand with these,' Trevor offered when Pam cleared their starter dishes.

'There's no need.'

'I'd like a word with the landlord anyway.'

'We're in the middle of dinner, Trevor,' Peter prompted.

'I'll be back in a couple of minutes.' Trevor heaped the last of the cocktail dishes on Pamela's tray and picked it up, leaving the pate plates for her. He followed her down the passage.

'Tim doesn't allow guests or the public into the kitchen,' Pamela warned. 'I'll take the tray as soon as I've dumped these.'

When she returned, Trevor said, 'Do you remember telling us Alan Pitcher kept his more valuable stock in his cellar?'

'That's no secret,' she murmured guardedly.

'You also said something about the house he'd just cleared.'

She nodded. 'The Harvilles' place, the old rectory. Now they had money – the Harvilles. Old inherited wealth going back hundreds of years. The family lived in the castle until the 1940s when the war office requisitioned it. They never moved back. My gran used to clean for the Harvilles and she told me Mrs Harville insisted she'd never known what it was to be warm until she moved out of the castle and into the rectory. When they left the castle, the Harvilles took what they could fit into the rectory and sold the rest. They had beautiful paintings, sculptures and antiques. Mrs Harville was the last of the family. She went ga-ga, poor thing. There wasn't even a will. Her entire estate went to the crown. Shame really. Alun Pitcher was going to bill the auction of the rectory contents "the sale of the century" and it would have been. There aren't many families who have possessions dating back eight hundred years.'

Patrick succeeded in banning current "shop talk" from the dinner table. Instead he and Ted Gant regaled everyone with stories about cases they had worked on together and, separately. As an entertainer, Patrick outshone Ted; as the Irish inevitably do in less expansive company.

'… there we were, in this mortuary in the hills of central Ruritania. Rumour had it as an early design by the architect who built Stonehenge. Problem was; it had deteriorated over the centuries. The floor and walls were crumbling and we were up to our ankles in rubble and puddles from the leaking roof. "We" being the legendary Norman Robbins, me and a poor lamb of an attendant who looked as though he should be adding up sums in junior school, not laying out the dead. Poor child had never seen a body more than a week old, never mind an exhumation. Norman gave the gravediggers the order to drop the coffin next to the only slab, a piece of granite that had been left out in the rain since St Patrick had preached to the heathen English.'

'St Patrick was Welsh and the only preaching he did was to the heathen Irish.' Ted cut into a roast potato.

'So you English say, we Irish know better. Anyway ... Norman found a stretcher and gave the poor boy a hand to lift out the contents ...'

'Dead long?' Jenny splattered her plate and the tablecloth with blood when she cut into her steak.

'Fourteen months in a cheap pine coffin.' Patrick contemplated a piece of liver he was ferrying to his mouth.

'Embalmed?' Ted checked.

'No.'

'Ripe then?' Jenny carried on eating her raw steak.

'Very,' Patrick took a moment to chew his liver. 'This kid went ballistic when he saw the maggots. They were wriggling and squirming as maggots do when they sense freedom. He was yelling his head off about them fouling his nice clean mortuary. Norman spotted a can of paraffin in a corner. The Lord only knew what it was doing there; probably they used it to heat the place in winter. Norman told the boy to sprinkle it in a circle around the corpse and light it. Everyone knows that even after the fire dies down the maggots won't go beyond the limits of the circle.'

'Everyone?' Peter looked around. 'I didn't.'

'Now you do. That's the point of life, Peter, you live and learn.' Patrick winked at Trevor. 'By the time the boy'd finished his sprinkling, the maggots were off the slab, out of the coffin and looking for new territory to colonise. The boy must have thought that one of the places they were making for was him, although maggots only like dead meat … come to think it perhaps …'

'Get on with it, Patrick,' Jen played the long suffering colleague, although she had worked with Patrick for less than a year.

'The boy lit a match, dropped it. Pouff!' Patrick grinned, his dark, aquiline features appearing even more sardonic in the flickering candlelight. 'But the poor lamb had sprinkled the circle around himself. He was caught in the middle of the fire. He panicked and climbed on top of the corpse. And did he stink afterwards? Mother of God, even the rats ran when he approached.'

'And the corpse?' Ted's professional interest was aroused.

'Straightforward poisoning, all we needed was the stomach contents and they'd been taken out at the first PM. Found them in storage in a rusty old freezer. If someone had taken the trouble to look we needn't have bothered with the exhumation. It was the usual story of country life. Miserable, miserly old farmer, lusty young wife. Young wife preferred virile cowhand but wouldn't give up farm so she flavoured the farmer's stew with weed killer. Murders in rural areas are so predictable.'

It was past midnight when Trevor and Peter returned to their cottage.

'Does the thought of Patrick getting his hands on your corpse bother you?' Peter grabbed the whisky bottle and a clean glass before laying claim to the sofa.

'With luck he'll have retired before I go. I intend to live long enough to see my great grandchildren.'

'Trust you to be wishing your life away. I haven't even considered the impact a child will have on Daisy and me. Grandchildren! Marty's not even a year old.'

'He soon will be.' Trevor went to the fridge and retrieved his glass of whisky.

'I suppose there's no point in worrying about it. They're all the bloody same.'

'Who's all the same?' Trevor murmured absently.

'Pathologists. Have you ever known a sane one?'

When Trevor didn't answer, Peter picked up the whisky bottle. 'Top up?'

'No thanks.' Trevor opened the curtain and looked out of the window. The stables backed on to the lane that ran at the rear of Main Street, and he could see nothing beyond the stone wall.

'Any murdering arsonists out there?' Peter asked.

'They've long gone,' Trevor left the window and sat in an easy chair opposite Peter. 'The question is where?'

'My guess is to ground in the town.' Peter poured a generous measure of whisky into his glass.

'Then you don't think Larry Jones killed the Pitchers?'

'I'm not saying he didn't have anything to do with it but much as I dislike agreeing with the Snow Queen …'

'Inspector March?' Trevor interrupted.

'That's what they call her. Who did you think I was talking about?'

'Superintendent Moore,' Trevor suggested.

'Local station is full of bloody frigid women trying to grow balls. "Nanny knows best",' Peter mocked. 'Ice Drawers – that's Reggie's nickname – and Snow Queen who both talk to everyone as if they are two years old. But the Snow Queen made some valid, if completely bloody obvious, points. We need to find the motive. When we've the motive we'll be halfway to finding the killer.'

'And the jewellery in Larry Jones's pocket?'

'Given the state of him, I think Larry Jones was set up as the fall guy. What better way to stitch him up than plant jewellery on him. And if that was the case, given the value, I think we can discount robbery.'

'Unless the thief or thieves were after something even more valuable,' Trevor observed.

'What did the luscious Pamela tell you when you helped her with the dishes?'

'That the house Alun Pitcher recently emptied of valuable antiques belonged to a family called Harville and they owned artefacts dating back 800 years.'

Nursing his glass, Peter sprawled on the cushions. 'So, emptying houses is what dealers do.'

'The house was called Llwynon Rectory. The three Pitcher boys bought the place with the intention of turning into apartments.'

'Who sold it?'

'The crown. The last owner died intestate.'

'Given we're in Wales I'd lay a pound to a penny that somewhere along the line it's a fiddle that's plumped several bank accounts. Man like Alun Pitcher, lived here all his life, local businessman and antique dealer who does house clearances, probably hand in glove with all the estate agents, local council officers and whoever represents the crown and tax man in Wales. You know what they say "England's corrupt but,"' Peter paused and adopted an exaggerated Welsh accent, "'Wales is beyond corrupt".'

'Even if it was a fiddle I don't see where it fits in with the murders.' Trevor sipped his whisky.

'We don't know and probably will never know what was in Pitcher's cellar.' Peter held out the bottle.

'No thanks, I know your measures.'

'Yours are skimpy.' Peter thought for a moment. 'If someone was jealous and wanted the contents of the rectory for themselves …'

'They wouldn't have set fire to Alun Pitcher's cellar,' Trevor declared.

'They could have taken the valuables first.'

'No one heard or saw a van despite the number of people who seemed to be out and about in the early hours. The landlord of the Angel, the fisherman who reported the fire, Michael Pitcher, his girlfriend, the two constables …'

'The nosy neighbour and Larry Jones,' Peter broke in. 'What's your point?'

'Lot of people around.'

'Some people prefer to make trouble than lie peacefully in their beds. They enjoy annoying overworked constables who live in hope of a quiet shift.'

'I'm going for a stroll.' Trevor set his untouched whisky on the table.

'Now who's going wandering in the middle of the

night?'

'I'm not asking you to come.'

'I wouldn't if you begged me on bended knee. Once the PM and forensic reports come in we're going to be working all hours, day, night and then some. I'm for one more drink then bed.' Peter picked up the TV remote. 'Turn on the TV on your way out. I like to be reminded of life in the real world before I go to sleep.'

CHAPTER TWELVE

Trevor left the cottage and crossed the yard of the old coaching inn. He went to the archway that connected with Main Street, leaned against the wall and looked up and down the street. Lamps burned in the darkness, lights shone out from behind screened and curtained windows. A fox slunk out from an alleyway that ran beside one of the larger houses on the opposite side of the road. It headed swiftly down towards the bridge and the river. Music blared, muted by distance but still raucous and irritating. If Trevor'd had to make a guess he would have said it was the theme tune of one of the dumbed-down reality TV shows Lyn and he couldn't stand and swiftly switched off.

He looked up towards the Pitchers' house. The accountant's offices between the pub and the house would have been unoccupied on the night of the murders but there were lights on across the road in what appeared to be residential properties. Had one or more of the Pitchers screamed when they'd been attacked? Or had they all been overpowered and silenced before they could make a sound? If one of them had cried out why hadn't anyone reported hearing them?

The kitchen door of the pub opened behind him. Tim Pryce walked out. He dropped a bag of rubbish into one of the wheelie bins in the yard, closed it and joined Trevor. 'You're standing where we left Larry Jones that night. If I'd known then what I know now I would have killed the bastard.' There was venom in his voice.

'You're that certain he's guilty?'

'You buggers have arrested him.'

'Not for murder, only arson, handling stolen goods and breaking parole. And, it's innocent until proven guilty,' Trevor said flatly.

'Stupid bloody maxim where the Garth Estate Joneses are concerned. You've heard of the rotten apple? Well the whole bloody barrel of Larry's family are rotten; every single one of them and, to the core. It'd be a favour to society to drown them at birth.'

'Did you convert the old stables into cottages?' Trevor didn't have to hear any more about Larry Jones's family to picture them. There were families like them in every town and city in the country. It was easy for a less than scrupulous copper to pin all the crimes within a ten-mile radius on them. He'd rather not think about how many files had been closed by officers using the simple expedient of bribing a none-too-bright "Larry Jones" clone to sign a list of "past misdemeanours to be taken into consideration" with false promises of leniency in court.

'My predecessor converted the stables but he didn't go in for mod cons. Most of his customers were the outward bound, camping sort who regarded a roof as a luxury. The cottages didn't even have inside lavatories when I arrived. I built the kitchen and bathroom extensions. Do you have everything you need in yours?' he asked Trevor defensively.

'Apart from a few more inches of headroom in the bedrooms and living room.'

Tim smiled. 'They're fine for people five feet eight and under. Claustrophobic for anyone around five ten and uncomfortable for anyone over six foot. Problem is, the stables, like the pub, are listed buildings. I wanted to dig out the floors to gain a couple of inches, but the builder warned me the foundations might not take the disturbance.'

'You reported the fire, didn't you?'

'Within a minute or two of Ken's call.'

'Where were you when you saw it?'

'My private living quarters and I heard it before I saw it.' Tim eyed Trevor. 'I suppose you want to see my place?'

'Please,' Trevor answered. 'If only to check how overlooked the Pitchers' yard is. It would help to know what risks the killer took of being seen.'

'As we're both here now, may as well get it over with.' Tim opened the back door to the pub. 'I warn you, it's a route march from here, and the ceilings are even lower in places than the cottages.'

'I'm ducking already.' Trevor followed him inside.

Tim locked the outside door before leading the way through the kitchen into a passageway that ran at the back of the bar. They walked past a function room behind the dining room.

'That,' Tim pointed to his right, 'leads to the wing that has the letting rooms, all full thanks to your forensic people. Although of choice I would prefer the Pitchers to be alive and the rooms empty.' He indicated a stone archway to his left. 'This leads to the back of the building and my accommodation. The arch is reputed to be medieval so duck even lower.'

He opened a door and Trevor stooped before finding himself in a small paved open air courtyard. Sensor-activated lights flashed on, momentarily blinding him. When he recovered he saw a simple art deco, ironwork garden set, matching planters filled with white flowers – and only white flowers – and a stone staircase that led up to a door about four feet from the ground.

Tim ran up the steps and opened a door. Trevor followed him into a large stone-walled room, furnished with two four-seater brown leather sofas, oak coffee tables and a bookcase filled with leather-bound volumes. An oak shelving system held a TV and speaker system. The walls were covered with original pastels, oil paintings and sketches. Mainly portraits with a fair sprinkling of male and a few female nudes.

'Who's the artist?' Trevor asked.

'I dabble. Most of those are the work of friends.' An open plan staircase led up to a mezzanine. Tim walked up the stairs and beckoned Trevor forward.

Wooden framed chairs were grouped around French doors, behind them was a king size bed and a massive antique wardrobe.

'Nice place you have here,' Trevor complimented him.

'I converted this old barn and turned the owner's living accommodation into guest rooms when my daughter married. It'd be no good for a family but it suits me.'

'No thoughts of marrying again?'

'Running a pub that offers food and

accommodation leaves no time for a private life. But then I've never had much of one of those. I used to be in your line of business. My wife couldn't put up with the hours I worked.'

'That was hard on you.'

'Spoken like a happily married man,' Tim said drily.

'I wasn't always.'

'And I wasn't always alone. But there comes a time in life when you have to sort your priorities. I intend to make enough money to retire to the South of France and paint while I can still enjoy life and art.'

'And in the meantime you have little time for yourself,' Trevor guessed.

'Only what I manage to steal from the recommended eight hours. But, as you see, I've indulged myself by creating comfortable surroundings. In summer I sleep with the door open.' Tim slid the glass doors open to reveal iron railings. 'Architects call these Juliet balconies. I would have preferred to have built out but the town's planning committee wouldn't budge. The pub and its outbuildings have Grade Two listed status, which precludes changing the outer appearance. I only managed to update the cottages after the Welsh Tourist Board stepped in on my behalf.'

'I was surprised to see balconies on the back of the Pitcher house,' Trevor said.

Tim rubbed the side of his nose knowingly. 'Alun made a point of making friends with every councillor in town. When the planning application went in a few years ago, he listed all three balconies as extensions

161

to the fire escape. The planning committee conveniently ignored that every one was wide enough to hold tables and chairs.'

'The Pitchers might not have had a garden but they certainly made the best of the view from the back of the house. Did they sit out there often?'

'Not that I was here to watch them. But occasionally I saw Alun and Gillian out on the kitchen level late on a summer evening. The boys generally used the higher balconies when they had friends in.'

'Was that often?'

'I believe so. They were a sociable and well liked family. Sit down. Unless I've an early delivery in the morning, I usually relax here for half an hour or so when I've finished for the day.'

Trevor sat in a comfortable chair that had been positioned to give a fine view of the river. When he turned his head, he found he also had a comprehensive view of the Pitchers' yard. 'You said you were in bed when you heard the Pitchers window explode?'

'You've read my statement?' Tim questioned.

'I've glanced at most of the information that has come in.'

'I was asleep. The explosion woke me. I ran to the window, saw the flames, dialled 999, dressed and went out. Frank Howell arrived in the yard a couple of minutes after me. I could barely see him for smoke. It was blinding. But not so blinding you couldn't see the flames. The fire was blazing in the cellar, the kitchen and the two top floors where the family slept.'

'Did you see the fire in the cellar from this window?'

'I don't think I looked past the flames shooting out of the kitchen window when I telephoned the emergency services. I certainly saw it when I reached the yard. I couldn't miss it.'

'Did you speak to Frank?'

'We shouted at one another but I couldn't hear him above the breaking glass and roaring fire. I wanted to do something but the truth is, even at that stage I think both Frank and I realized it was hopeless to attempt to get near the house. When the fire tender turned up a minute or two later the officers ordered us around to the front of the house. I was angry because I wanted to stay and help, but even as I argued with the officers I knew there was no way I could do anything the firemen couldn't.'

'From what the technicians said, the fire took hold quickly. The fact they were brought under control relatively swiftly was down to the calls you and Ken made.'

'Little enough.' Tim shrugged. 'Frank and I went into Main Street hoping that Alun, Gill and the boys had escaped that way. Couple of minutes later Ken turned up.' Tim gave a grim smile. 'After reporting the fire, worried sick about Alun and the Pitcher family, he'd still remembered to pack his gear, bring his dog and his catch of fish. He had a plastic carrier bag full.' Tim clenched his fist impotently. 'What none of us knew at the time, was that it was already too bloody late. They were all probably dead.'

'We won't be sure until we get the PM reports. I'm sorry,' he sympathised. 'They appear to have been a nice family.'

Tim went to a drinks tray on the shelves. 'They were. I never drink in the bar, seen too many good landlords become alcoholics that way. But I always have a nightcap back here. Join me?'

'No, but thank you for the offer.'

'You're on duty?'

Trevor saw Tim watching him. He shook his head. 'No. This is an informal chat.'

'In that case, a small brandy won't hurt you.'

'As long as it's a small one,' Trevor replied. 'I had one after dinner, and that coupled with what I drank with my meal is usually my limit before a busy day. And, tomorrow will be busy.'

'The bodies were moved out of the house earlier weren't they?' Tim enquired.

'Yes.'

'The forensic teams expecting to finish soon?' Tim handed Trevor a brandy a quarter of the size of one of Peter's measures.

'You'd have to ask them.'

'I have. One of them mentioned he was hoping to check out at midday.'

'Then you know more than me.' Trevor changed the subject. 'You said you sit here in the evening after you close the pub.'

'When I'm not too tired.'

'The night of the fire?'

'No. After Ken left for the river I served one of the constables, Dai Smith, in the bar. He'd just come off shift, and wanted a pint and a chat about the nosy parker across the road.'

'Mrs May Williams.'

'You've done more than glance at my statement,' Tim eyed Trevor with new respect.

'How long did Constable Smith stay?'

'Twenty minutes, maybe half an hour. I wasn't watching the clock.'

'Do many constables drop into the bar after their shift?'

'Some do, some don't. Dai and another constable had answered a call to check on May's report of a disturbance. May heard Larry Jones shouting when I evicted him from the pub and phoned the police station to complain. Woman has nothing better to do than sit in her window overlooking Main Street day and night, and watch the comings and goings of everyone in town.'

'You find her irritating?'

'Very, especially when she telephones the police to complain about the noise my customers make when they leave. I think she'd like to see them tiptoe home in their socks. Not that it would make any difference to her whether they made a noise or not. Judging from the number of calls she makes to the police I don't think she sleeps.'

'What did you do after Constable Dai Smith left?'

'Locked up, checked the doors and windows, came up here, opened the window and went straight to bed. Without looking at the view or having a nightcap.'

'What time was that?'

'Ten past one.'

'You're very sure,' Trevor observed.

'I set the alarm because I was expecting a delivery from the brewery at six. As it happened the driver had to turn back. After the fire the police closed off all access to Main Street and the back lane for two days.'

'But you opened this window that night?'

'Yes. When the Pitchers' window exploded, the noise was shattering. I thought a bomb had gone off in the room.'

'Did you see anyone in the Pitcher yard when you opened the window before you went to bed?'

'I don't think I looked in that direction,' Tim said thoughtfully. 'But I did see Ken's dog racing around the riverbank. I remember the moon was so bright it was almost as clear as day.'

'And Ken? Did you see him?'

'No. But he always sits in a copse of trees to fish, so I wouldn't have noticed him in the shadows. The dog was in the open field.'

'You didn't look in the direction of the Pitchers' yard at all?'

Tim frowned with the effort of remembering. 'I might have, but if I did nothing out of the ordinary registered.'

'You sure?'

'I've replayed every minute of that night in my mind a dozen times over and more, searching for clues as to who could have killed Alun and his family.' He sipped his brandy. 'I wish I'd dumped Larry Jones in the middle of the road when I'd had the chance, so a car could have turned him into jam. The Pitchers were nice people.'

'So everyone says.' Trevor left his chair and went to the window so he could take a closer look at the Pitchers' yard. The smell of smoke and burning hadn't lessened, just somehow grown colder and more unpleasant. Floodlights had been set up illuminating every corner and the two uniformed constables standing guard where the yard opened into the lane. Shadows moved behind the blinds in the mobile HQ parked behind the house.

'Like most coppers, including me when I was in the Met, you have a problem with nice people, Inspector Joseph. It took retirement for me to realise they do exist.'

'Were you in serious crimes?'

'Drug Squad.'

'I don't have a problem with nice people, Mr Pryce. But when a rogue is murdered there's always a list of enemies to work through. Process of elimination usually generates one or two leads worth investigating. My job is never easy but it's impossible when I've nothing to work on.'

'I see what you mean.'

Trevor turned his back to the yard leaned against the railings and faced Tim. 'Alun Pitcher was a businessman. In my experience, businessmen make enemies.'

'Not Alun,' Tim said emphatically. 'No one else in the town sells antiques or has an auction house so he had no competition, or money worries as he inherited the business debt free from his father. I recall him telling me once that his great-great-great grandfather came here from Carmarthen in the eighteenth century and opened a furniture and carpentry shop.'

'Buying and selling antiques is a risky business. People who don't know the difference between the genuine article and fakes can pay over the odds, and people who sell can be short-changed,' Trevor argued.

'Not by Alun. He was as honest as the day is long. If he knew the value of a piece, he'd buy it from you at book price less ten per cent handling and I never heard anyone complain about the ten per cent. When it came to house clearance, he preferred to put everything up for auction, sending out catalogues to buyers well in advance. People came from as far as Scotland and London for the larger auctions he organised. If anyone in the town wanted something in particular, he'd scout for it and try and get it at a fair price.'

'What about the boys?' Trevor asked.

'Craftsmen every one and, hard working. Not that they didn't play hard.'

Girlfriends?' Trevor suggested.

'The youngest Michael has been courting Alison Griffiths since they both went into the comprehensive when they were eleven. Nice girl, nice family. The older two, Lee and James changed their girls as often as they changed their socks.'

'They were ladies' men?'

'The ladies loved them,' Tim confirmed. 'My barmaids fell over themselves to serve them every time one of them came into the pub.'

'Please don't take exception to this question. I'm looking for a motive for these murders. Did either of the Pitcher boys include married women or women in steady relationships among their girlfriends?'

'If they did they wouldn't have flaunted them in front me and everyone else in the pub.'

'Point taken. You never heard rumours or gossip

about any of the Pitcher boys or Alun – or Gillian?'

'Alun and Gillian, never,' Tim replied. 'But one or two jealous types blamed Lee and James for the break up of their relationships. Lee came in once with a black eye. Pam said a disgruntled husband gave it to him but Lee never said who, and Pam never found out. Which means no one else in the town other than Lee and whoever gave it to him knew. A few months ago there was a rumour that Dai Smith's wife …'

'The constable who was here at midnight on the night of the fire?' Trevor interrupted.

'That's the one. There was a rumour that Dai's wife and Lee had an affair. I didn't pay much attention to it and never saw any animosity between Lee and Dai. In fact they both drank together here, in the bar on dart match nights.'

'Dai's wife's name?'

'Marianne. She's French and visiting her parents in Paris at the moment. But it's a holiday. They have three-year-old twin girls Dai dotes on. I wish I hadn't mentioned the rumour now. Given Dai and Lee's behaviour towards one another there couldn't have been anything other than the gossipmongers putting two and two together and making twenty-five.'

'Other than the suggestion that Lee Pitcher had a wandering eye.'

'Do you really think the Pitchers were killed by a jealous husband?' Tim asked.

'The beating Lee was subjected to was savage.'

'A crime of passion as the French say.'

'At this stage I'm not discounting anything. Thank you.' Trevor finished his brandy and handed Tim the glass.

'Inspector, I'm sorry I bit your head off at lunchtime. But Alun was a good friend as well as neighbour. I'm going to miss him.'

'You known him long?'

'Since I moved here six years ago.'

The words were trite and overused, but they were all Trevor had. 'I'm sorry for your loss.'

'Thank you.'

'If you hear a noise outside, it will be me. I want to get a feel for the back lane and the Pitchers' yard at night.'

'Turn right at the bottom of the steps and you'll see a wooden door. There's a light operated by a sensor and a key code lock. Punch in 9876. The door leads directly into the back lane. From there it's only a few steps to the yard. I hope you catch the bastards, Inspector.'

'I'll do my best, Mr Pryce. Goodnight.'

CHAPTER THIRTEEN

'Don't tell me you forgot your key, you silly bugger,' Peter shouted when he heard a light tap on the cottage window. Heaving himself from the sofa, he went to the door and opened it.

'Switch the light off, quick. Before someone sees me.' Carol March slipped inside. She dropped the hood of her black sweater and the long blonde hair she'd worn in a knot while in uniform tumbled to her waist.

She was the last person Peter wanted to see. But when he saw her hair, he had to stop himself from reaching out and stroking it … it would have been easy … so easy …

He tightened his fists until his nails dug into the palms of his hands. 'What do you want?'

'I'd have thought that was obvious.'

'Not to me.'

'Come on, Petey, you know why I'm here.'

'I don't. And don't call me Petey.'

'Someone else calls you that now?' she murmured huskily.

'The people I'm acquainted with have more sense.'

'Acquainted with? You only have acquaintances and colleagues,' she probed. 'No one closer.'

Ignoring her question, he checked the blinds were closed before turning the light back on. 'I hope you can't see through those from outside.'

'You can't.'

'How do you know?'

'I tried before I knocked.'

'Trevor is living here too.'

'I saw him go into the pub with Tim Pryce twenty minutes ago.'

'You were watching the yard?'

'Yes.' She sat down.

'Carol …'

'Don't try telling me that you haven't missed me, Pete.' She looked up defiantly at him. 'Because if you do, I won't believe you.'

Trevor found the gate. It was oak, protected by close wrought iron-work, seven foot high and set in an even higher stone wall. Tim Pryce was more cautious with the security of his property than Alun Pitcher had been. But, the key code worked and Tim hadn't been wary of giving it him, which said something for an ex-copper's respect for the local police.

The light flashed on but Trevor didn't need it. Tim had mentioned how bright the moon had been when he'd seen Ken Lloyd's dog by the river. Trevor doubted it could have been any brighter than it was at that moment. He opened the latch and stepped into the lane. The stench of smoke grew even stronger bringing tears to his eyes and rawness to his throat.

Tim was right. Only a few feet of tarmac separated the back of the pub wall from the Pitcher's yard. He closed the gate and spotted the arc of a glowing cigarette. The pin prick of light moved closer.

'May I ask what you're doing here, sir?'

'Checking out the crime scene, Sergeant Howell.' Trevor stepped out of the shadows.

'Sorry, sir. Didn't recognise you.'

'You're still on duty?'

'We're short on manpower. I volunteered a double shift. At the moment I'm relieving Constable Murphy so he can grab a cuppa. It's not easy keeping the public out of an open access without a gate. The super wants the area watched round the clock until the forensic teams move out.'

'You seem to have discovered the secret of living without sleep, Sergeant Howell.'

'Goes with the job. And it's not only me. All the locals want Larry Jones to go down and we're prepared to do whatever it takes to get an airtight case that will see him put away up for life.'

Trevor wondered just how far "the locals" would go to get a life sentence for Larry Jones. He'd heard officers say "Whatever it takes" before, and seen the results in mistrials and cases thrown out because of tampered evidence. None of which had reflected well on the investigating force. He changed the subject. 'Have many people tried to get into the yard today?'

Frank indicated a mound of flowers that had been heaped to the right of the entrance. 'When we ran out of room on the pavement at the front of the house, the Pitchers' friends and neighbours came to pay their respects here. Those who knew the family were no trouble, just handed the tributes over to us, but it hasn't been easy keeping the reporters and TV news crews at bay. Some turned aggressive when Tim Pryce and the accountant's refused to allow them access to their back windows. We intervened but the bastards kept citing free speech – and "the public's right to know". Then they hung around here all day filming people crying. We've also had a few ghouls standing and staring. A couple even asked if the bodies were still in the house, sick sods. But then, they were either from the Garth Estate or outsiders.'

Trevor reflected there was no one like a beat copper for pigeonholing people into "good" and "bad". 'No one else?'

'That was enough for us to cope with in one day, sir.'

'I'm back, Frank. Thanks for covering.' Jim Murphy left the mobile HQ and joined them.

'Want to come into the HQ for a cuppa, sir?' Frank offered.

'Has any new information come in from the public in the last few hours?' Trevor asked Jim.

'No, sir. It's not for the want of people trying to help, but they can't report what they didn't see. We've still no sightings of anyone just before the fire started or when it was burning, other than Ken Lloyd's of a person on the fire escape. And he was too far away to identify Larry Jones.'

'The jewellery and matches we found on Larry might not be enough for a conviction of murder or even arson – only receiving stolen goods and burglary as we've no evidence that proves he was in the Pitchers' house. In my opinion the super was right to send for you.' Frank spoke as though he was the only officer in the force who agreed with Reggie Moore's decision.

'As there's nothing new I'll forgo the tea, Sergeant Howell, and take a look around the yard and fire escape.'

'Want to get the feel of the place, sir?'

'Yes,' Trevor conceded.

'Want me to come with you, sir?'

'Thank you, it would be useful to have the viewpoint of a local who knows the area.' Trevor approached the back of the house, looked around and went to the building where Larry Jones had been found.

'Bastard picked a good place to sleep it off. Even with the doors off it's not easy to see inside in daytime. Night time it's impossible,' Frank peered into the dark interior as if he wanted to prove what he'd said.

Trevor stepped inside and exchanged the stench of smoke for something more unpleasant. 'You'd either have to lose your sense of smell or be desperate to hide to go inside.'

'The place honks,' Frank concurred.

'Is there a sewage problem or is it being used as a lavatory?'

'There's no sewage pipes or manholes inside. I watched forensic check it out this morning.'

'Someone mentioned that a vagrant broke into the pub and the accountant's. Do they congregate around here?' Trevor asked.

'The one who broke in was old Mitch and that was a long time back, sir. We've a few hopeless homeless cases in the town. Mainly addicts and drunks but we've had no complaints about them hanging round here. They mostly congregate around the old bus station. If Alun or Tim had seen them in the lane they would have chased them away.'

'Then why this stink?' Trevor demanded.

'I don't know,' Frank admitted.

'It might be worth finding out who has been using this place as a toilet and how long it's been going on.' Glad to step away from the building and into the yard, Trevor went to the fire escape and began climbing, stopping every few steps to check the view of the surroundings. When he reached the kitchen floor, he walked along the balcony and stared down towards the river. On the far side a black dog was racing around moon-silvered fields.

'Ken's been out fishing every night since the fire. His wife has put him in the doghouse for sure,' Frank stood alongside him.

'I gather she disapproves.'

'Of everything Ken enjoys.' Frank looked sideways at Trevor. 'The whole town is upset about what's happened to Alun and his family, but Ken's devastated. He and Alun were close.'

'I heard.' Trevor left the balcony and continued to climb. Passing the balcony on the next floor he carried on until he reached attic level. 'This is the part of the fire escape Ken Lloyd saw someone on after the fire had broken out, isn't it?'

'He said he saw someone descending from the attic stairway to the next level down.'

'But the first firemen, you, and Tim Pryce saw no one when you arrived.'

'That's right. Tim was in the yard when I turned up. Minutes later the officers on the fire tender arrived and sent us out front to Main Street.'

'Tim's already told me he saw no one else here. Did you see anyone in the street on your way from the station?'

'Dr Edwards, he lives at the end of Main Street in

the old Manor. He came out after hearing the explosion. He thought his professional services would be needed.'

'Tim said the fire officers sent you to the front of the house for safety reasons.'

'It was bedlam here. The back of the house was ablaze, the yard full of smoke, windows were shattering, glass splinters raining down.'

'Yet Larry Jones slept through it all?'

'He must have,' Frank countered.

'Don't you think that's odd?'

'Not when you consider how drunk he was.'

'Some might think he was too drunk to murder anyone.'

'I've seen the photographs of the bodies of the Pitchers, sir, and with all due respect to your rank, I think someone would have to be drunk to do something like that to another human being.'

Sensing he would get nowhere if he suggested Larry might not have acted alone – or might even be innocent – Trevor changed the subject. 'So, when you, Tim and the fire officers arrived none of you thought to check the buildings in the yard.'

'Given the severity of the fire all the fire officers were concerned about was controlling it. They knew another tender was on its way. They'd spoken to the officer in charge and asked him to tackle the blaze from Main Street. They were also concerned about the safety of the residents of Main Street which is why they asked me to evacuate the area.'

'Who reached here first, you or Tim Pryce?'

'Tim was here when I arrived.'

'What time was that?'

'3.12.'

'You're very precise.'

'Call came into the station at 3.03 am. I alerted everyone on duty and directed them to the front of Main Street, ordered Jim Murphy to call in everyone else then ran down here. I glanced at the time when I arrived.'

'And the first fire tender?'

'Arrived a couple of minutes after me at 3.14. It will be on the timeline.'

Trevor walked up to the attic floor and gazed at the view. 'I understand why the Pitchers built the balconies. This was quite a house.'

'Alun made the best of it, although it was Lee's idea to add balconies to the fire escape. I think he wanted some privacy. Understandable in someone his age still living with his parents. He rarely bothered with the front door, always used to walk up and down here. I often saw him climbing up when I was on night patrol.'

'Foot patrol?' Trevor checked.

'In a town this size, not likely, but when you drive into the centre from the bridge end you get a good view of the back of these houses. Anyone climbing the fire escape or sitting out on one of these balconies is in plain view. I've often seen Lee here in summer in the early hours.'

'With anyone?' Trevor turned and studied the door that led into the attic.

Frank thought for a moment and more or less repeated what Tim had said. 'Every time I saw one of the two older Pitcher boys they had a girl with them and rarely the same one twice. With Michael it was always Alison, but the older two …' He smiled wryly. 'Every man in town envied their power to attract. If only it was as simple as the advertisements would have us believe. Wear the right aftershave and it can happen to you.' There was envy in Frank's voice.'

'So Lee played the field?'

'And James. You know what youngsters are like these days. My sons were the same when they were single. They'd fit four girls into twenty-four hours if they could. In my day it was one at a time and none of this experimenting with sex.'

Trevor deftly steered the conversation back on track. 'There are only two chairs on this attic balcony. Was Lee usually with a female or male friend?'

'Both, but generally men in the early hours. It's a pleasant place to sit with a mate and have a few drinks after the pubs close. If a woman was with him, chances were they'd be inside and in bed.'

'Could Lee have annoyed someone's partner?'

'There's no way Larry Jones moved in the same circles as Lee Pitcher if that's what you're thinking.' Frank gazed at Trevor. 'Surely you're not looking for someone else. The jewellery tells us that Larry Jones killed the Pitchers. All we need is a few more pieces of evidence. My gut tells me it's there, waiting for us somewhere in the house. I'm sure of it.'

'If it is, the forensic teams will find it.'

'They seem to know what they're doing,' Frank agreed grudgingly. 'I just wish they'd hurry up about it.'

'You married, Sergeant Howell?' Trevor asked as they began the long descent.

'Twice. Never again. My first wife left me over twenty years ago with two boys under three and moved in with a plumber from Carmarthen. If my mother hadn't taken us in I don't know how I'd have managed. I swore I'd never get caught again but five years later I met another girl. I thought we were happy but after twelve years she went out on a hen night and met an Australian. A month later she took our two girls and went to Oz. That was three years ago. I've seen the kids once since. I flew out there but my missus and her new bloke, made it clear they didn't want me around.'

'What about your daughters?'

'They barely remembered me. I managed to swap my flight and came home early,'

'I'm sorry.' Trevor was; before Lyn his personal life had been a disaster. They reached the yard. 'See you at the changeover briefing in the morning?'

'As it'll be the tail end of my double shift I'll be there. Super's put everyone on twelve-hour shifts until further notice.'

'If hard work counts we'll get the breakthrough we need, Sergeant Howell.'

'Call me Frank, guv, we don't go in much for titles around here.'

Trevor made his way back to the Angel via the end of the lane, turning left into Main Street and stopping beneath the archway that led into the old stable yard. He walked at normal pace and timed himself. Nine minutes. How much longer would it be for a man as drunk as Larry Jones had been?

He stood for a moment staring at the spot Tim

Pryce had pointed out. Larry Jones's disappearance from the yard entrance was one more thing to check on the timeline. Had he woken of his own accord and walked around to the Pitchers' yard with the intention of breaking into the house? No one disputed that Larry Jones was drunk, but the question was how drunk? Had Larry been capable of walking to the Pitchers' yard or had he been carried and dumped there?

Had the valuable pieces of jewellery been planted in his pocket? Had there been any other valuable pieces in the house? Surely a relatively wealthy man like Alun Pitcher would have bought his wife expensive jewellery. Yet there'd been no mention of any by the forensic teams.

Trevor spotted movement in an upstairs window of a house across the road. A blind moved but the room behind it was in darkness. Mrs May Williams?

One more person to interview. How much could he delegate to the locals? How far could he trust them? Bill Mulcahy wouldn't be pleased if he contacted him less than twenty-fours hours after he'd arrived asking for more personnel. Why was Frank Howell so determined to ignore Larry Jones's condition at the time of the murders and nail him at all costs?

Trevor's mind worked overtime, sorting facts into compartments and formulating a list of priority interviews. He took his key from his pocket and went to the front door of the stable cottage. He turned the key in the lock and pushed the door. It slammed into Carol March who was standing in front of Peter in the passage. Her arms were wrapped around Peter's neck, her mouth glued to his.

Peter pushed her away.

There was an embarrassing silence before Trevor said the first thing that came into his head. 'Thought you were having an early night.'

'I intended to,' Peter growled.

Trevor acknowledged Carol. 'Inspector March.'

'Good evening, Inspector Joseph.' She picked up her handbag from the hall table. 'See you tomorrow, Pete.'

Peter didn't wait for her to cross the yard. He slammed the door as soon as she was through it and turned to Trevor. 'The last thing I need is a bloody lecture from you.'

'I wasn't about to give you one.' Trevor went to the fridge and fetched his whisky.

'One day you'll actually drink that.'

'I keep trying.'

Peter topped up his own glass. 'Don't tell Daisy?'

'Tell Daisy what?'

'Don't play stupid, Joseph. About the Snow Queen.'

'Your life is your business, but I won't lie for you,' Trevor warned.

'I don't expect you to.'

Trevor moved the conversation on to what he felt was safe ground – the case. 'I went to the pub and saw Tim Pryce's private quarters. There's a good view of the back of the Pitchers' yard and house from there.'

'Did he see anything on the night of the murder?'

'No.'

'Then his view of the crime scene was wasted.'

Trevor picked up his glass. I'll finish this upstairs. See you in the morning.'

Peter sat sullenly in his chair. Trevor didn't press him. Experience had taught him that Peter would only talk to him on his own terms and when he was ready. Not before, no matter how hard he was pressed.

CHAPTER FOURTEEN

'Everything OK?' Trevor asked Lyn.

'Why wouldn't it be?' she replied, 'Marty and me can manage without you, darling. We're quite self sufficient.'

'Didn't doubt you were, not too sure about me though. Miss you,' Trevor murmured.

'Miss you too. Just because we manage without you, doesn't mean we want to,' Lyn qualified. 'What's wrong?'

Trevor reflected that in the comparatively short time they'd been together Lyn had learned to read him like a book. 'Just the case,' he lied. 'It's foul. Almost an entire family wiped out and we've virtually no leads and even less evidence.'

'How's Peter?'

'Being Peter.'

'Poor you.'

'How's Daisy?'

'Starving. She's craving everything but unable to keep anything down. I keep telling her it will be worth it but I'm not sure she believes me.'

'You didn't believe it when you were told the same thing.'

'I suppose I didn't. But she only has to look at Marty …'

'You're a doting mother.'

'And you of course are a strict, stern father.'

'Who has to go and interview a man.'

The vista from Trevor's window was more limited than from Tim Pryce's private quarters but it did overlook part of the riverbank and he had spotted a man walking along the path carrying fishing gear, a black dog trotting at his heels.

'At …' Lyn checked the time. 'Six fifteen in the morning.'

'I'm in the sticks. They get up earlier here. Love you.'

'Love to you from both of us. Don't work too hard. What am I saying, you always work too hard.'

Trevor met Ken as he was leaving the river path for the road. He'd stopped to slip on his dog's lead before crossing the bridge into town. His rod, fishing tackle, and a plastic carrier bag of wet fish were heaped at his feet.

'Mr Lloyd, Ken Lloyd?'

Ken squinted up at Trevor. 'Who's asking?'

'Inspector Trevor Joseph.'

'The incomer hot-shot policeman. You're up bright and early.'

'I wouldn't describe myself as a hot-shot but incomer is apt.' Trevor crouched down and patted the collie. 'Friendly dog.'

'Mars is the best I've trained and I've trained a few in my time.' Ken fastened the lead and rose to his feet.

'I know you're tired after fishing all night, but I was hoping to have a word.'

'I've told the local police all I know and made an official statement.'

'I haven't had a chance to read the statements in detail and I know this is difficult for you. Superintendent Moore told me you and Alun Pitcher were close friends.'

'We've been neighbours since the day I married but I knew him before. We were both in the rugby team in our younger, fitter days. Got on as kids and adults. Some people never change. Alun was the kindest, most easy-going man anyone could wish to meet. He's going to be sorely missed by the people in this town. If anyone was in need and Alun heard of it he found a way to provide, and usually anonymously. Few discovered the identity of their benefactor.' Ken's eyes were suspiciously damp. 'Even with his house burned to a shell across the road from mine I can't believe I'll never see him again.'

'Can I help you carry something?'

'You could take my rod. Don't pick that up, not if you don't want to stink of fish all day,' Ken warned when Trevor reached for a plastic bag. 'I've gutted them and they're dripping. The tackle bag's not much drier.'

'A chat with you now could save me hours of work,' Trevor coaxed. When he sensed Ken hesitating, he added, 'I need all the help I can get to bring whoever killed Alun Pitcher and his family to justice. Is there anywhere I can buy you breakfast?'

'Nothing in town will be open until nine. There are a couple of truckers' cafes on the outskirts but they wouldn't allow Mars inside.'

'In that case, would you mind coming back to the cottage we're renting in the Angel? I saw a pack of ground coffee in the cupboard and there's a cafetiere.'

'That depends on whether or not the wife is up. If she is, I'll have to go in because she'll have breakfast

186

on the table. But I was going to call into the Angel anyway and give Tim the fish, unless you'd like a couple of trout.'

'Can you spare them?'

'I had a good catch. Half a dozen decent sized ones and I did well yesterday too. My freezer has more fish in it than I can eat and the wife won't touch them. If you take two I'll still have four for Tim.'

'In that case, thank you.' Trevor waited until Ken picked up all his gear and walked across the bridge with him.

Ken glanced across the road when they drew close to the Angel. Trevor noticed that all the curtains were closed in the front windows of the house he had looked at.

'I'll probably be able to spare you half an hour or so. It's looks as though the wife's still in bed.'

'Thank you.'

'The breakfast chef's in and cooking,' Ken commented when they reached the arch and smelled the extractor fan blowing out the aroma of bacon and sausages. 'I'll give him the fish then I'll be with you.' Ken knocked on the pub's kitchen door.

'I'll leave our front door open and put the coffee on. It's the last cottage on the right facing you.'

Trevor went in, brewed the coffee and laid out cups and saucers on the table in the living room. The french doors behind it opened on to a small patio but although the sun was shining he decided it was too cold to sit out at that time of the morning. He searched the kitchen. There was nothing in the fridge, freezer or cupboards except sugar, a carton of long life milk, salt, pepper and a bottle of brown sauce.

Given the hours he and Peter worked when they were immersed in a case he made a note to pick up a couple of frozen pizzas.

'Hello?'

'In the living room, Mr Lloyd.'

'Ken – no one calls me Mr Lloyd, not even the bank manager.' Ken walked into the living room, Mars was off the lead, trotting at his heels. 'The chef gave me half a dozen bacon and sausage baguettes in exchange for the trout.' He set a plate of steaming rolls on the table.

'That was good of him and you. Thank you. Help yourself to coffee, I'll get plates.'

'So, what would you like to know?' Ken asked when Trevor returned with two plates and knives.

'Superintendent Moore told me you worked for Alun Pitcher.'

'The odd day here and there,' Ken admitted warily. 'I admit it was always cash in hand …'

'I'm not a tax inspector, Ken. All I'm interested in is anything that was in Alun Pitcher's house that might provide a motive for killing him and his family.'

'But they caught Larry Jones with valuable antique jewellery. I assumed it was an open and shut case which is why I found it odd …'

Trevor said what Ken couldn't bring himself to say. 'That Superintendent Moore asked for the help of officers from outside the local force?'

'As you've mentioned it, yes.'

'Superintendent Moore decided there were a few odd aspects to the case that warranted more investigation that she had spare man hours,' Trevor said tactfully. 'You reported the fire at three in the morning. You saw Larry Jones at midnight when you helped Tim Pryce move him from the pavement to the archway. According to Tim he was comatose. Do you think Larry could have recovered sufficiently to have left the archway walked around to the Pitcher house and killed all four family members in three hours?'

'I don't know,' Ken replied. 'All I can tell you is that Larry Jones was certainly out of it at midnight. Do you think someone else was involved?'

'I'm looking into the possibility, which is why I'm trying to find out what, if any, valuables, apart from the jewellery that was found on Larry was in the house. Someone mentioned the Pitchers had recently acquired the contents of an old Rectory.'

'Llwynon Rectory. The boys bought the house. They are … were … converting it into flats.'

Trevor didn't pursue the Pitcher sons' purchase of the rectory. He'd already filed it away for future reference if it should prove relevant. 'Apparently there was some antique furniture in the rectory that had been in the family for centuries.'

'There was. I helped Alun move the pieces into his cellar.' Ken put a baguette on the plate Trevor handed him and sliced it.

'Do you think it's possible the fire was lit to cover up the theft?'

'One man couldn't have lifted most of the pieces. It took four of us to carry some of the heavier items into that cellar. And, if they were stolen, they'd have to be loaded on to a van and driven away. Larry wasn't in a fit state to drive. In fact I don't know that he even has a licence. He's been up for stealing cars …' Ken thought for a moment. 'So that's why you think that Larry might have had an accomplice.'

'Was there any single piece that might attract a thief?'

'I'm no expert, not in the way Alun was, but he did say some of the furniture was unique and the paintings and sculptures irreplaceable.'

'Could you make a list of the cellar's contents?'

'No need, Alun always kept an up-to-date stock list both for the cellar and the warehouse in his fireproof safes. He was meticulous about records. I saw him updating both ledgers when we cleared the Rectory. Although the estate was going to the Crown he needed a detailed inventory.' Ken fed Mars a piece of sausage before heaping sugar into his coffee.

'Where are these safes?'

'The one for the cellar is in the house.'

'The office is damaged and the floor burned away.'

'The safe was sunk into the cellar floor. Under the Belfast sink in the washroom. The other one was sunk into the floor of the office in the warehouse. Look under the desk. It's hidden by a rug. If his wife, Gill, had time she would have inputted the items on the stock list in the ledgers on to the computer.'

'Thank you, that's useful to know. I'll ask one of our experts to check the computer in the warehouse. Did you put it in your statement?'

'No, because no one asked about the safes or the stock list.' Ken continued to feed his dog more titbits than he fed himself.

Trevor scribbled a note on the writing pad next to

him. 'What packaging materials did Alun store in the cellar?'

'The usual. Wooden chests and containers for shipping. Packing cases and rolls of protective felt for the larger items. Newspaper for smaller items, bubble wrap for china, string, plastic sheeting …'

'Brown paper?' Trevor interrupted.

Ken frowned. 'I don't remember seeing any in the cellar.'

'Are you sure?'

'There wasn't any with the packing materials and I often packed furniture and smaller items before they were transferred to the warehouse for auction.'

Trevor heard sounds of movement upstairs. Peter was unpredictable at the best of times. After last night's episode with Carol March, he didn't even want to try to second-guess Peter's mood. He moved on swiftly. 'Did Alun have any enemies that you knew of?'

Ken was emphatic. 'None.'

'No arguments, quarrels with anyone over an item he sold or bought?'

'I can't think of an instance. If there had been I would have heard of it. Gossip of that sort travels quickly around the town.'

'So Alun Pitcher was a businessman who always satisfied his customers?'

'Alun's policy was simple and he drummed it into the boys and everyone who worked for him. "Happy customers spread the word; unhappy customers can send a whole town full of potential customers to another dealer." If someone was dissatisfied with something they'd bought from Alun he'd take whatever it was back, no questions asked and give them a full refund. When it came to buying antiques he always gave the seller list price less ten per cent handling charge.'

Ken's revelation confirmed what Trevor had already heard but he still had difficulty believing it. 'In my experience a generous nature lends itself open to abuse.'

'One or two customers took advantage of Alun. But he never allowed it to worry him.'

'Can you give me an example?'

'A certain lady in the town refurnished her house with valuable antiques when she was hosting a weekend party for some important business clients of her husband's. She rang Alun on Monday morning after her guests left and said the furniture wasn't suitable.'

'He took it back?'

'Every piece and gave her a full refund. But the story got around town. I think Alun decided that was punishment enough for the person concerned.'

'Alun spread the story?'

'Alun never said a word. His employees weren't as tactful.'

The more questions Trevor asked about Alun Pitcher the more he came to the conclusion that the man had been a saint, or the entire town was in collusion to make him one, or what appeared to be most likely, Alun Pitcher had been a genuine, honest businessman admired and respected by everyone he'd had dealings with.

Peter walked in and glanced from Trevor to Ken to the baguettes. 'Breakfast.'

'Courtesy of our guest.'

'May I?' Peter didn't wait for an answer before picking up a baguette.

'Plates in the kitchen,' Trevor reminded him.

'Good point. As no one's mentioned housekeeping we may have to do our own hoovering.'

'Coffee's made, so bring in a mug as well.'

Trevor waited until Peter returned before introducing him to Ken. 'Mr Ken Lloyd, Sergeant Peter Collins.'

'The fishermen who reported the fire.' Peter filled his coffee mug and added milk and sugar.

Ken left the table. 'If there's nothing else, Inspector Joseph, I must be getting home. The wife will be up by now and wondering where I am.'

'Thank you for the trout, the breakfast but most of all your time, Ken.' Trevor offered him his hand and Ken shook it.

'If there's anything else you think I can help with …'

'I'll be in touch,' Trevor broke in.

Mars rose on his haunches and trotted to the door as soon as Ken opened it. Ken turned and looked back at Trevor. 'You will find out if anyone besides Larry Jones was involved in the murder of Alun and his family?'

'We'll do our best to find whoever's responsible for the deaths of the Pitcher family, Ken,' Trevor assured him. 'I promise you that much. I'll see you out.' Trevor waited until they reached the front door before asking his last question. 'Can you describe the figure you saw on the fire escape when the house was on fire?'

'I was half a mile away, concerned with phoning the emergency services …'

'Tall, thin, short, fat? Hair colour?'

Ken closed his eyes for a moment. 'Tall,' he declared when he opened them. 'Tall and slim and wearing a dark hat.'

'Thank you, Mr Lloyd, you have been most helpful. Did you put that description in your statement?'

'No, because no one asked.'

'Begs the question as to how they interview people here,' Peter commented when Trevor returned to the living room.

Trevor picked up his notebook and sat at the table. 'You heard.'

'I did. Our fisherman gave us a few things to think about. And food. Great baguettes, great sausage and the bacon's not too bad either.' Peter took a large bite.

'He gave us a couple of trout as well.'

'Why?'

'He said he caught too many.'

'If he's on your list of suspects he could be trying to poison us.'

'He's not on my list of suspects.' Trevor picked up his pen and a pad of scrap paper.

'Why?'

'He reported the fire …'

'Could be a blind.'

'His dog was seen racing around the fields by the riverbank at one in the morning. And, when he turned up outside the Pitcher house he was carrying his catch in a plastic bag.'

194

'Who's to say how long it took him to hook them?'

Tired of bantering, Trevor said, 'Give me Ken's Lloyd's motive?'

'All right, seeing as how he organised breakfast I'll leave him off the list of suspects for now. I take it you're going to interview the nosy parker across the street from the Pitchers who reported the ruckus when Tim Pryce ejected Larry Jones from the Angel.'

Trevor referred to his notes again. 'Mrs May Williams.'

'How much are we delegating to the locals?'

'Let's look at what we need to do ourselves first. We'll call in on Mrs Williams on our way to the station.'

Peter sat forward and tried to decipher Trevor's scrawl. 'Who else is on your list?'

'Larry Jones.'

'Obviously.'

'Don't suppose you'd like to wade through his file …'

'I already have.'

'When?' Trevor asked in surprise.

'Last night. And before you say anything about Inspector March …'

'Your personal life and what you do in your own time is your business, not mine. We have a murder investigation to conduct.'

Peter stared at him. 'And if I want to explain?'

'It can wait. Did you come to any conclusions about Larry Jones?'

'He's what he looked like in the interview. A thug, drunkard, occasional user of illegal substances – I say occasional in the broad sense. I noted the name of the prison he'd been released from on the morning of the day before the fire. Unlike some, it has a good record of keeping drugs to a minimum. Four per cent of the prison population in the last shakedown. I've no doubt that on the night of the murders Larry Jones was drunk out of his skull, but I can't see a small-time nuisance breaking into the Pitcher home to steal valuable antique jewellery. For a start how did Larry know it was there? Or where it was kept? Given what we know about Lee Pitcher I doubt he left it lying around for a casual burglar to pick up. Antique jewellery like all unique objects is difficult to dispose of.'

'It could have been an opportunist theft. Newly released prisoners are generally broke,' Trevor finished his baguette.

'He had money on him.'

'Money he said he'd been owed and collected earlier that day but he didn't say who he'd collected it from,' Trevor said. 'He could have owed someone himself and needed more.'

'I'll grant you that if Larry had broken into the Pitcher house and seen the jewellery lying around he could have taken it to sell it on to some small dealer who'd prize the stones from their setting and melt down the gold. But break-up value on a delicate piece like the one we saw wouldn't be more than a hundred or so to the taker. Not enough in my book to want to kill four people.'

'So you think Larry's innocent?'

'I think he's nasty, boorish and violent. But much as I hate to agree with the Snow Queen, I can't see

196

the drunken lout getting into the Pitcher house because I can't see him being steady enough to pick the lock or them opening the door to him.'

'He could have smashed his way into the cellar.'

'And stumbled up four flights of stairs without leaving a fingerprint or any DNA?' Peter challenged.

'He could have wiped them off.'

'In his state of inebriation?'

'So you don't think he was ever in the house?' Trevor stacked his plate and coffee cup.

'The jewellery could have been planted on him. As could the ashes and smuts,'

'They could.' Trevor wiped the grease from his hands in a tissue he took from his trouser pocket.

'Given that there's four witnesses including two coppers prepared to swear that the bloke couldn't even stand three hours before the fire you don't believe any more than I do that Larry Jones killed four healthy Pitchers, three of them strapping fit men.'

'Something still tells me we can't rule him out. Not yet.'

'Because you think he could be connected to the killer or killers who set him up to take the blame?'

'It's possible.'

'If he was working with someone, he's not talking.'

'Yet,' Trevor glanced at his notes again.

'So we interview nosy parker …'

'Refer to her as Mrs May Williams or you may end up calling her Nosy Parker to her face.'

'You want me there when you talk to her?'

'Yes.'

197

'Don't trust yourself to pick up everything.'

'It helps to have another pair of eyes especially when you're making notes or recordings.' Trevor scanned the list he'd made.

Peter looked over Trevor's shoulder. 'Mrs May Williams, the two police officers who answered the call of a disturbance outside the Angel. Michael Pitcher ...' Peter raised his eyebrows. 'You expect them to let us into the loony bin.'

'Psychiatric hospital,' Trevor corrected. 'Not yet, but in time.'

'And there's me hoping we'd be done with this case in a week and on our way home.'

'Do you believe in fairies as well?'

For once it was Peter who kept the conversation strictly business. 'What about Ken Lloyd and Tim Pryce?'

'After we've interviewed May Williams you can go through the statements they've made. But first, you telephone the duty officer in the station and get May Williams's exact address in Main Street.'

'You sure there's someone here to open the door?' Trevor stood next to Peter on the doorstep of the house next door to Ken Lloyd's in Main Street.

'Constable Paula Rees, the one with the figure …'

'Watch those sexist remarks, you're not on home territory now,' Trevor warned.

'Whatever,' Peter dismissed airily. 'She told me that Mrs May Williams is house bound but carers go in four times a day to bathe her, dress her and get her meals. She said the first ones call at eight. She also gave me the code for the key box.'

'Which we can't use without Mrs Williams's permission.' Trevor read at his watch. 'If the Constable is right, the carers should have gone in ten minutes ago.'

Peter pressed the doorbell a second time, keeping his finger on it.

A sash window opened above them and an angry voice rasped down. 'Keep your hair on. I'll be down when I can.'

It was another five minutes before they heard the thunder of footsteps on the stairs. The door was wrenched open and a red-faced, flustered middle-aged woman glared at them.

'Yes?' she demanded.

'Inspector Trevor Joseph.' Trevor took his warrant card from his pocket and held it up, 'and Sergeant Peter Collins. We'd like to ask Mrs May Williams a few questions about the call she made to the local police station a few hours before fire broke out in the house across the road.'

'We're getting her up. She's not dressed yet and we won't be taking her into the living room for another quarter of hour.'

'We can wait.' Trevor stepped inside, precluding a dismissal.

'It's important you speak to her?' There was belligerence in her voice.

'It is,' Trevor answered.

'Then I suppose you'd better come in,' she conceded ungraciously. She turned and walked up the stairs.

'Thank you,' Trevor followed her and Peter closed the door.

'You've visitors, Mrs Williams.' The carer called out when she reached the top of the stairs. 'The police. They say it's important.'

'About time.' The patient was even brusquer than the carer.

The carer, who didn't bother to introduce herself, lowered her voice a fraction but not enough so it wouldn't carry into all the upstairs rooms. 'She's crippled by arthritis. Can't move an inch without help which is why she never goes downstairs. Social Services said they'd put in a stair lift but the man they sent took one look at the staircase and said it couldn't be done with the stairs curving the way they do. And because the house is Grade 2 listed it can't be altered. So she's trapped upstairs.' The carer walked along the landing towards the front of the house and opened a door. She showed Trevor and Peter into a large room with two floor-length bay windows that overlooked Main Street. The smell of dried lavender was overwhelming. Half a dozen bowls filled with potpourri were scattered about and, as if they weren't enough, two vases were filled with the dried distinctive grass shaped flowers.

Both windows were screened by three sets of blinds, one for each window pane, and angled so they didn't interfere with the view of the pub, the yard behind it and practically the entire street, depending on where you stood.

'That chair is Mrs Williams'.' The carer pointed to an electrically operated recliner in prime position in one of the bays. 'You can sit on the sofa or one of the other chairs. I'll help my colleague finish off Mrs Williams and bring her in. You can talk to her while we make her breakfast.'

'Thank you.' Trevor left his laptop case on the floor beside the sofa and walked into one of the bays.

Peter sat in the reclining chair that the carer had warned them off. He adjusted it until his feet were almost level with his head and looked around. 'I can see why the locals and the neighbours say nothing goes on in Main Street without Mrs Williams knowing about it. She has a front row view.' Peter looked at his watch. 'What time's the briefing?'

'I don't recall setting a time other than "first thing". I should think about nine o'clock.'

The door opened and the carer they hadn't met pushed Mrs Williams into the room in a wheelchair.

Trevor walked towards her and held out his hand at chair level. 'Mrs Williams, I'm Inspector Trevor Joseph?'

'Haven't seen you about before. You're not local, are you?' she barked suspiciously.

'We've been brought in to assist with the investigation into the fire and murder of the Pitcher family. This is my colleague, Sergeant Peter Collins.'

May's response was an unintelligible 'Hummph!'

Peter left the chair as soon as May Williams and the carer entered. But unable to lower the seat quickly enough he had jumped from the seat which was still raised.

Tutt-tutting, the carer reached for the controller and returned the chair to a forward upright position, ready to receive its occupant.

Trevor studied the elderly woman the carer half-helped, half-carried from the wheelchair into the recliner. She was certainly crippled by arthritis; her claw-like hands and swollen joints bore testimony to damage the disease had wrought. But her eyes were bright. A deep, intelligent, inquisitive blue Trevor suspected missed little.

The carer draped a blanket over May's legs. May tore it away and dropped it to the floor. 'For pity's sake, woman, you've wrapped me in cashmere trousers and a cashmere sweater. The sun is shining out there. You trying to roast me to death?'

'Trying to take care of you,' the carer rebuked her.

Trevor retreated to the sofa. Peter took one of the easy chairs.

'What do you want for breakfast?' the carer asked.

'The usual,' May bit back.

'Which is?'

'How long you been coming here, woman?'

'It seems like centuries.'

Peter stifled a smile.

'Coffee, toast and orange juice. And these

policemen would like coffee too. And mind you make it a decent strength for once.' May reached for the controller for the chair and adjusted it. Trevor noticed that if May moved her head slightly to the left she had a better view of the street than she did her TV.

'No coffee for us, thank you,' Trevor refused, 'we've had breakfast.'

'You were up early, Inspector Joseph,' May commented.

'We have a great deal of work to get through.' Trevor waited until the carer left the room and closed the door behind her before poising his pen over his notebook. 'We'd like to ask you about the call you made to the police on the night the Pitchers' house burned.'

'And, I'd like you to tell me why the local police haven't made the follow-up visit that was promised by Dai Smith, until now?' May questioned.

'They've all been working flat out on the investigation into the fire and the murders,' Trevor said in their defence.

'None of the local officers know what work is. Dai Smith and Paula Rees answered the call that night. And Dai had time enough to go into the Angel with Tim afterwards – and stay there thirty-seven minutes. Drinking when he should have been on duty.'

'He'd finished his shift.' Trevor explained.

'Had he now?' May challenged. 'If he'd used common sense he would have stayed with Larry Jones and watched what he got up to when he came round.'

'No officer can work 24/7, Mrs Williams.'

'So why did the local force send for you two? None of them up to the job of bringing Alun and his family's murderer to justice?'

'It's a question of manpower,' Trevor continued diplomatically. 'Superintendent Moore felt she needed more people to work on the case. Preferably ones who hadn't known or been acquainted with the Pitchers.'

'Everyone in Wales is aware of the dangers of over-familiarity, and the corruption it can lead to, Inspector. You in charge or is Reggie?'

Trevor realised May Williams was interrogating him and he needed to redress the balance. 'Superintendent Moore has total authority over local policing, Mrs Williams.'

'But you're in charge of the case?'

'I'm heading the investigation because I've had more experience of serious crimes.'

May adjusted her chair until her feet were raised. 'I suppose Reggie Moore sent for you because of what I saw.'

'What you saw, Mrs Williams?' Trevor reiterated.

'On the night of the fire.'

The carer knocked before wheeling in a trolley, loaded with coffee pot, sugar bowl, butter dish, marmalade, milk jug, three cups and saucers, a jug of orange juice a glass and a rack of toast.

'Thank you, you can go now,' May Williams ordered imperiously.

'And the washing up? I suppose you're going to do it.'

'The midday carer can.'

'And if she's short of time?'

'My cleaner's in tomorrow, she's used to clearing the mess you lot leave.'

The carer slammed the door behind her. May leaned forward and reached for the trolley.

'Allow me.' Trevor left his seat and pushed the trolley, the same time May grabbed it and pulled it next to her chair.

'I may be incapacitated, Inspector Joseph but I am capable of buttering my own toast and pouring my own coffee.'

'I apologise. I'm used to helping my wife. She obviously needs more assistance than you.' Trevor returned to his seat. 'You were telling us what you saw on the night of the murder.'

'You know why I telephoned the station?'

'You heard a disturbance outside the Angel,' Trevor prompted.

'Tim Pryce was frogmarching Larry Jones out of the door of the pub and making a din about it.'

'They were both shouting?' Peter asked.

'No, only Larry Jones.'

'Your recognised him,' Trevor said in surprise.

'I taught in this town for nearly forty years. Larry Jones wasn't one of my pupils, but his useless, promiscuous grandmother was. And I recognised the boy from his photograph in the local paper. The only time he's not on the front page is when he's in prison.'

'What was Larry Jones shouting?' Trevor shook his head when May held up the coffee pot.

'Absolute rubbish,' May replied.

'Was he in pain, was Tim Pryce hurting him?' Peter looked past May and out of the window. A dustcart was moving slowly up the street, the men picking up plastic bags from the side of the road and tossing them into the back.

'All Tim was doing was steering Larry Jones out of his pub. If he'd given the idiot the thump he deserved, Larry wouldn't have made enough noise to disturb decent folk at that time of night or murder innocent people later. You have arrested Larry Jones?'

'He's in custody for breaking his parole,' Trevor informed her.

'And for arson, killing and robbing the Pitchers I hope,' May retorted. 'He had antique jewellery that Lee Pitcher had been working on, in his pocket. What more proof do you need?'

'Who told you he had jewellery in his pocket?' Trevor asked.

'As I only see my cleaner and the carers it must have been one of them. Whoever it was, said it's all over town.'

Trevor caught Peter's eye. Just as Peter had warned, the people in the town knew more about developments in the case than the officers working on the investigation.

'So you haven't arrested him for killing the Pitchers,' May commented.

'We only arrived in town yesterday,' Trevor tried not to make the revelation sound like an apology.

'I saw. You had lunch in the Angel.'

'Do you know what we ate?' There was amusement, not malice in Peter's question.

'Judging by the time you were in there I'd say it was a snack not a full roast.' May's eyes sparkled with mischief.

'You'd be right. I had burger and chips.'

'I had you down as eating unhealthily from the weight you're carrying.'

'There's only ever time for snacking in this job.'

'Rubbish. You could have ordered a salad.'

'I could say unkind things about you,' Peter retorted.

May set down her toast. 'I was active enough to burn off the calories until this damned arthritis crippled me. Since it set in, my only pleasure comes from watching others. Can you blame me? Look at this room. I hate it. Not the room itself but the wallpaper. My late husband picked it out. He loved roses. I don't. But I knew why he chose it. It reminded him of his mother's bedroom. She died when he was small so I let him have his way. Now he's long gone and I'm left suffering the roses. So if I do spend my days looking out of the window instead of at the walls you'll have to forgive me.'

'We'll forgive you anything you want in exchange for information,' Peter offered.

'Well, you'll get the truth the whole truth and nothing but from me, Sergeant,' May lectured him in a schoolmistress voice.

'I'm glad to hear it.'

Trevor sat back and allowed Peter to take control. For the first time since he and Peter had entered the room, May Williams was smiling and she was smiling at Peter. Contrary to his expectations Peter had established a rapport with the old woman. He sympathised with her predicament. He would hate to be trapped within four rose strewn walls. It was little wonder she spent so much time monitoring the doings of her neighbours. He doubted that anyone beside her carers visited her. Loneliness hung heavier than the smell of lavender in the room.

'So, if you'd thrown Larry Jones out of the Angel, you would have got physical with him?' Peter teased.

'The trouble with this country today, is that people who have the tiniest bit of authority are full of PC nonsense. When I was teaching, we were given canes and we used them. Larry Jones should have been given a good thrashing when he was younger. If he had, he would have learned right from wrong and wouldn't have spent the last ten years in and out of prison. Tim Pryce treated the stupid boy as if he were made of porcelain. He and Ken Lloyd lifted him up and carried him under that arch when they should have pushed him into the gutter.'

'What happened after they left Larry under the arch?' Peter enquired.

'Michael Pitcher drove past with his girlfriend Alison. He stopped and chatted to Ken and Tim for a couple of minutes. One of my carers told me Michael's been spending his nights with Alison at her house while her parents are away. In my day they would have been the talk of the county.'

'Why?' Peter was mystified.

'Not a wedding ring in sight and as good as living together – at their age. My father would have horsewhipped me …'

'And after Michael Pitcher and Alison left?' Peter prompted.

'Dai Smith and Paula Rees finally turned up. Not that they called to see me, although they have the code for the key box. Dai and Tim waved to me from the pavement. No doubt they think of me as an interfering old busybody. Paula didn't wave but then she's a nice girl from a good family. I taught her father thirty-five years ago. They talked for a few minutes then Paula drove off in the squad car. Ken walked off with his dog and fishing rod and Dai went into the pub with Tim. As I told you, he came out about thirty-seven minutes later. After Dai left, Tim locked up the pub and put out the lights.'

'Did you see Larry Jones leave the archway?' Trevor interrupted.

'No.'

'You went to bed.'

'No. The carers try to get me to bed at seven. I'm not a child. I'll go to bed when I damn well please and, if I want to stay up all night in the chair, I will. It's a sight more comfortable than my bed I can tell you. And I can adjust it any way I want.'

'So you stayed in the chair all that night,' Peter frowned at Trevor.

'I did,' she confirmed defiantly.

'And you slept?'

'Now and again but I woke around one o'clock. A squad car was driving down the street.'

'Routine patrol?'

'They drive past all hours.'

'Have you any idea of the time Larry left the archway?'

She thought for a moment. 'He was still there at one o'clock. The squad car slowed as it went by and I remember thinking they were checking on him. Criminals get more care and attention in this town than their victims. But he wasn't there at twenty past two.'

'How can you be sure?' Peter scribbled a note in his book.

'Because I was woken by the officer walking down the street at twenty past two.'

'What officer?' Peter sat forward on the chair.

'I don't know what officer but I heard footsteps and saw the top of his cap quite clearly.'

'It was a man?' Trevor checked.

'I assumed it was but I suppose it could have been a woman. Whoever it was was wearing trousers and carrying a bag and, walking quickly.'

'In which direction?' Trevor asked.

'Towards the police station.'

Trevor saw Peter watching him. He knew the same thought was in both their minds. Towards the police station was also towards the lane that led around the back of the Pitchers' house.

'Was it a large bag?' Peter asked.

'About the size of a weekend case.'

'And you didn't recognise whoever it was?'

'The street lamps were lit, the moon was bright but he or she was walking in the shadow of the houses. I told Dai Smith all this when he called the morning after the fire.'

'Constable Smith?' Trevor checked.

'He wanted to know if I'd seen or heard anything. I told him what I've just told you. That I didn't see Larry Jones leave the archway but I saw a police officer in the street at two twenty. Other than that, the street was quiet until the fire tenders and police cars arrived after three o'clock. Then chaos broke out, with the police evacuation. They wanted to move me, but I wouldn't go. The wind was blowing in the opposite direction so there was no danger of sparks hitting my roof. Ken Lloyd's wife went. That woman will do anything to get attention.'

'You're certain you spoke to Constable Smith.'

'My body may not work too well, but there's nothing wrong with my brain, Sergeant Collins. I'm not ga-ga yet,' May snapped. 'Dai Smith made notes and said he'd be back with a colleague. When you turned up this morning, I assumed you'd spoken to him.'

'The rate information is coming in it must have been overlooked.' Trevor couldn't disguise his annoyance. 'Can you think of anything else that happened that night that might help us?'

May shook her head.

Trevor took a card case from his pocket and handed her a card. 'If you do, this is my mobile number. If you recall anything, no matter how trivial, that you haven't mentioned, ring this number, any time day or night.'

'You mean that, knowing the hours I keep, Inspector Joseph?' she questioned mischievously.

'He means it, but he won't enjoy a call from you as much me.' Peter left the chair and gave her one of his own cards.

'Call in any time. If the carers aren't here you can make yourselves – and me – coffee. The key code is 1960. One of the best years of my life.'

'When life was swinging,' Peter joked.

'You don't know your ancient history, Sergeant Collins. That was the last year before life began to swing. When women still wore gloves and a hat when they went out to buy a pound of sugar. People were polite to one another, life was pleasant and drunks weren't left to soil the street. They were locked up overnight and brought before the magistrates the morning after, to be fined and shamed by having their names printed in the local paper. No one in their family would have been able to hold their heads high for at least a year. But in those days people had pride. They cared for their friends and neighbours and no one was murdered in their beds or had their house burned down around them.'

CHAPTER SIXTEEN

'I want to see Constable Dai Smith in my office immediately,' Trevor informed Tony Sweet as he walked into the station foyer.

'He's not available, sir.'

'I assumed all leave had been cancelled.'

'It has, sir.'

'Then why isn't Constable Smith available?'

'You'd have to ask Superintendent Moore that, sir,' Tony Sweet replied.

'Problems, Inspector?' Reggie Moore eased past officers who were shifting furniture between rooms in the corridor that housed the offices.

'No problem.' Trevor looked her in the eye. 'I need to see Constable Dai Smith urgently.'

'Could we discuss this in the office we've cleared for you and Sergeant Collins? I trust you don't mind sharing?'

'It won't present a problem provided interview rooms are available,' Trevor replied.

'As we have over a dozen interview rooms that shouldn't present any difficulties.'

Peter followed Trevor and Reggie into the office and collided with Carol March who was carrying a stack of files.

'Sergeant Collins.' Hands full, she nodded to him.

Conscious of Trevor watching him, Peter took the files. 'Where do you want them?'

'I've moved in with Sergeant Howell next door.'

Trevor looked around the room. It was a square box with one desk under the window opposite the door and another set on the left-hand wall. Both had been positioned far enough from the walls to leave room for a chair. Two upright "guest" chairs, an empty bookcase and filing cabinet completed the furnishings. 'I trust we're not putting you to too much trouble.'

'I'm sorry we're so cramped at present. We're moving to new premises in two months. If you're still here I'm sure we'll be able to come with something better.'

Peter returned. 'Inconsiderate of the Pitchers' murderer not to wait.'

Trevor was accustomed to Peter's quips, but he saw that Reggie was irritated. He went to the window and looked out before sitting on the sill. 'Constable Dai Smith?'

'He's missing.'

'Missing as in vanished?' Trevor checked.

'No one's seen him since the morning after the fire.'

'Was he called in to help evacuate people from Main Street?' Trevor questioned.

'Yes.'

'What time did he arrive?'

'Around 5 a.m.'

'Wasn't that late?' Trevor frowned. 'I understood Sergeant Howell delegated someone to call everyone in shortly after three o'clock.'

'He did,' Reggie confirmed. 'Constable Smith said he went to bed when he reached home after his shift and slept heavily. He was woken at four thirty by his mobile buzzing with the message asking him to come in. He helped search Larry Jones when he was brought into the station. The last officer to see him was Constable Rees. He told her he was going to interview Alan Pitcher's neighbours in Main Street.'

'What time was that?'

'Constable Rees said it was before nine o'clock.'

'He conducted at least one interview,' Trevor revealed.

Reggie was surprised. 'How do you know?'

'Because I spoke to a witness he interviewed that morning,' Trevor divulged. 'Why didn't you tell me Constable Smith was missing?'

'I didn't think his absence relevant to the investigation.'

'It could well be relevant given the information Sergeant Collins and I've received. Did Constable Smith turn in his notes that morning?' Trevor watched Peter try out the chair behind the desk in front of the window.

'No.'

'You're certain.'

'I checked.'

'Did you make any effort to contact him when he disappeared?'

Reggie erupted. 'Of course I did. We've tried ringing his mobile. It's been switched off since ten o'clock that morning. I sent Constables Rees and Howell to his house.'

'Why them?'

'Paula Rees has worked with Dai Smith for six months. She knows where he keeps a spare key for emergencies. They searched his house. As far as they could ascertain the only thing missing was his car from the garage. His clothes are in the wardrobe. His passport in a drawer. They did find his wife's parents' telephone number in France.'

'Did you phone them?'

'I spoke to his wife. She told me she wasn't interested in her husband or his whereabouts and asked me not to call again.' She eyed Peter. 'Leave us, Sergeant Collins.'

For once Peter didn't argue. He closed the door behind him, leaving Trevor wondering if he'd followed Carol March into her office.

'Constable Smith has personal problems,' Reggie confided.

'He discussed them with you?'

'His timekeeping had deteriorated. I was considering instigating disciplinary proceedings but before I set things in motion I called him in for an informal chat. For ten years he'd been an exemplary officer with a clean service record. I couldn't understand why he'd begun to turn up late for his shifts. I knew his colleagues were covering for him. And I also knew there were times when he couldn't be raised, not even on his mobile.'

'What was his response when you challenged him?'

'He said he was depressed because his wife had left him and taken the children.'

'You didn't know his marriage was in trouble?'

Reggie hesitated. 'Constable Smith's wife is French. He'd told people she'd taken the children to France to visit her parents. I think he believed the story himself until I forced him to face facts. She'd been gone over ten weeks when I called him in.'

'Marriage break-up is a common problem with

police officers.' Trevor crossed his fingers behind his back. It was hard enough being separated from Lyn and Marty because of work. He couldn't bear the thought of having to live permanently apart from them.

'Dai Smith is besotted with and devoted to his three year old twin daughters.'

'Did he say why his wife had left him?'

'No.'

'You didn't ask?'

'It was none of my business.

'Although he'd been shirking his duty for over ten weeks?'

'It was four weeks before his behaviour was brought to my attention.'

'When his shift finished at midnight on the night of the fire, he asked Constable Rees to return the squad car to the station. Presumably he also asked her to turn in the end of shift report. Or is that done on the next day here?' Trevor questioned.

'The end of shift procedure depends on the preference of the duty sergeant and the level of activity in the town.' Reggie couldn't contain her curiosity a moment longer. 'Who did Constable Smith interview the day after the fire?'

Trevor briefly related what May Williams had told him and Peter.

'And Mrs Williams was certain that this person she saw at two twenty carrying a bag was a police officer?'

'She saw the top of his hat,' Trevor confirmed, 'and given the amount of time she spends looking out of her window at passers-by, including police officers, I'm inclined to believe her.'

'Do you think the sighting could be connected to the Pitcher murders?'

Trevor voiced what Reggie appeared to be reluctant to. 'Have you considered that the destruction of forensic evidence suggests the Pitchers' murderer having a certain amount of professional knowledge?'

'We can't be certain it was all destroyed.'

'Yet,' Trevor qualified, 'but early indicators are that someone had a damned good try to clean up the crime scene.'

'You can't possibly believe the Pitchers were murdered by one of my officers ...'

'No more than I can believe they were murdered by one of the forensic team working in the Pitcher house,' Trevor interrupted. 'Are you certain Constable Smith didn't report back here after he interviewed May Williams?'

'Not to my knowledge and I've read every witness statement that's come in.'

'Can we go to his house?'

'Now?'

'As this is the first lead we've had, I believe it's worth looking into immediately.'

'It'll mean postponing the briefing.'

'We may have more to report.'

'I'll pull his file and ask Inspector March to check if there's been any recent activity on his phone and banking records.'

Peter knocked on the door and entered. He handed Trevor and Reggie files, keeping one back for himself. 'The updated timeline I thought you'd like to see it before the briefing.'

Reggie took it from him. 'The briefing is postponed. If you'll excuse me I must see Inspector March.'

'I'll accompany whoever goes to Constable Smith's house,' Trevor said.

'I suggest Paula Rees as she knows the location of the key. Carol March and myself will go with her.'

'If it's an outing, can I come?' Peter chimed.

Reggie gave him a withering look and left.

'Stop winding up the locals,' Trevor ordered. He sat behind his desk and started reading.

11.55 pm Call logged at station. Mrs May Williams, Main Street complained of disturbance outside Angel Public House. Constables Smith and Rees contacted and ordered to attend.

12.05 a.m. Tim Pryce, landlord of Angel and Ken Lloyd deposit Larry Jones (comatose drunk) in archway leading from Main Street into Angel yard. Tim Pryce and Ken Lloyd talk to Michael Pitcher and Alison William, who are driving to Bryn Houses on outskirts of town to hous- sit Alison's parent's house.

12.10 a.m. Michael Pitcher and Alison Williams drive out of Main Street. Constables Smith and Rees arrive. Constables check Larry Jones who is unconscious and breathing normally. Larry Jones has history of drunken violence, decision is made by Constables Smith and Rees to leave Larry Jones in yard to sleep off effects of alcohol.'

Trevor looked at Peter. 'Would you have left Larry Jones where he was?'

'If the only option was putting him in a squad car that I had to clean – probably.'

'Knowing he had a history of violence when drunk?'

'It was never a question for us when we were on the beat. We used to send for the van. And it was simple enough to hose that down.'

Trevor recalled one memorable incident when a newly appointed Constable Peter Collins had hosed down the van – or drunk tank as it was known in the station – with the pick-ups inside. They'd had a rude awakening. Peter defended his action by insisting the passengers were so heavily soiled by vomit, urine and faeces they would have posed a health risk to the officers in the station.

To the admiration of every other rookie Peter had been given a caution and verbal reprimand – nothing more.

Constables Smith's and Rees's shifts finished at midnight. Constable Smith enters Angel with publican Tim Pryce to discuss Mrs May Williams's complaint. Constable Rees returns car to station prior to going off duty.

'No mention of putting in an incident report,' Peter commented.

'Reggie admitted the report system here is lax. She told me it depended on the preference of the duty sergeant.'

'Lazy sods. I wonder how long Tim Pryce and Dai William's "discussion" of May Williams complaint took. If they talked about it all, I bet it was no more than a casual "interfering old bat".'

'Now you've answered your own question, can we finish reading this?' Trevor turned the page.

12.15 a.m. Constable Rees leaves Angel in squad car. Constable Smith and Tim Pryce enter Angel. Ken Lloyd leaves Main Street to walk to river.

2.53 a.m. clock stops in attic of Pitcher house. Due to fire?

2.55 a.m. Ken Lloyd sees flames in attic (fifth floor from back of house) of Pitcher house from bank of river. Sees and hears fire blow out window in kitchen of Pitcher house (third floor from back of house). Sees someone descend fire escape.

2.57 a.m. clock stops in cellar of Pitcher house. Due to fire?

3.00 a.m. Ken Lloyd calls emergency services from river bank on his mobile.

3.02 a.m. Tim Pryce calls emergency services. Woken by blast and glass falling from Pitcher house, sees fire in attic and kitchen of Pitcher house from window of private living quarters in Angel.

3.04 a.m. Emergency services call local police station and fire station. Sergeant Frank Howell responds and sends all available officers to Main Street. Sergeant Howell leaves to make assessment of fire at back of Pitcher house.

3.06 a.m. Tim Pryce enters back lane behind Pitcher house.

3.12 a.m. Sergeant Howell enters back lane behind Pitcher house. Meets Tim Pryce. Fires are burning on cellar, attic and kitchen floor (at back of house – ground, third and fifth floor). Situation volatile and dangerous. Windows blowing out.

3.13 a.m. ambulance and paramedics park in Main Street at safe distance from Pitcher house.

3.15 a.m. 1st fire tender arrives in back lane. Officers assess situation and order evacuation of street. Sergeant Howell and Tim Pryce go to Main Street to implement evacuation of neighbouring houses and Angel pub.

3.18. a.m. Fire tender 2 arrives in Main Street. Officers axe front door of Pitcher house and proceed to fight fire. Tim Pryce and Sergeant Howell arrive in Main Street. Dr Edwards (local physician) offers professional service. Dr Edwards waits in Main Street with police officers, paramedics and Tim Pryce. Evacuation of street underway. Sergeant Howell acts on information given by Tim Pryce and sends for Michael Pitcher. Short of officers he enlists help of respected local medical consultant.

3.25 a.m. Ken Lloyd arrives in Main Street, informs Police and Fire Officers of likely location of family in Pitcher house. Fire Officers act on information.

3.30 a.m. Sergeant Howell asks Tim Pryce to set up rest centre for Fire Officers in pub.

3.32 a.m. Fire Officers enter master bedroom on second floor front of Pitcher house (from Main Street) discover one corpse, later identified as Gillian Pitcher.

3.40 a.m. Chief Fire Officer Huw Thomas arrives in Main Street.

3.50 a.m. Superintendent Moore arrives in Main Street.

4.25 a.m. Michael Pitcher and Alison Griffiths arrive in Main Street. Driven in by Henry Clarke consultant surgeon (neighbour of Alison's parents).

4.40 a.m. Larry Jones found asleep in derelict stable at back of Pitcher House.

4.50 a.m. Larry Jones's hands and feet bagged. Matches, cigarettes, lighter, cash, gold clip and jewellery taken from attic of Pitcher house (according to Michael Pitcher's statement) found on his person.

'No mention of police officers carrying weekend bags.' Peter set his file aside.

'Did you expect there to be?' Trevor asked.

'I live in constant hope of my fellow officers being as efficient as me and in constant disappointment when they fail to live up to my standards. What we need is a timeline covering the movements of every officer in this station that night.'

'Thank you for volunteering to draw it up.' Trevor looked at him over the edge of his file.

'I didn't and I won't, because a wise man once told me never to volunteer for anything.'

'And another man – if not a wise one – told me that he didn't want to stay in Wales any longer than he had to. Unless, that is, you've seen something here to change your mind?' Trevor said archly.

Peter didn't take the bait. 'I suppose you do need someone from outside the station to draw it up.'

'You've been talking to the locals …'

'What's that supposed to mean?' Peter broke in testily.

'The file.' Trevor tapped his. 'You brought them in, remember? Is there any news on Michael Pitcher?'

'No one's mentioned him.'

'I'll bring his condition up at the briefing.' Trevor opened his laptop case, removed a pad and scribbled a note.

'Sir.' Paula knocked on the door and carried in a tray of coffee and biscuits. 'Sergeant Collins said you drink your coffee black. And you prefer chocolate digestives to plain biscuits.'

'What Sergeant Collins meant, Constable Rees, is that he prefers chocolate biscuits to plain.' Trevor set the timeline on the desk.

'And you don't?' Peter picked up one of the cups of coffee from the tray and added sugar.

'Superintendent Moore's put the briefing back until twelve o'clock, sir, so you can go to Constable Smith's house. She told me to tell you that she has some calls to make but hopes to leave in ten minutes. And, Mr Gant's asking if you'd like him to make a preliminary report on the findings in the Pitcher house during the briefing. He said he should be free at midday.'

'Yes please to Mr Gant. I take it you're coming to Constable Smith's house with us?'

'The Super asked me to, sir.'

'You knew him well.'

'Only through work. I'll get a message to Mr Gant, sir.'

'Thank you, and after you've done that could you come back here and answer a few questions, Constable.'

'Bring your own coffee when you do and thank you for this.' Peter handed Trevor a cup, black without sugar the way he drank it.

'Sir.'

Peter watched her leave. 'Do you want me to go to Smith's place with you?'

'Yes. Another pair of eyes is always useful.'

'Do you think Smith's involved in the murders?'

'It's a possibility.'

'The locals are in this up to their necks. That's why Ice Drawers sent for us. The only question I'm asking is this: does Ice Drawers hope we'll discover the truth or does she want us to play dumb and go along with the Larry Jones charade so murdering coppers can continue pounding the Welsh beat?'

CHAPTER SEVENTEEN

Paula appeared nervous when she returned to Trevor and Peter's office. Peter pushed a chair in between Trevor's desk and his own and she sat down.

'Does Dai Smith live far from the centre of town?' Trevor shook his head when Peter offered him the biscuits.

'About a ten-minute walk,' Paula answered. 'He lives in a converted barn on the hill behind Main Street.'

'You get on with him well?' Trevor reached for his coffee.

'Reasonably well, sir. We've been working together for about six months and this is a small station.'

'Do you know his wife?'

'I've baby-sat for them on occasions, but I wouldn't really say that I was friendly with her.'

'You usually do the driving at work?' Peter chipped in.

'Not always,' Paula replied. 'Dai and I take it in turns.'

'Have you any idea where Dai Smith could have gone?' Trevor monitored her reaction.

'No, sir. We work together but we're not that close.'

'You never socialised with him or his family?'

'As I said, I baby-sat for him and his wife occasionally, on special occasions, like their wedding anniversary and birthdays. And I saw him sometimes outside work, in a pub or one of the restaurants in town.'

'Who was he with?'

'Usually a group of men.'

'Not his wife or another woman?' Trevor persisted.

'No man would go out with a woman in this town who wasn't his wife, sir. The gossips would have him in the divorce courts before he even got home.'

'So who were these men?'

'Fellow officers or men from the town. Dai was in the darts team and he used to play ruby but he gave it up after his daughters were born.'

Trevor referred back to the timeline. 'When you went to the Angel with Dai Smith to answer the call Mrs May Williams made, you were off duty as your shifts had finished at twelve o'clock.'

'It was the last call of the day and we knew it wouldn't take long.'

'Why's that?' Peter took his fourth biscuit and moved his chair closer to Trevor's desk.

'If there'd been a real problem in the Angel the landlord would have telephoned us himself,' Paula said defensively.

'There'd been trouble there before?' Peter suggested.

'No, sir, Tim Pryce has a cool head. He avoids problems by banning troublemakers.'

'He's never asked the locals for help?'

'As far as I know, only when the pub's been broken into but I've only been a constable for a year.'

'If Tim Pryce had been busy dealing with the disturbance he might not have been able to telephone the station. So how could you be so sure that the call wouldn't take much of your, and,' Peter glanced at the timeline again, 'Dai Smith's time?'

'We shouldn't prejudge situations, sir, but the complaint was made by Mrs Williams. She phones the station at least a dozen times a week. In fact she telephoned the morning before the fire. I took the call. She reported a cat sitting on the roof of the Pitcher's house.'

'Did you call the Fire Brigade?' Peter lifted an eyebrow.

'No, sir. But Mrs Williams rang an hour later to say that the cat had disappeared.'

'Did you take credit for spiriting it away?'

Paula looked bemused, as people generally did when they were exposed to Peter's odd sense of humour.

Trevor took control of the conversation. 'As you're here, Constable Rees, it might be as well to go through your movements on the night of the fire. You haven't seen Constable Smith since the morning after the fire, is that right?'

'Yes, sir, but I'd rather you discussed Constable Smith's absence with Superintendent Moore, sir.'

'I'm checking facts, not asking for speculative comment about Constable Smith's absence. When you and Constable Smith arrived at the Angel, you saw Larry Jones lying under the archway that leads into the yard of the Angel Hotel?'

'He wasn't lying down, sir. Tim had propped him against a drain pipe. He said he was concerned that Larry might vomit and choke.'

'A publican who knows how to look after his regulars.' Peter helped himself to yet another biscuit.

'Larry wasn't a regular at the Angel. Tim Pryce banned him and his mates before they reached their eighteenth birthdays for trying to drink under age.'

'Then why did Larry Jones go to the Angel that night?' Trevor asked.

'I've no idea, but I recall thinking it odd at the time. Tim said that Larry turned up drunk at closing time and demanded to be served. When Tim refused as, even drunk, Larry must have known Tim would do, Larry started shouting. Tim escorted him outside where Larry passed out.'

'Courtesy of the fresh air or the landlord.' Peter looked quizzically at Paula.

'There were no marks on Larry, sir, and he stank of booze.'

'What kind of alcohol?' Trevor asked.

'Beer, sir.'

'Where had he been drinking?' Trevor made a note on the pad in front of him.

'We don't know, sir.'

'Find out,' Trevor ordered. 'He must have bought his alcohol from a pub, supermarket or off-licence.'

'There's no supermarket in town, sir. Only outside but I'll look into it.'

Trevor returned to the timeline. 'So, after checking that Larry Jones was breathing you and Constable Smith went off duty?'

Paula shifted uneasily on her chair. 'There was some discussion as to whether or not we should take Larry Jones to the station and put him in the cells.'

'But you decided not to?'

'I know what you're thinking …'

'You do?' Trevor sipped his coffee.

'This is a quiet town, sir. It's not like the city.'

'You think we don't know that constables are reluctant to put drunks in squad cars because they're likely to throw up?' Peter asked.

Paula looked embarrassed but remained silent.

'You don't have a secure vehicle that can be hosed down to transport drunks?'

'We use it at weekends and whenever there's a festival or special event. But we didn't have any drivers free that night,' Paula explained. 'If the people in this town knew just how few officers man the night shifts they'd be horrified.'

'And the burglars would make whoopee,' Peter suggested.

'So, knowing Larry Jones had a history of violence when drunk, you and Constable Smith left him to "sleep it off" next to a public thoroughfare.'

'It wasn't like that, sir.' Paula's hands shook.

'Then what was it like?' Trevor questioned.

'Larry Jones was unconscious …'

'We've established that,' Trevor interrupted.

'I'm sure that none of us …'

'Us, being Constable Smith and yourself?'

'And Tim Pryce and Ken Lloyd, sir. None of us thought that Larry Jones presented a danger to the public. We assumed he'd sleep until the early hours, then go home.'

'How far is home for Larry Jones from the Angel – walking not driving?'

'The estate is about three miles away, sir.'

'A good hour's walk, longer for someone with a hangover.'

'I suppose it would be, sir.'

'So, knowing Larry Jones's record of violent and anti-social behaviour when drunk you left him in your terms "sleeping it off" in the centre of town at midnight and when he woke, facing an hour's walk during which he could have assaulted an innocent passer-by going about his or her legal business?' When Paula didn't reply, Trevor continued. 'You drove the squad car to the station?'

'Yes, sir.'

'Did you go into the station?'

'Yes, sir.'

'Did you make a report on Larry Jones?'

'Only in my notebook, sir. But I told Sergeant Howell that we – that is Constable Smith and myself had left Larry Jones in the archway of the Angel.'

'He made a note of it?' Trevor finished his coffee and pushed his cup away.

'I assume so, sir.'

'You didn't see him writing anything up?' Trevor checked.

'No, sir.'

'Then what did you do?'

'I left the keys to the squad car at the station and went home.'

'Did you drive your own car home?'

'No, sir. I live in town, less than five minutes' walk from the station.'

'Handy.' Peter commented.

'Did you go out again that night?' Trevor held his pen poised over his notepad.

'Yes, sir. As soon as the fire was reported Sergeant Howell left the station but before he went he asked Jim Murphy to call in everyone whether they were on- or off-duty and direct them to Main Street to help with the evacuation from the buildings that were under threat.'

'You spoke to Jim Murphy, or did he leave a message on your voice mail?'

'I spoke to him.'

Did you note the time?'

'It was around three fifteen. I remember looking at the clock. He asked me to contact Damian Howell and Tony Sweet to speed things up, rather than make all the calls himself.'

'So Damian Howell and Tony Sweet weren't on duty that night?'

'I don't believe so.'

'Who was on duty?'

'When I brought in the keys to the squad car Sergeant Howell was manning the desk. I didn't see anyone else but as Jim had called me I assumed that he was also on duty. There are generally two or three officers on the night shift.'

'Two or three?' Trevor questioned.

'More usually two, as I said, sir, staffing has been a problem on the night shift since our budget has been cut.'

'And after you were called by Jim Murphy, you did what?' Trevor continued.

'Made the calls he asked me to, dressed and ran to Main Street, where I stayed with the people who'd been evacuated in the church hall until the fire service brought the fire under control.'

'To go back to when you left the Angel. You drove the squad car directly to the station car park?'

'As directly as the one-way system will allow,

sir.'

'Did you see anyone when you were driving around the town?' Trevor asked.

'A few stragglers leaving the Commercial. It mainly caters for people from the housing estate.'

'Did you recognise any of them?'

'Most of them, sir.'

'Were any headed towards Main Street?'

'Not that I saw, sir. They were walking in a crowd in the direction of the estate.'

'So you saw no one apart from a few stragglers walking back from the pub when you drove through the town?'

'No one I can recall, sir.'

'And when you walked home from the station?'

'No one, sir. The streets were quiet.'

'How about when you left your flat after you received the telephone call from Jim Murphy?'

'The streets were busy then, sir. Between police, bystanders ...'

The telephone rang and Trevor picked it up. He glanced at his watch then said, 'We'll meet you there ... Constable Rees is with me now, I'll ask her for directions ... we'll need sterile suits, caps and overshoes ... we're on our way.'

'To Dai Smith's house, sir?' Paula asked.

'Correct. You can give us directions?'

'Yes, sir.'

Peter handed her a sheet of paper and a pen. 'Draw me a map from the Angel, my car's parked in the yard.'

Paula drew a rough sketch of the town and arrows to indicate the route.

Peter studied it. 'Excellent: an idiot should be able to find the place from this.'

She left her chair and gathered their cups back on to the tray.

'Constable,' Trevor called to her just as she was about to leave the room. She turned.

'I asked awkward questions but no more awkward than you'll be confronted with by anyone looking into the way this investigation was conducted from the outset. You did well, Constable Rees.'

She finally smiled. 'Thank you, sir.'

Peter and Trevor found Dai Smith's house without difficulty. It took precisely twenty minutes to drive there from the station by Trevor's watch and it would have been considerably less if Peter hadn't had to adhere to the convoluted one-way system. As the roof of the house was visible from the yard of the Angel Trevor doubted that it would take a fit and active man more than a few minutes to walk there from the pub.

Peter parked alongside the squad car on the gravelled drive at the side of the house. Reggie, Carol and Paula were already climbing into white paper boiler suits, and bonnets they'd taken from the boot. Trevor left Peter to lock the car and joined them. Reggie handed him two white suits.

'The largest we have.'

'Thank you.' He passed one to Peter, pulled on the other and looked around. The house had obviously begun life as a barn, but the conversion was imaginative and no expense had been spared. Practically the whole of the stone wall at the front of the barn that faced the town had been replaced by glass. Trevor stepped up on to the terrace that ran the full length of the house and looked inside, but cream blinds obscured his view.

He looked back towards the town. The view of the surrounding hills was magnificent.

'Nice spot,' he said to Reggie when she joined him, overshoes in hand.

'Dai Smith's father owns most of the land around here. His farmhouse is at the top of this hill – and before you ask – no he hasn't heard from his son. He's frail, elderly and very concerned because Dai's disappearance is totally out of character.'

'Father and son are close?'

'As close as most fathers and sons.'

'Did you have any luck with Dai's phone or bank statements?'

'There's been no activity on his phone since the night of the fire when he called back into the station. And, as it no longer goes straight to message when you ring the number I assume the battery has run down. The only outgoing activity on his bank account is payments of standing orders and direct debits.'

'I'll get the key, Super,' Paula called out.

'Wait, I want to see where it's kept.' Trevor ran up to her and Peter followed. Together they walked on the stone paved path that ran around the house.

'Expensive conversion and landscaping.' Trevor noted a pond at the back of the house that fed a small waterfall.

'Dai did a lot of the work himself to keep down the cost.'

'Nice kitchen.' Peter looked through the large picture window. The blinds were open and anyone sitting at the table or working at the sink would look out at the waterfall.

'James Pitcher made it. He fitted most of the new kitchens in the town.'

'Did Dai Smith know James Pitcher?' Trevor asked.

'Well, most of the furniture in the house is either antique, bought from Alan Pitcher, or made by James to order to fit various alcoves in the house. This is where Dai keeps the spare key.' She stopped in front of the waterfall. 'This isn't a water feature. It's a natural spring. Dai dammed it to make the pool and had a drain and culvert constructed to carry away the overflow.' She picked out a pebble that looked no different to the others placed among the plants behind and around the fall, and handed it to Trevor. 'It opens at the back.'

Trevor turned it over and swivelled a metal plate. He upended the pebble and a key fell into his hand. 'And this is a police officer's house? How many other people know where he keeps his key?'

'I should think most of his friends. But …'

'Don't tell me, this is a small country town where everyone knows everyone else.'

'And no one is murdered. And houses never get burned down by arsonists,' Peter muttered.

'Which door does this open?' Trevor asked.

'The one to the kitchen.'

He looked at the box over the door. 'There's a burglar alarm and CCTV.'

'The CCTV is never on and I know the code for the alarm.' Paula donned her overshoes, opened the back door and, ignoring the bleeping of the alarm, stepped directly into the kitchen which looked even more expensive than it had done through the window. The worktops, cooker and fridge were stainless steel, the cupboards black ebony and the floor and walls tiled in multi-coloured ceramic squares.

Paula went to a box behind the door and tapped in a code. Peter, Trevor, Reggie and Carol slipped on their own overshoes and followed.

Reggie shouted, 'Hello.' When they were greeted by silence, she looked at Trevor. 'This is your search. Where do you want to start?'

'To save time, I suggest Inspector March and Constable Rees start upstairs, you and I downstairs. Sergeant Collins can take the garage and outbuildings.'

'What are we looking for?' Reggie asked.

'I have absolutely no idea, Superintendent,' Trevor answered.

'But you'd better hope that we recognise it when we see it.' Peter eyed the keyboard screwed to the wall next to the kitchen door. Selecting keys marked "GARAGE", "SHED" and "WORKSHOP he lifted them down, pocketed them, slipped off his overshoes and returned outside.

CHAPTER EIGHTEEN

Trevor left Reggie in the kitchen and went into the hall. Light streamed in through the glass front door, illuminating four doors on his left and two on his right. The first door opened into a marble-walled and -floored shower room. There were no cupboards, only an open set of white wickerwork shelves that held towels, a bowl of soaps and various cosmetics. Trevor was no expert but the packaging looked expensive. He lifted out the towels, shook them and returned them to the shelf before checking the glass shower cubicle. It was empty, clean and smelled of bleach.

The second door led into a walk-in cupboard that held a Dyson cleaner, mop, brush, and shelves of cleaning materials. The third was a wardrobe, racked on one side for shoes. Trevor noted there were no children or women's coats and shoes, only those suitable for an adult male of forty-four-inch chest and size eleven feet.

The fourth door opened into a study. Shelved on three walls, it held a substantial collection of books, DVDs and CDs. A leather-topped desk dominated the centre of the room, a swivel leather chair behind it. The mock brown leather in-tray held half a dozen unopened letters, all from utility companies and banks. A matching penholder contained two biros, a pencil, and a small notepad. A plain wooden frame held a photograph of what Trevor assumed to be Dai Smith's family. A good-looking dark haired man had one arm wrapped around an attractive blonde woman's shoulder, the other around two small blonde girls perched on his knees.

Two matching leather armchairs were set either side of a leather topped coffee table in front of the glass wall and door that opened on to the patio.

Trevor went to the bookshelves. He found what he was looking for on a high shelf in the back left-hand corner. He pulled away a false frontage of leather-bound volumes to reveal a safe. He went to the desk. The drawers were locked. He reached for his penknife and flicked open a long thin blade. In less than a minute he'd succeeded in opening all six drawers.

One held computer disks. He removed all the boxes and piled them on the desk. Another held photographs. A quick glance established that most, like the photograph on the desk, were family snaps of the small girls at various stages from birth to toddler. The widest and slimmest drawer held pens and biro refills, pencils, rubbers, rulers, paper clips and, address labels. Another was full of receipts and bills, all marked paid. One contained a file of bank statements.

Trevor flicked through them. The savings account held rather more than he'd expect to find in a constable's account, but he recalled Paula Rees telling him that Dai Smith's father had owned both the land and the barn, so his mortgage only reflected the cost of the conversion.

The last two drawers held the usual household files of insurance policies, guarantees on appliances, wage slips etc. Trevor thumbed through them and noticed there was only one driving licence – Dai's.

After a final and fruitless search for keys, he returned to the safe and examined it.

It was fireproof. He knew because he'd bought a similar model to store his and Lyn's documents. He hadn't been impressed when unable to find the key; Lyn had opened it with a paperclip. The lock proved even easier than those on the desk drawers.

Inside were a couple of leather cases and a single passport. He opened the passport and turned to the back. It was recognisable portrait of the same good-looking man in the photograph on the desk.

Setting the passport aside, he lifted out the smallest leather case. It contained four credit cards. Beneath it was a larger leather case that held a removable external hard drive for a computer and half a dozen USB computer storage pens. He placed the case and passport on top of the disk boxes on the chair before replacing the credit cards in the safe and locking it.

He went to the desk, took a pen from the holder and scribbled a note on the pad.

Passport, hard drive and USB pens removed from safe, disk boxes from drawer. Taken by police officers concerned for the safety of Dai Smith. Photograph may be used for public appeal. Please contact station, ASAP, Inspector Trevor Joseph.

He closed the door, switched on the computer and inserted one of USB pens into the computer. It was password protected but, courtesy of the computer expert, Sarah Merchant, in his home station he knew about passwords. It had been wiped clean but he also knew how to retrieve information from deleted files. Less than five minutes after inserting the pen, he'd seen enough.

He looked up when the door opened. Reggie was standing in the doorway. He closed down the computer and removed the pen.

'Have you found something?' she asked.

'Possibly, but I need more time than we have right now. You?'

'Kitchen equipment in the kitchen and, silverware and porcelain in the cupboard in the open plan living space. I had no idea people could be so tidy and well organised. You seem to have had more luck.'

'Time will tell.'

'We have a computer expert at the station.'

'No need.' Trevor picked up the disk boxes, hard drive and pens. 'It will give me something to do this evening.'

Peter walked through from the kitchen. 'There's something you should see outside.'

'I'll be with you in a moment.' Trevor unzipped his suit, pocketed the storage pens, hard drive and passport and picked up the disk boxes.

Reggie looked at Peter but he didn't extend the invitation.

'You could check how Paula and Carol have fared upstairs,' Trevor suggested pointedly.

Reggie went up the stairs. Trevor followed Peter to the back door where they both slipped off their overshoes.

'The garage?' Trevor asked, seeing the door open.

'Is well organised, neat, clean, tidy and the car, a BMW, is missing, just as Paula said.'

How do you know it's a BMW?'

Peter pointed to a manual on a shelf.

'This is as clean and well organised as the house.'

'Not at all a scruffy copper's lair.' Peter observed.

'There's scruffy and organised in all walks of life, and this garage could be yours.' When they had first started working together Peter's addiction to minimalism, order and cleanliness in all things domestic had astounded Trevor.

'This is what I wanted you to see.'

A reel was fastened to the wall below a tap. 'A hose reel.'

'Exactly.'

'The hose?' Trevor asked.

'Nowhere to be found and the car's missing. What does that suggest to you?'

After checking that Paula and Carol had so far drawn a blank in their search of the upstairs of Dai's house, Trevor and Peter left them and Reggie to finish the task while they returned to the station.

'Did you find anything on Dai Smith's computer pens and hard drive?' Peter asked as soon as they were in the car.

'Partial photograph.'

'Anything interesting?'

'Gay porn with Dai Smith in a starring role.'

'Could explain his wife going off in a huff.'

'It could, but let's not read too much into it until we know more. Do me a favour,' Trevor asked as Peter parked, 'check if anything new has come in? Then, get hold of the time sheets and records for the station, starting at midnight on the night of the fire.'

'You're phoning the cavalry.' Peter guessed. It wasn't a question.

'I should have gone with my instincts and done it this morning.' Trevor entered the building, nodded to Tony Sweet who was manning the foyer, went down the corridor and into his office. He closed and locked the door before unlocking his briefcase. Its combination lock was more sophisticated than the locks on Dai Smith's desk drawers and safe. He placed the disks, hard drive and USB pens inside, spun the lock and sat behind the desk before ringing Bill Mulcahy's private number on his mobile. Bill picked up on the third ring.

'I need Merchant.'

'Problems?'

'Being cautious.'

'Cautious is good. Locals involved?'

'Too early to tell.'

'Want another beside Merchant?'

'If one's available.'

'Merchant's other half mopes when they're separated. I'll send them to you this afternoon.'

'Undercover. Ask Merchant and her other half to try to book into one of the stable cottages in the Angel or a room in the pub. If they succeed they don't know me or Peter. Tell them to wait for us to contact them.'

'Understood. Tread carefully.'

'Like a ballerina.' Trevor ended the call, stripped off his boiler suit, bonnet and gloves, tossed them into his waste bin, unlocked the door and returned to reception with his briefcase.

Peter was talking to Tony Sweet at the desk. 'The gorgeous Jen phoned. Patrick wants us in the mortuary.'

Trevor glanced at his watch.

'They can't start the briefing without you,' Peter reminded him.

'Where's the mortuary?' Trevor asked Constable Sweet.

'In the general hospital, sir. About a mile out of town. Turn right when you leave the car park and follow the road. A Victorian building fronts the road, but it's only used for admin, the wards are behind it in the grounds. The mortuary is at the top of the hill. The last building on your left.'

'Phone and tell them we're on our way.'

'And the briefing, sir?'

'You have my mobile number. Phone me when Superintendent Moore returns.'

Jen was waiting for them in the ante-room with paper bonnets and white coats.

'You found something?' Trevor asked.

'No "Good morning, Jen. I'm sorry to nag you for reports before you and Patrick have time to write them. How conscientious of both of you to start work at six this morning".'

'Want a kiss in compensation?' Peter teased her.

'Not from you,' Jen retorted. She winked at Trevor. 'Maybe your boss.'

'Stop flirting with the plods, Jen, and get them in here,' Patrick shouted from inside.

Trevor slipped on the white coat and entered the mortuary. He'd been in dozens of morgues and seen more post mortems than he cared to remember but he'd never become accustomed to the smell of formaldehyde.

Patrick was sipping coffee from a specimen beaker while studying a partially dissected charred corpse. He'd cut through the chest and removed the baked lungs, heart, stomach, liver and pancreas. The skull had been severed from the body and the brain lay in a dish above the crown. The extremities were so badly burned it was impossible to see the individual finger and toe bones.

'Which one is this?' Peter asked.

'The youngest victim.' Patrick checked his chart. 'James Pitcher.'

'Cause of death?' Trevor asked.

'Smoke inhalation. But, the fractures in his skull suggest he was unconscious at the time.'

'Poor bugger,' Peter said feelingly.

Trevor struggled to keep his equanimity. 'What am I looking for?'

'On the slab behind you.'

Trevor and Peter turned and saw a motley collection of objects. Fragments of brown paper, singed at the edges, two partial dentures, both for the upper jaw, blackened pieces of jewellery, two wedding rings, one labelled GILLIAN PITCHER, the other ALUN PITCHER. There was a blackened chain-link bracelet labelled LEE PITCHER, and a chain necklace labelled JAMES PITCHER. A clutch of bones was lying in the centre of the slab apparently closed over something. Trevor peered closer.

'It's a medallion.' Jenny snapped on a clean pair of rubber gloves and lifted the top bones. 'This was Lee's hand, I cut through it earlier,' she explained. 'The medallion is blackened by soot, the chain's snapped and the broken ends have been melted by the heat. But I cleaned off the dirt. The inscription's legible.' She held it in front of Trevor.

'LARRY AND DEBS FOREVER,' he read. 'Larry Jones?' he looked at Patrick.

'That, Inspector Joseph, is for you to determine,' Patrick crowed. 'Bag it for them, Jen.'

'If Lee pulled it off Larry, it would explain the red mark on the side of Larry's neck in the interview we saw,' Peter murmured. 'But isn't that like Larry himself – just too easy?'

'Anything else?' Trevor pressed.

Jen handed Trevor a pair of gloves from a box. When he'd slipped them on she gave him the hand.

'Can you feel it?' she asked.

'A coating. Burned skin?'

'Look carefully. The coating's been shrivelled by the heat to almost nothing but there's still traces.' She handed a pair of gloves to Peter, after he'd put them on Trevor passed over the bones.

'It feels like cellophane,' Peter said.

'Close. It's Sellotape,' Jen explained.

'Then the murderer was anxious for us to think that Lee had pulled the medallion from Larry's neck,' Peter murmured.

Trevor turned to Patrick. 'Were there any marks on the hand to indicate that Lee had tugged at the chain and broken it?'

'Not that I've found, although it's difficult to say whether there were or weren't given the degree of damage. It's possible the chain was wrapped around the fingers and fastened there by the tape to ensure that it wouldn't fall from the hand during the fire.'

'Who else knows about the medallion and tape?'

Trevor asked.

'Jen, me, and now you and Peter.'

'Let's keep it that way. DNA, fingerprints …'

'The medallion was clean,' Jenny assured him.

'Wiped?'

'I found smudges.'

Trevor turned back to the assortment of objects on the slab but he knew better than to touch them without changing his gloves. 'Anything on the brown paper?'

'It's thick, good packing quality.'

'Used by?'

'Butcher, baker, candlestick maker? Your guess is as good as mine. The only thing I can say with any certainty is that it isn't used by me or any pathologists of my acquaintance. But I did ask Ted Gant about it. As of this morning he hadn't found any paper like it in the cellar of the Pitcher house, or in any of the other rooms, but that's not remarkable. You saw the place. Paper has no chance of surviving an intense blaze and given the amount of ash it could take weeks to sift through looking for traces.'

'The bed bugs?' Trevor asked.

'You really think I'm a miracle worker, don't you? It would have been a first to have extracted DNA from baked bugs. I tried, but no go.' Patrick finished his coffee and handed Jenny the specimen jar.

'You didn't find any live ones?' Trevor persisted.

'No, only a way to get them out of your house. Burn it down,' Jen said cheerfully. 'We're thinking of posting the advice on the internet.'

'Do you have cause of death on the others?'

'All four were battered, but the only sign of smoke inhalation was in James Pitcher's lungs. Jen examined the others this morning after I did his PM. She found nothing, so I think I can safely say they died from trauma. Three were definitely killed by the metal hoe found at the scene. I've found impressions of the handle and slice marks made by the edge of the hoe in Lee, James and Gillian Pitcher's heads.'

'Alun Pitcher?'

'A single massive fracture to the top of his skull. The most damage was inflicted on Lee and Gillian Pitcher.'

Jen referred to a chart. 'Fifty-seven fractures on Lee Pitcher's body, fifteen to his head. Four blows to James Pitcher's head. Twelve separate wounds on Gillian Pitcher, eight to her head.'

'And Alan Pitcher?'

'Something large flat and extremely heavy was dropped on the top of his head, possibly as he ascended the attic stairs. I mentioned the bronze Dying Gaul when you were in the house. Ted Gant's team found Alun Pitcher's blood and hairs on the base. If there's more, they'll put it in their report.'

'And your reports?' Trevor asked hopefully.

'If you stop badgering us we may find time to write them.'

'You sent for us,' Trevor reminded him.

'Did I?' Patrick enquired absently.

'I take it that's a dismissal,' Peter said caustically.

'We've been up so long my stomach thinks it's lunch time. Jen, we'll take our break now. Fetch the sandwiches.'

Jen opened a drawer in the body bank. 'Want to

stay for coffee and sarnies?' she invited Trevor.
'They're ham and tomato.'

'Thank you for your help and thank you for the
invitation but we have a briefing to attend.'

'Whisky's on you tonight,' Patrick warned.

'Sure you won't stay for coffee?' Jenny rinsed two
specimen jars under the tap and carried them over to
the electric kettle in the corner.'

'We'll take a rain check.' Peter stripped off his
white coat and followed Trevor to the car.

'Are the cavalry on their way?' Peter asked as
they drove off.

'Yes.'

'Who?'

'Merchant and Brookes.'

'Why Brookes?' Peter demanded. 'I can
understand a computer expert to work on the pens
and drive you found in Dai Smith's house. And we
may well need help to decipher the station's record
system ...'

'The record system is complicated?' Trevor asked.

'I couldn't make head or tail of it.'

'Merchant likes having Brookes around and he's
good at legwork. But as they won't be here until this
afternoon I'd like you to walk around the shops in
town and find out which ones, if any, use brown
paper. Hopefully there won't be too many as I'd like
you to buy something so we can match the wrapping
without arousing anyone's suspicions.'

'You keeping Merchant and Brookes undercover?'

'Yes.' Trevor confirmed.

'You going to do anything about Dai Smith?'

'Get the locals to look for him.'

'They haven't found him so far.'

'But have they really been looking?' Trevor questioned.

'It's possible they don't want to find him.'

'That thought has occurred to me,' Trevor concurred.

'With Merchant doing the computer work and Brookes the legwork, what's left for you and me?' Peter drove off when the lights turned green.

'I'll carry on supervising, but don't worry; I'll find something interesting to occupy your mind after your shopping trip.'

'Like?' Peter pressed.

'Studying all the serious crime files in the station that cover incidents of rape, murder and violence, during the last …' Trevor reflected for a moment. '… twenty-five years.'

'To look for officers, who've worked closely with pathologists and forensic experts, witnessed their methods and who might, just might, know enough to destroy the physical evidence at a crime scene.' Peter drove into the police station yard, parked the car and turned off the ignition.

Trevor smiled. 'And to think people wonder why I work with you.'

'I'll start when you're in the briefing. I take it the official story is we're looking for suspects who've graduated to arson and murder.'

'Do you need to ask?'

'Just making sure you're as cunning as me.'

CHAPTER NINETEEN

Trevor was crossing the foyer on his way into the briefing room when Reggie walked in with Carol and Paula. She drew him aside.

'Nothing except Dai's clothes and a few toys. By the look of them, ones the children had outgrown. Even the posters from the children's walls and the bed linen had been stripped from their rooms. There were no single duvet covers or sheets in the airing cupboard. When a woman packs to that extent, she has no intention of returning.'

'Thank you for being so thorough. Briefing in ten minutes?' he asked.

'As soon as we've stripped off our boiler suits, we'll be with you.'

Trevor entered the conference room and found Frank Howell fixing photographs to a Perspex screen under the direction of Ted Gant.

'Any news on the PM, sir?' Frank asked.

'You knew I'd been to the mortuary, sergeant?'

'Can't keep anything quiet on this case, sir,' Frank informed him. 'Too many officers knew and liked the Pitchers. We've all been hoping for some hard evidence.'

'Sorry to disappoint you, Sergeant.'

'Just want to see justice done, sir.'

'As long as it is justice, not a stitch-up, Sergeant.' Trevor looked at the photographs Ted had chosen to illustrate the devastation in the Pitcher house.

'This is the last one, Frank,' Ted Gant squinted at a print and turned it sideways before handing it over.

'That's the right way up.'

'Inspector,' Frank began. 'This conference …'

'Is a routine briefing, sergeant,' Trevor looked at his watch. 'It would be helpful if you could round up the others so we can begin on time.'

Frank took the hint and left.

'You found anything?' Trevor asked Ted, although he knew from the expression on Ted's face what his answer would be.

'Nothing.'

'You're doing tests?'

'What do you think?' Ted snapped. 'We're doing everything we can think of.'

'I wasn't being critical. This is my first clean crime scene.'

'Mine too,' Ted replied, slightly mollified. 'Do you want a run down before the briefing?'

They heard the sound of approaching footsteps. 'Save your voice. You may as well inform all of us of your progress at the same time.'

'Or lack of it,' Ted corrected. 'Hi Reggie.'

'Do you have anything for us, Ted?'

'I told Ted to save it for the briefing.' Trevor pulled a table to the side of the screen, so it wouldn't obscure the view of the photographs from the rows of chairs facing it.

Gradually the room filled with officers. Peter beckoned to Trevor from the doorway. Trevor joined him outside.

'I've volunteered to man the desk.'

Trevor didn't ask if Peter had the station computer passwords. He knew from the expression on his face he did. 'I'll update you after the briefing,' Trevor said loudly for the benefit of the local officers who were filing into the room.

'Don't worry I'll hold the fort.' Peter winked at Paula who pretended she hadn't seen him.

Trevor returned to the room, lifted three chairs behind the table and waved to Reggie and Carol, indicating they should join him.

Tony Sweet lurched in last, tripping over his own feet.

'Anyone behind you, Constable?' Trevor took his seat.

'No, sir.'

'Who's manning the desk?' Reggie demanded.

'Sergeant Collins volunteered.'

Reggie frowned disapproval. Trevor rose to his feet.

'Close the door, Constable Sweet.' He faced the assembled officers. 'For reference, you have files on your chairs containing, among other papers, the timeline that fixes events, movements and locations of people on the night of the murders. Mr Gant has volunteered to deliver an update on the examination of the Pitcher house. Mr Gant?' Trevor gave Ted the floor.

Ted stood to the side of the screen. Using a laser pointer, he indicated the photographs on the lowest line. 'These have been placed in order of the rooms of the house. The ones on the lowest level are of the cellar, above them the office floor, above that the Pitchers' living room and kitchen, then the bedrooms, finally the attic. They are here for later reference only. If you'd look to your left.' He switched on a computer and laptop and the photograph in the bottom left corner of the Perspex screen filled a whiteboard beside the screen.

'Some of you have seen the cellar, if you haven't it was gutted by the fire. We have established it was arson. The glass panel in one of the doors was smashed and bottles filled with petrol thrown in. We have retrieved splinters and neck fragments from three separate green glass bottles. We're attempting to match fragments to a brand but so far without luck. There's no sign of fuses so I'm guessing paper. As for the rest of the cellar, we've found a few surviving fingerprints, all belonging to the Pitcher family and employees. Nothing that shouldn't have been there apart from the remains of the petrol bombs. There's no evidence to suggest the cellar was broken into. The doorframe was in place and locked from the inside, as were all the windows.'

'Did you find the remains of any petrol cans that could have fed and accounted for the severity of the fire?' Reggie asked.

'No. But, we found the remains of various containers that had held chemicals.' Ted flicked on to more photographs. 'According to Alun Pitcher's employees, metal tools and tin trunks were stored in the cellar alongside the furniture. It's going to be a long job to sift through all the debris. But we are making headway, just not at the speed you'd like us to.'

'The petrol bombs were made outside the cellar,' Trevor suggested.

'In my opinion, yes.'

'Could the petrol have been siphoned from the Pitchers' cars?' Trevor questioned.

'We found no alien prints on the cars.'

'But you found evidence the cars had been wiped clean?'

'Yes.'

'Have the petrol tanks on the Pitcher cars been checked?' Trevor persisted.

'They will be now,' Ted said drily. 'The office floor. The fire in the cellar burned through the floor in what had been the conference room and two of the other offices. The room Alun Pitcher used as his office was comparatively undamaged because it was at the end of the house and the furthest from the door and windows which were the sites of the seat of the fire. As far as we can ascertain this floor wasn't touched by anyone outside of the family and Alun Pitcher's employees. Alun Pitcher's office has been examined and, documents, cash and jewellery retrieved from his safe. Nothing appears to be missing but we haven't received confirmation from Alun Pitcher's surviving son. There were fingerprints on the front door and staircase rail leading from the office floor to the living quarters above but only those of the family.'

'So it wasn't wiped clean?' Trevor clarified.

'Unlike other areas of the house, it wasn't,' Ted confirmed, 'which suggests no one entered the area that night. The kitchen.' Ted flicked on to slides of the next floor. 'Propellant was used to start the fires, in this case cooking oil. But in every room in the living quarters, including the halls, stairs and landing, flammable items had been piled up and set alight. Alcohol was used to feed the fires in the living room, perfume, deodorant, after shave and cologne in the bedrooms. We have smudges that suggest rubber gloves were worn. We've found very few prints, all of the family, and fewer of those than we'd expect to find in a family home.'

'So, to get this right, the murderer broke into the Pitchers' house, killed the family then cleaned up the evidence before setting fire to the house?' Jim Murphy clarified.

'If you're asking if there's evidence of thorough and professional cleansing, the answer's yes. The most obvious example is that of the bucket of bleach and water we found containing the unscrewed sink and bath traps from the attic bathroom. We also found diluted traces of Lee Pitcher's blood around the plughole in the shower which suggests the murderer showered after killing him. Given the extent of Lee Pitcher's wounds the killer would almost certainly have been heavily sprayed with his blood.'

'What about the murderer's clothes?' Carol asked.

'We found fabric ashes in the attic and bedrooms. There's evidence of bloodstains but not enough to determine type or extract DNA. Wardrobes had been emptied and fires lit, destroying most of the clothes. It's possible the murderer burnt his clothes together with the Pitchers and left the house wearing their clothes. But it would be impossible to prove what, if anything was missing even if we had a list of the victims' clothing because there isn't enough left to determine what was burned. So, there's no evidence that the killer burned his clothes and walked away in those of his victim but neither is there evidence he didn't.' Ted spoke in the careful pedantic manner of a scientist accustomed to dealing with police pressure.

'What about Larry Jones's clothes?' Carol asked.

'I examined them and found no blood stains, other than on the bag containing the jewellery. That blood is Lee Pitcher's. The only fingerprints on the bag were Larry Jones's,' he added.

'Wouldn't Larry Jones's clothes have been bloodstained if he'd killed the Pitchers?' Carol ventured.

'I examined Larry's clothes and found no blood stains,' Ted reiterated. 'Anyone who rained the blows on Lee Pitcher would have been spattered with his blood. One of my assistants checked with the prison Larry Jones was released from that morning. When you arrested him he was wearing the same clothes he'd worn on his release. Those are the facts.'

'Have you found any evidence that could convict Larry Jones, Mr Gant?' Frank Howell asked.

'We found Lee Pitcher's blood on the plastic bag containing the jewellery in Larry Jones's pocket. Nothing else.' Ted coughed.

Trevor poured him a glass of water from the jug on the table and handed it to him.

'Nothing?' Frank repeated.

'Nothing,' Ted repeated. 'You will have to wait for Patrick Kelly's report to establish cause of death but I can show you the positions the corpses were found in.' Ted flicked through the slides until he came to a graphic close-up of Gillian Pitcher's body. 'Mrs Pitcher's body isn't as charred as her head because whoever wrapped her in paper and set fire to her piled a duvet and bedspread from the bed on top of her body. Both acted as fire blankets and smothered the flames. Blood splashes indicate that, just as her sons were, she'd been beaten about the head, shoulders and torso. You may ask me questions about the rooms and the blood spray but not about the victims' injuries. They are in Patrick Kelly's jurisdiction. For the record we also found smudges in the bedroom, but no alien prints, which suggest gloves were worn.'

'Were the bedrooms cleaned like the attic and bathrooms, sir?' Paula Rees asked.

'Bleach had been poured on the carpets around the bodies and in the doorways, one theory – and there is no proof to substantiate it – the purpose was to dilute bloody footprints. Alun Pitcher's blood was found on the landing.' Ted flicked through the slides again until he came to the photograph he wanted. 'Next to the stain is the weapon that killed him. A Victorian bronze of the Roman Dying Gaul. From the position of the body the most likely scenario is that Alan Pitcher was hit with the bronze as he entered the attic. The blood could well have come from the bronze as it fell outside the door.'

'Was the bronze thrown or brought down with force?' Reggie asked.

'That's a question for Patrick Kelly.'

'But the blow killed him?' Jim Murphy asked.

'Again, that's for Patrick Kelly to ascertain. The attic and the last two corpses.' Ted paused to allow the collective gasp to die. Over familiarity with gruesome crime and accident scenes hardened officers and forensic scientists. But Lee Pitcher's corpse was barely recognisable as human.

'Questions?' Ted flicked through the close ups.

'Were they alive when they were burned, sir?'

Tony Sweet stammered.

'That's for the pathologist to determine, Constable.'

'You've found no evidence to suggest that anyone other than family entered the house that night?' Carol asked soberly.

'Other than the obvious, no,' Ted replied.

'The obvious,' Carol reiterated.

'The Pitchers couldn't have inflicted the injuries on themselves because all four bodies were wrapped in brown paper and string. Therefore we have discounted a triple murder and suicide scenario.'

Trevor asked the next question but he didn't look at Ted. Instead he scanned the faces of the officers around him. 'Did whoever murdered the Pitchers deliberately clean all evidence from scene?'

'Someone certainly scoured the crime scene, yes,' Ted answered briefly.

'How long would you estimate it would take one person to do that?'

Ted hesitated. 'Difficult to answer. We've found traces of bleach on several surfaces, including, as I've already said, the shower, bathroom, outside rails of the fire escape and balconies and some of the internal stair rails and walls. In my opinion – and it is only an opinion – I would say that it would have taken one person with considerable scientific knowledge at least two hours to clean the bathroom and inside stair rails alone. And that's without taking the other things into account.'

'Like wrapping the bodies and setting the fires. How long would that take?' Trevor persisted.

'One person acting alone, I'd say another two

hours.'

Trevor referred to the timeline. 'When Michael Pitcher and his girlfriend Alison left the Pitcher house at midnight, his parents and brothers were alive.'

'Can we be sure of that, Inspector?' Ted Gant played devil's advocate.

'Tim Pryce and Ken Lloyd saw Alun Pitcher throw a set of keys down to Michael Pitcher a few minutes after midnight. All three appeared normal and neither Ken nor Tim saw bloodstains on Michael or Alison's clothes. So to answer your question, Mr Gant, yes, we can be sure that all four Pitchers were alive at midnight. And no one reported anything suspicious until Ken Lloyd saw flames in the attic of the Pitcher house around three o'clock.'

'Which means that all four Pitchers were murdered, the crime scene cleaned and the fires set in three hours,' Ted mused.

'So Larry Jones must have had an accomplice.' Frank was clearly reluctant to relinquish Larry Jones's status as prime suspect.

'I suggest you run that past Mr Gant, Sergeant.'

'Given the time-frame, I'd suggest that more than one person was involved in the crime, more than that I cannot say,' Ted answered cautiously.

'The only person in custody is a man who was drunk and unconscious at midnight and still asleep when he was found at 4.40 a.m.' Trevor rose to his feet. 'Are there any more questions for Mr Gant?' He looked around the room. When no one spoke, he offered Ted his hand. 'My thanks to you and your team for a professional job.'

Ted switched off the projector and closed his

laptop.

'I'll visit the house again later if I may,' Trevor added.

'We'll expect you,' Ted left the room.

'Larry Jones could have worn one of the Pitcher's coats when he killed them,' Damian argued. 'So I don't know why we're bothering to look for anyone else when we've got him in custody. I'll grant we may need more evidence than the jewellery …'

'I'd like to remind you, Constable, and all the rest of you, that even a Garth Estate Jones is innocent until found guilty. And, we have no hope of convicting Larry on the evidence of the jewellery alone. As you know, Larry Jones insists it was planted on him, and without bloodstains on his clothes that argument could stand up in court.'

'You saw him being searched, Super …' Frank began.

'I did, but who's to say who was with him or what happened before the fire officers found him in that outbuilding,' Reggie interrupted.

'You have the timeline. You've seen photographs of the crime scene. You've copies of the witness statements. Take a few minutes to go through them,' Trevor ordered.

Everyone obediently and diligently turned to their files.

Trevor waited ten minutes before speaking again. 'Anyone have any comments?'

'Has the figure Ken Lloyd saw on the fire escape outside the Pitcher attic been identified, sir?' Paula asked.

'No.'

'There was only one figure?' Jim checked.

'Ken Lloyd only saw one,' Trevor confirmed.

'Do we know if the murderer or murderers entered by the fire escape?' Paula asked.

'You heard Ted Gant. The outside rail was cleaned.'

'Right down to ground level, sir!' Tony exclaimed.

'The entire length was examined and nothing found.' Trevor sat back in his chair. 'I know you've all been out and about interviewing potential witnesses. Have any of you come up with sightings you haven't yet written into the files; no matter how trivial or apparently innocent?' Greeted by silence, Trevor added. 'Nothing within a half mile radius of the Pitcher house between midnight and 3 a.m.?' He looked around expectantly. 'Nothing?' he reiterated.

He shuffled his papers together. 'Back to work everyone.'

CHAPTER TWENTY

The briefing ended, Tony Sweet returned to his desk and Peter and Trevor went to their office. Trevor dropped his briefcase on his desk and sat down. 'Shut the door.'

Peter did as he asked before sitting behind his own desk. 'I scanned the officer rotas for the week of the fire and e-mailed them to you.'

Trevor switched his computer on and began downloading them.

'Anything come up at the briefing?' Peter asked.

'Damian Howell ...'

'Blond Einstein.'

Trevor looked over the top of his laptop screen at Peter.

'That's his nickname in the station.'

'He doesn't strike me as bright,' Trevor agreed.

'He's not. In Welsh terms he's dim but pretty; which is why they call him blond Einstein.'

'Who told you that?'

'Tony Sweet. We had a chat before I persuaded him it was essential he attend the briefing. I told him the desk officer has to be well informed to sift through all the information the public bring in. Otherwise they won't be able to tell the difference between time wasters and statements that move the case on.'

'What else did Tony Sweet tell you?' Trevor asked.

'This and that, you know station gossip.'

'Frank's nickname?'

'Bow How.'

'After Howell, very funny.' Trevor smiled wearily.

'Did you know Damian's his son?'

'I hadn't made the connection but it might explain what I was going to say about his refusal to take Larry Jones's state of inebriation into account and his fixation on Larry being the murderer. Like father like son.'

Trevor pushed the printer cable into his lap top and printed off two copies of the file he'd downloaded. He handed one to Peter. 'You had a chance to go through this?'

'The briefing wasn't that long. Neither can I read at Superman's speed. I looked through past cases on Holmes 2.' Peter referred to the updated version of the "Home Office Large Major Enquiry System" that collated all the files pertinent to serious crimes in the UK. 'Regina Moore's worked on eight murder enquiries one as a sergeant, seven as an inspector. A fatal shooting during an armed robbery on a jeweller's; the rape and murder of a teenager out clubbing; a child abduction that turned out to be no such thing. The mother murdered the child and concealed the body. Another two were random attacks on innocent bystanders by drunks. I saved the best until last. Three were related murders of pensioners in their own home by a junkie. He was convicted on forensic evidence left behind in the houses. Her clear-up rate is impressive. One hundred per cent. So much for Ice Drawers being out of her depth on the Pitcher case. I'm surprised upstairs allowed someone with her record to send for the cavalry.'

'The three OAP's. Were they here?'

'South Wales, none in this town.'

'Frank Howell?'

'Worked on two domestic murders here. A farmer was killed by his wife on Christmas Eve. She hit him with a frying pan, cut up his body, parcelled the joints in plastic bags and Christmas paper and stacked them in a disconnected freezer in the barn.'

'You're joking?'

'I kid you not. You should see the evidence photographs. But as she turned herself in the following May and made a full confession, which incidentally Frank and the duty officer here didn't believe, I can't commend Frank's investigative skills. Poor woman had to fetch her solicitor before they sent someone to search the barn.'

'And the second murder?'

'Two brothers fought over a girl. One killed the other. There were eyewitnesses. On the plus side, he has worked on a few burglaries where convictions were made on forensic and DNA evidence.'

'Inspector Carol March?'

Peter busied himself with the printout. 'Clever girl. Fast tracked up the promotion tree because she has a degree in law and a masters in psychology. Worked on nine murders, none in this town. But you're barking up the wrong tree there. My money's on the Snow Queen, Frank, Dai Smith, or Tim Pryce.'

'Tim Pryce the landlord. May Williams saw …'

'Someone in a police hat. It's possible he didn't turn his in when he retired from the Met with the rank of inspector. He was …'

'Drug Squad.'

'You knew?'

'He told me.'

'He also worked on cases that warranted forensic searches of the crime scene.' Peter pulled out his cigar case. 'But we still don't have a motive.'

'You were the one who mentioned crime of passion. Carol March is attractive. Both Pitcher boys were good-looking womanisers, but you ruled her out. Why?'

Peter was curt. 'Because I know her.'

Trevor had a vision of Daisy, pale pregnant, vomiting while Carol March kissed Peter in the background. It infuriated him. 'And because she fancies you and you haven't the sense to send her packing.'

Peter looked at Trevor and then back at the printed sheets. 'The day before the fire; four till midnight shift. Dai Smith and Paula Rees. Paula signed out at twenty past twelve.'

Knowing he'd overstepped the mark, Trevor took his time over squaring his own copy on the desk in front of him. 'Paula told us she talked to Frank Howell when she dropped the keys to the squad car back in the station.'

'Frank Howell and Jim Murphy were on ten till six in the morning.'

'Carol March and Damian Howell worked midday until eight, and Grant Williams and Tony Sweet nine till five.'

'Lucky buggers,' Peter murmured. 'Civilized hours.'

Trevor looked down the rest of the list. 'So we can

take it that while the Pitchers were being murdered, Frank Howell was in the station, Jim Murphy was out in the squad car …'

'Signed out at twelve thirty, back at two thirty.' Peter looked up at Trevor. 'He could have laid the fires and carried a bag around the town.'

'Did he fill in a report?'

'Reports are at the back,' Peter turned back the pages of the printout.

'Drove around outskirts, checked isolated houses. Stopped speeding car – registration number …'

'At one ten,' Peter commented. 'Then nothing until he clocked back in at two thirty.'

'Fires took hold from two fifty-three,' Trevor reminded him.

'He could have had an accomplice.' Peter returned to the sheet.

'What about Frank's movements?'

'According to this he didn't leave the station until after the fire had been reported,' Peter continued to flick through the pages.

Trevor turned to the telephone records. 'Nothing came into the station between May Williams's call at midnight and the emergency services a couple of minutes after three. So there's nothing to prove that Frank was there the entire time.'

'The lack of calls surprise you?' Peter asked.

'Not midweek in a country town. But we'll need to check exactly where all the officers in the station live, how long it would take them to get to Main Street from their homes and how long it took them to get there after they were called in on the night of the fire.'

'You looking at me?'

'I can't ask the locals to do it because there's no way they'd incriminate themselves or one another. But check on the brown paper first, will you? I've a feeling the origin of those sheets could prove interesting.'

Peter sat in his chair. 'Much as I hate to say it, May Williams might not have seen a copper. It could have been a security guard – a traffic warden …'

'And the destruction of evidence,' Trevor interrupted.

'Could be down to a technician. Ted Gant or any one of his team would have the knowledge.' Peter took his cigar case from his shirt pocket.

'The fact that Alun Pitcher was killed with a bronze and the others battered to death with a hoe suggests more than one killer, but when it comes to the destruction of evidence, you'd only need one person with the knowledge to instruct one or more accomplices.'

'This is turning into an Agatha Christie denouement,' Peter grumbled. 'Next thing you'll be pinning an announcement on the board of the incident room? "Would the following suspects … "'

'You have a list?'

'Every officer in the station who doesn't have an alibi that covers midnight to 3 a.m. on the night of the murders will do. We'll ask them to congregate in the conference room, where you can then proceed to reveal the killer or killers.'

'You've been watching way too much bad television.'

'Comes of living with Daisy. She's too exhausted

after a day in the hospital to do anything else.'

'Doesn't the bronze Dying Gaul suggest something to you?'

'Bad Victorian taste.'

'Nothing else?' Trevor pressed.

Peter stared for a moment. 'Gays …'

Trevor's mobile phone rang and he answered it. 'Thanks for ringing back. I want you to look for a car. Silver BMW model 116i, registration number …' Trevor swivelled his chair to avoid the look Peter was sending his way. '… All the neighbouring counties … Check CCTV images at ports and airports … If it's still in the locality I believe it'll be parked up off the road somewhere out of mainstream traffic … The edge of a country park, or private road … I'd be grateful if you could get back to me on this number … don't phone the station direct … thank you.'

'You've asked the neighbouring forces to look for Dai Smith's car?'

'It has to be somewhere,' Trevor said.

'Why not in this county?'

'The locals say they've looked.'

'You believe them?'

'As it happens, yes,' Trevor said carefully. 'Dai Smith is one of them.'

'Was he suicidal?' Peter questioned.

'Reggie told me he was depressed.'

'Poor sod, having his wife walking out on him was bad enough but taking the kids with her … that's enough to tip any man over the edge.'

'I never thought I'd hear that from you after all the things you said about your first wife and the day she walked out on you. I believe "happiest day of my life" was one of the hackneyed phrases.'

'We were kids. Shouldn't have married in the first place,' Peter growled. He changed the subject. 'So, what makes you think Dai Smith is in a neighbouring county?'

'If he was depressed enough to kill himself, I lay odds on him doing it out of his colleagues' beat.'

'You're right, if I was out to top myself I wouldn't want the people I worked with poking around my corpse and that's without the local O'Kelly carving me up.'

Trevor picked up his briefcase and went to the door. 'I have the computer disks I found in Dai Smith's house to work on.'

'I thought Merchant's on her way.'

'She is.' Trevor glanced at his watch. 'But I'm not expecting her for another three or four hours. I'm hoping to make some headway before she gets here.'

'You're going back to the stables?'

Trevor didn't answer. Instead he opened the door quickly. Frank Howell was outside.

'You heard me before I even knocked, sir.' Frank's laugh was forced.

Trevor glared at him.

'We've found a witness,' Frank said unabashed. 'Mitch. He's a vagrant. He said he's been sleeping nights in the building in the Pitcher's yard. I've put him in interview room six. I didn't want to show him in here. He stinks to high heaven.'

There was no warmth in Trevor's, 'Thank you, sergeant.'

'He can be unpredictable, sir. You'll need a

couple of strong men who know him when you talk to him. Damian's watching him and I'm free at the moment,' Frank volunteered.

Peter left his desk, 'I'll get on with the chores and leave you to your computer disks. See you back at the stables.'

'The fridge is empty, pick up some food,' Trevor reminded him.

'You're worse than a nagging wife.'

'A couple of frozen pizzas, water – sparkling …'

'I know,' Peter cut in impatiently. 'What you regard as essentials. Pork pie, crisps, beer … what about fresh fruit, cheese, bread, malt whisky …'

He was talking to an empty room. Trevor had walked away with Frank.

In his younger days Trevor had worked undercover in hostels for the homeless but he reeled at the stench emanating from what appeared to be a bundle of rags perched on a chair in the interview room. There was no sign of hands or feet, just a mass of filthy grey-black fabric. The bundle moved and Trevor saw two beady dark eyes peering out from beneath a thatch that was so low-growing it could have been hair or eyebrows. The few bits of skin that could be seen were as black and grey as the ribbons of cloth wound around the body.

A grubby hand emerged from the rags and scooped four Rich Tea biscuits from a plate on the table. A second hand grabbed a mug of tea. Both retreated back into the rags.

'Mitch, this is Inspector Trevor Joseph.' Frank sat beside Damian on one of the chairs across from

Mitch. Without remembering that all the chairs were bolted firmly to the floor he attempted to push it back from the table and away from Mitch. His boots scraped the floor.

Trevor went to the window, propped his briefcase on to the floor and leaned on the sill facing Mitch.

'Sergeant Howell tells me you were in the Pitcher yard on the night of the fire, Mitch?'

Mitch stared at Trevor over the rim of his mug.

'Is that right?' Trevor persevered.

Mitch withdrew a hand from his rags and slurped a soggy biscuit.

'Tell the Inspector what you told PC Howell,' Frank prompted.

Mitch made a noise somewhere between a frog's croak and a cat's growl followed by sucking when he lowered his head to the cup concealed in his clothes.

'Did you see anyone?' Trevor was beginning to wonder if any information Mitch had was worth extracting. He was finally rewarded with a nod.

'Who did you see, Mitch?'

Mitch looked blank as if he had spoken in Swahili.

'Was it a man or a woman?'

Same uncomprehending look.

'A man or a woman?' Trevor reiterated.

Mitch nodded warily.

'A man or a woman?' Trevor repeated impatiently.

Mitch crammed his mouth full of biscuit before holding up a finger.

'You saw one person?'

Trevor had hoped for a more lucid response he was disappointed when Mitch shrugged.

'Did you recognise whoever it was?'

'Just one but he was normous. Half the size of a house. And all black. Soon as I saw him going up the steps I ran.' Mitch pushed the empty plate towards Trevor. 'More.'

Trevor picked up his briefcase and jerked his head towards the door. Frank accompanied him into the corridor.

'Get some more biscuits, Frank.'

'You're as soft as the super, sir.'

'Comes with promotion.' Trevor said. 'If you get anything worthwhile out of him, which I doubt, let me know. Anyone wants me I'm on my mobile.'

'If you need someone to work on the computer disks you found in Dai Smith's house, sir, Damian here is our expert ...'

'I'll manage, thank you.'

'And if we need to send a car for you, sir?'

'You won't,' Trevor said shortly. His mobile rang. He answered it. When he ended the call he knocked on Reggie's office door.

'Dai is dead?' Reggie repeated.

'His car was found in woodland outside Carmarthen.'

'Another county.' Reggie slumped back in her chair.

'There was a hose pipe connecting the exhaust to the interior of the car. No suspicion of foul play. It's outside your jurisdiction.'

'Dai must have wanted it that way.' She looked up at Trevor. 'Did they say how long he'd been there?'

'Probably since the day he disappeared. I'm

sorry.'

'So am I. I should have done more …'

'You did what you could for him. He had problems, you listened. You have nothing to reproach yourself with.'

'I wish I could believe that.'

Trevor hesitated before he realised there was nothing more he could say to ease her pain. 'If I'm needed, I'll be on my mobile.'

She nodded and he closed her office door behind him.

Trevor walked the short distance to the stables. He dumped his laptop on the table in the living room and switched it on. Hungry, he went into the kitchen and opened the fridge. To his amazement there was a bottle of sparkling water on the shelf and a couple of cellophane-wrapped fresh pizzas.

He looked at the clock, almost one. He took the last of the bacon and sausage rolls that Ken had brought around that morning and stuck it in the microwave for thirty seconds. It came out slightly rubbery, but he carried it and the bottle of water and a glass into the living room. Unlocking his briefcase, he set up his laptop and inserted the first of the disks he had taken from Dai Smith's house.

It took him a few minutes to retrieve the same fragment of photograph he had viewed on Dai Smith's computer. Unable to progress further, he phoned Sarah Merchant's mobile.

Peter walked purposefully down the shopping end of Main Street and into the square. He been walking in and out of shops for over an hour and seen absolutely no sheets of paper, let alone the thick brown variety he and Trevor were hoping to find. He stopped at the town's bookshop and went inside.

The choice of books was bewildering and all in a language he could neither read nor understand. He looked at the sign swinging from the ceiling above them.

'Do you only stock Welsh books?' he asked a young woman with spiked silver and purple hair who was stocking the shelves from a trolley.

'English section is through the arch. Are you looking for something in particular?'

Peter thought back to his own childhood and tried to recall the first books he'd taken notice of.

'Are you?' she slid half a dozen Welsh Quick Read books on to a shelf.

'A picture book for a young child.'

'English or Welsh?'

'As I don't speak Welsh I suppose it'd better be English.'

'You're never too old to start. They run evening classes in the tertiary college.'

'Definitely English.' Peter said flatly.

She abandoned the trolley and walked through the arch showing him half a dozen shelves of children's books.

'Can you recommend any?'

'Alphabet, Numbers? Is the child going to learn to read phonetically …'

'I was thinking of a fun bedtime story.'

'Age?'

'Under a year.'

She proceeded to pull them off the shelves. 'Nursery rhymes, classic children's fairy tales, Winnie the Pooh ...'

Peter made his choice purely on the illustrations, familiar titles and the thought of the amusing voices he could adopt when reading them to his son – or daughter. He smiled at the thought. A son would be wonderful, a daughter even better because she'd look like Daisy.

He picked up Jack and the Beanstalk, The Billy Goats Gruff, The Three Little Pigs and – the Snow Queen. 'I'll take these four.'

'The Snow Queen is beautifully illustrated but frightening. Hardly suitable for a young child.' The girl sounded like a Sunday school teacher.

'It's what I want.'

'Yes, sir.' The assistant obviously didn't subscribe to the view that the customer was always right. 'The till is this way.'

To his disappointment she slipped the books he'd chosen into a paper carrier bag.

'You don't wrap the books?' he asked.

'We have a gift wrapping service ...'

'When I was a kid and my father used to buy us books they always came wrapped in brown paper.'

'And no doubt one of the assistants used to carry his purchases behind him when he left the shop.'

Peter took out his wallet. 'How much?'

'Sixty-eight pounds ninety-nine pence, sir.'

'What!'

'Children's books of this quality are expensive, sir.'

He handed over his credit card.

'Even if he reformatted the disks and hard drive more than once some of the information will remain, sir,' Sarah explained down a line that was fading in and out as Chris Brookes her "other half" drove towards Wales. 'It will just be scrambled. Are you sure you can't wait? We'll be there in two hours.'

'I need to check something urgently.'

'First you have to find out if he's just deleted his files or used one of the software programmes that clean up the drives and disks. Pressing delete or dragging it to a wastepaper basket will scatter the data, not obliterate it. The file stays. Information about that data, along with the data itself, will be left on hard drive in temporary files and registry entries. If we're in luck you may find the original file still intact. Start by checking the time stamp information. It will show if and when any files were deleted and what the properties of those files were.'

Trevor listened intently to the instructions Sarah Merchant fed him down the line. He poured a glass of water and took a bite out of the roll. The bread crunched but it was edible and all he wanted was to stave off hunger pangs. He followed her directions.

'Now we're reinstating the parameters, sir …'

The fragment of photograph slowly, gradually grew in size.

He stared at it then blinked. The room appeared to be moving around him. He could no longer focus. He heard Sarah's voice but it seemed to be coming from a great distance.

'Sir …'

'Sarah …'

'Sir …'

It was no use, he simply couldn't keep his eyes open. He fell, knocking over the glass of water. The last thing that registered was that he wasn't alone.

'Peter?'

White-gloved hands took his computer and emptied his briefcase … then there was only darkness.

CHAPTER TWENTY-ONE

Peter was in the baker's watching an assistant wrap a loaf of bread in a sheet of white paper that looked so thin it could almost be tissue when his mobile rang.

'Peter?'

'Sarah, so looking forward to seeing you,' he greeted her expansively.

'I've just been talking to Trevor.'

'He cracked the computer yet?'

'He started mumbling,' she broke in impatiently. 'He sounded ill. He didn't end the call for some time but all I could hear was breathing and footsteps.'

'It's probably the line. We're in the depths of deepest darkest Wales.' He gave the assistant, who was listening in, a bright artificial smile.

'I think something's wrong.'

'This is a sleepy Welsh town.'

'Please, go and check he's all right,' she pleaded.

'For you, darling, anything. And while I'm at it I'll shake out the red carpet for your arrival.'

'We're undercover.'

'Then I'll paint it black.' Peter handed over a ten-pound note, pocketed his change and took his bag of baguettes, sausage rolls and doughnuts. He left the shop, and sheltered in the doorway; turning up his collar against a sudden squall of rain.

He looked up and down the road. To his left was a marble-fronted interior designer's that reeked of quality – and expense. The sort of place he usually walked past at speed. On one side of the window a tiffany lamp stood next to a bowl of silk orchids on a revolving Edwardian bookcase. The other was filled with a display of linen upholstery fabrics. The rolls cascaded artistically from a mahogany dining table. But Peter didn't see the cloth, only the thick brown paper on the floor that the cloth was resting on.

The bell clanged as he opened the door, just as it had done in every other shop he'd entered in town making him feel as though he'd walked through a time warp.

'Can I help you, sir?'

An elegantly dressed woman with silver hair left a desk behind the counter and joined him.

He looked around. One of the rolls of fabric caught his attention. A pattern of fantastic animals, all smiling and all in improbable colours. Red giraffes gambolled with purple hippopotami. Green monkeys swung in lilac and orange trees above white-foamed water filled with pink-spotted blue whales and cream-and-black-striped crocodiles.

The woman saw what had caught his attention and rolled out the cloth. 'That is one of our most popular patterns, sir.'

'It's certainly colourful.'

'It will complement any nursery decor. It's a pattern adored by parents and children of both sexes and not tied into any commercial film, cartoon or,' she lowered her voice as though she were about to swear, 'television series.'

Peter thought it would look brilliant in the room Daisy had prepared for their baby. She'd already had the decorators in to paint the walls "sunshine yellow" and spent hours poring over nursery catalogues before deciding on plain whitewood furniture. He could imagine a duvet cover, curtains and even a small sofa and chair in the fabric. The room was certainly large enough to accommodate them.

'How much would I need for curtains and throws to cover a bed and chair, and to make cot and bed linen?'

'We have matching cot and bed sized duvet covers, sir, and the amount of fabric would depend on the size of the windows.'

He gave her approximate measurements and she talked him into buying twenty metres, plus three sets of cot and three sets of bed linen and then added, 'you do realise that once it's cut you may not be able to match it, sir. The dye batches can vary enormously.'

'Make it thirty metres,' he said rashly.

'It is forty pounds ninety-nine pence a metre and there's the linen …'

Peter blanched. This was one expense he'd never be able to claim back from the force. He could almost hear Bill Mulcahy shouting. "Forty metres. All you were after was a bit of bloody brown paper. Half a bloody metre would have done, Collins … "

For the second time in an hour he extracted his credit card from his wallet and handed it over.

The woman produced a long thin rod from beneath the counter. Working slowly and methodically, she unrolled the cloth and began measuring it. When she'd finished, she cut it carefully, folded it and the linen together, tore a large sheet of brown paper from a roll on the wall and covered the counter with it. Placing the linen in the centre of the sheet she wrapped and tied it into a neat parcel with string.

'You're an expert packer,' Peter complimented.

'A necessary skill for anyone who works with soft furnishings.'

He slipped his credit card into the machine and tapped out his number. 'Bet you don't get many orders that size in a town this small,' he said casually as they waited for the bank to accept it.

'You'd be surprised. Only two weeks ago we had an order for one hundred and twenty metres of fabric.'

'Someone professional?'

'You could say that. Tim Pryce is redecorating ten of the rooms in the Angel.'

Peter opened the door to the cottage and walked in. Dropping the parcel on the stairs, he called out, 'Honey, I'm home.'

When there was no answer he went into the living room. Trevor was lying on the floor, an empty glass and plastic bottle that had held water next to him. Peter knelt besides him, checked he was breathing and placed him in the recovery position. Only then did he notice that the patio doors were open. Trevor's briefcase was lying open and empty on the table. Next to it was the lead to his laptop. There was no sign of his computer or the disks he'd taken from Dai Smith's house.

Patrick ended the call to the emergency services and laid a reassuring hand on Peter's shoulder. 'The paramedics will be here in ten minutes and I bet you a bottle of oak-aged malt it's Gamma

Hydroxybutyrate.'

'Gamma what?' Peter asked testily.

'GHB to you, one of the classic date-rape drugs,' Patrick declared. 'Banned since 2002 in the UK. Easy to manufacture, beloved by users of the gym because it soothes muscle pain and gives the recipient a feeling of euphoria, or so I'm told. Almost odourless and tasteless although it's slightly salty; the perfect drug to slip into the drinks of unsuspecting women and men by would be rapists. It takes effect within ten to twenty minutes.'

'And Trevor?'

'If it is GHB he could be out for two to four hours depending on the dose he was given.' Patrick picked up first the glass then the bottle from the floor with his pen so as not to smudge any prints. He shook them in turn and a drop of liquid fell on to his finger from the bottle. He sniffed then tasted it. 'No salt. This has been rinsed out. As there's no way of knowing how much Trevor ingested he'll have to stay in hospital so he can be monitored until he comes round.'

'He'll hate you for it.'

'I'll risk his wrath as all I have as an aid to diagnosis is his current condition. He could slip deeper into a coma or even die if he's been fed too much. Or given something entirely new in the drug line. The chemists are coming up with variations all the time.'

Peter leaned over Trevor and adjusted the cushion he'd placed under his head.

Patrick pulled two evidence bags from the pocket of his white lab coat and wrapped the glass and bottle. 'He's not going to be a happy when he wakes and finds his computer gone.' Patrick looked at the lead and empty briefcase. 'You must be getting close to solving this mess?'

'What makes you think that?' Peter asked.

'The state of Trevor. He's obviously rattled someone's cage enough for them to drug him in order to steal his laptop.'

Tim Pryce walked through the patio doors and looked down at Trevor. 'How is he?'

'We'll know more when he gets to a practising doctor and away from a pathologist. Hopefully he'll live,' Patrick slipped his mobile back into his pocket.

'I'm so sorry,' Tim apologised. 'I've spoken to everyone in the Angel. The staff, the customers, the residents and people in the bar. No one has seen anyone hanging around the back of the cottages. Carol March and Reggie Moore are supervising the search of the property but I doubt they'll find anything. Whoever took Trevor's computer and disks is probably long gone. I've never had anything else like this happen to any of the Angel's guests before …'

'Just four people murdered two doors away,' Peter said scathingly. 'Looks like this street's going downhill.' He left Trevor's side at a knock at the door. 'That'll be the ambulance.'

'If it is, it's quick,' Patrick commented.

'They haven't far to come.' Tim closed the patio doors.

'Stay with Trevor, Patrick.' Peter answered the door. Ken was outside, Mars standing obediently at his heels.

'I've only just heard. Is Inspector Joseph all right?' Ken asked.

'We won't know until he gets to hospital.'

'I'm sorry this isn't a good time.' Ken backed away. 'I'll come back later.'

'If it's important, you can tell me,' Peter suggested.

'It might be nothing. It's just that working with Alun – he used to allow me to take some things home.'

'Like?'

'Waste paper: I use it to make bricks.'

'Bricks.' Peter's head was spinning. He leaned against the wall.

'To burn in the fire. I have a machine – you wet the papers, make a brick let it dry and then –'

'I get it,' Peter cut in sharply. 'You've found something in the waste paper?'

'As I said, it's probably nothing. But it's a will. Mrs Harville's will. Dated thirty years back around the time her husband died. It's signed by two witnesses …'

'Didn't I hear that she died intestate?' Peter took the envelope from Ken.

'That's what everyone said. But this is quite specific. She left everything to Mary Wells or in the event of Mary Wells' death, Mary's family.'

'Who's Mary Wells?'

'She was the Harvilles' cleaner for years and years.'

'Is she dead?'

'Yes, but her daughter Annie isn't and neither is her granddaughter, Pamela George. Look, can I leave

285

this with you …'

'You most certainly can.' Peter slipped the envelope into his inside pocket. An oversight, or proof that Alun Pitcher was in no way as squeaky clean as the image of him that the town wanted to project. He wasn't quite sure where exactly it fitted in with Pitcher case. But it was another piece of the puzzle. And one that didn't throw too good a light on the town's "honest" antique dealer.

'That's the ambulance. I'll be on my way.' Ken turned awkwardly.

'Ken, can you give me a couple of hours before telling anyone about this. Just until Trevor comes round?'

'As long as you like,' Ken stammered.

'Tomorrow morning the whole town will know about this. I promise you.'

'Know about what?' Tim asked as he passed the front door and saw Ken crossing the road and entering his own house.

Peter said the first thing that came into his head. 'Something about the man Ken saw on the fire escape. He wants to add to the description he made in his statement.'

The paramedics entered the house and Peter followed, deliberately closing the door in Tim's face.

Chris Brookes drove under the arch into the yard of the Angel just after the paramedics had loaded and closed the doors on Trevor.

'You're taking him to the local hospital?' Peter asked the paramedic.

'Initially, the doctor may move him after

assessment.'

'I'll follow you in my car.' Peter waited until they had driven away before walking over to Chris's car. He opened the door on the passenger side.

'We're supposed to be undercover,' Sarah hissed.

'Trevor's in that ambulance …'

'I knew it.' Sarah stepped out of the car. 'You're always putting him at risk. I told you something had happened to him. I knew it …'

Peter was taken aback by the tears in her eyes. He realised that Trevor was far more popular than him in their station but he had no idea that Trevor commanded this much respect – or affection – from their colleagues.

'He's been drugged. Patrick says he'll probably be fine. …'

'Patrick O'Kelly the pathologist?'

Peter nodded.'

'What would he know about a live patient …'

'We're here to do a job, Sarah,' Chris reminded her as she continued to round on Peter.

'Trevor has USB pens he wants me to work on?' Sarah looked expectantly at Peter as if she expected him to produce them immediately.

'When he was drugged they were stolen along with his computer.'

'Then there's nothing for me to do?'

Peter thought for a moment. 'There might be. Trevor tried the disks in the owner's computer. He's missing but I know where the key is to his house.'

'It's worth a try,' Sarah agreed.

'Follow my car. Chris you stay with Sarah; if anyone questions you, show your badge and give them my mobile number. After I've set you up I'll go on to the hospital. Just wait five minutes. I've a call to make.'

Peter sat in his car and punched in a number. 'Carol? Take Tim Pryce in for questioning and keep him in the station as long as you can ... now immediately ... ask him about brown paper ... yes ... the brown paper the Pitchers were wrapped in ... if you don't think it's enough use your imagination ... tell him a witness saw him planting water bottles and pizzas in our cottage ... that's not helpful. I can't ask Trevor if he put them there when he's unconscious can I ... I'll be in the station as soon as I know what's happening with Trevor.'

He ended the call, waved to Chris through the window and gunned the ignition.

Peter saw Trevor's eyelids flicker and moved his chair closer to the bed.

'Sleeping beauty waking up?'

Trevor tried to sit up, fell back on the pillows and groaned. 'What the hell happened?'

'According to Patrick and the duty doctor here, it was some kind of date-rape drug. Works in ten to twenty minutes. Someone fed you something, probably in a bottle of water?'

Trevor blinked hard and moved to a more comfortable position. 'My laptop ... the disks ...'

'Were taken.'

'I know.'

'Did you see who took them?'

'Hands wearing white latex gloves.'

'Given the number of people and officers working

in the Pitcher house that rules in at least seventy people.'

'As well as the catering staff in the pub. They wear gloves as well,' Trevor reminded him. 'I feel weird,' he complained.

Peter was never one to mince words. 'You look weird.'

'Update me?' Trevor sat up, rose gingerly to his feet and left the bed.

'I found the brown paper. It's used to wrap linen. Tim Pryce must have had a lot of it. He bought a hundred and twenty yards of material to refurbish the bedrooms in the pub. I asked Carol to take him in for questioning.'

'Good move.'

'What the hell do you think you're doing?' Peter grabbed Trevor as he swayed precariously towards the sink.

'Sticking my head under a cold tap. I need to think.'

'The way you're carrying on you're likely to fall and hit your head on the sink. Then you won't be capable of any thought for some time.'

Trevor ignored him, turned the mixer tap to cold, and splashed his face.

'Reggie's searching the Angel for your computer.'

'Tell her to stop and interview the blond Einstein instead.'

'On what basis.'

'Photograph on one of Dai Smith's USB pens. Gay porn. Damian Howell and Lee Pitcher on the bed. There was a mirror on the wall behind them. Dai Smith was filming them.'

'So, who cares about gays these days?'

'No one where we live. But if Dai Smith's and Damian Howell's wives found out, they might be put out.'

'Enough to leave their husbands,' Peter mused.

'Or enough to batter Lee Pitcher for cuckolding them.'

'You sure you haven't seen Tim?' Carol demanded of Tim's chef.

'I'm his employee, not his bloody keeper,' the man retorted. 'Now, if there's nothing else I've fifty chicken breasts to stuff with mushrooms and garlic butter.'

Carol returned to the yard. She looked up and down, then she heard a scream. Phyllis Lloyd ran out into the road. There was screech of brakes, a bang and she was flung headlong over the bonnet of a mail van.

Carol dialled the emergency services as she dashed towards her.

Phyllis's eyes were open. She pointed back to the house and murmured, 'Ken.'

CHAPTER TWENTY-TWO

Carol March left Phyllis with Reggie and went into
Ken's house with Jim Murphy. Tim Pryce was sitting
on the top of the steps that led down to the cellar. Ken
was lying at the bottom, his neck at an angle it could
never have achieved in life. Mars was whining
piteously and licking Ken's hand.

'I tried to grab Ken when he slipped but he just
carried on falling … I couldn't hold him. Phyllis
came to the cellar door, saw Ken lying there,
panicked and ran. I heard a bang and the sound of
brakes. She's not badly hurt, is she?' Tim looked
from Carol to Jim.

'She's dead,' Carol answered.

'I'm sorry. As a neighbour and wife to Ken she
was a pain … but poor Ken …'

'You have to come with me to the station, Tim.'
Carol took his arm.

'You can interview me in the pub …'

'In the station, Tim,' Carol said firmly. 'You have
to give a full statement, starting with the night of the
fire. It's so obvious. I don't know why I didn't think
of it before,' Carol declared. 'You were the first on
the scene …'

'I live next door,' Tim protested. 'I heard the
window blowing out.'

Carol recalled the telephone conversation she'd
had with Peter. 'Sergeant Collins asked me to
mention brown paper.'

'Now it's an offence to have brown paper in your
house?' Tim rose slowly to his feet.

'It is when it's used to wrap corpses up in before they're set alight,' Carol said.

'I need a solicitor.'

'I'll send for Judy,' Jim Murphy offered.

'Not Judy, one of the others,' Tim said sharply.

'Why?'

'I don't want her to hear what I have to say.'

'About Ken?' Carol questioned. 'This is Ken's house. He was used to climbing up and down the cellar steps. He was fit, healthy. There's no reason for him to slip and fall.'

'I told you, he slipped …'

'On what?' Carol looked around the top step.

'I don't know on what,' Tim countered testily. 'He just slipped …'

'Jim, get a photographer and scenes of crime in here, and the pathologist,' Carol ordered. 'We'll need a PM as soon as possible. And, while they're working, you and I are going to have a little talk in an interview room, Tim.'

'It wasn't murder.' Tim leaned back against the wall. 'I didn't want to hurt Ken, but Sergeant Collins told me that Ken was going to add a description to his statement.'

'What statement?' Carol removed her notebook from her pocket.

'The statement Ken made about seeing someone on the fire escape at the back of the Pitchers' house just after the fire had been lit. I confronted Ken but he denied he was going to change it. Lied to my face. Said he'd spoken to Sergeant Collins about something else. I didn't believe him …'

'And for that you killed him?'

'I told you I didn't mean to hurt him,' Tim reiterated insistently. He was so damned stubborn. I got angry. We were standing here …'

'You pushed him?' Carol questioned.

Tim stared at her and the look of utter despair in his eyes froze her blood. 'I didn't have any option. Don't you understand? It was me on the Pitchers' fire escape. I was leaving after I set the fires.'

Peter and Trevor went straight to Reggie's office when they returned from the hospital.

'You shouldn't be here,' Reggie admonished Trevor, who was swaying on his feet.

'I'm the investigating officer,' he reminded her, 'and this case is almost ready to wrap.'

'Tim's made a full confession.' She held up the disc. 'He killed the Pitchers, cleaned the house, set the fires and burned the bodies. He had the knowledge from his time in the Met. He's also confessed to pushing Ken down his cellar steps. A fall that killed him. Because of something you said to him about Ken's statement, Sergeant Collins?' She looked to Peter.

Peter blanched. 'That was something I made up. I didn't want him to know what Ken had said. He found a will, signed by Mrs Harville leaving everything to her cleaner, Pamela George's grandmother. I thought it could have been connected in some way with the Pitcher's murders …'

'A will?' Reggie interrupted.

Peter reached into his coat pocket and handed it to her.

Weak, Trevor sank into a chair. 'The will can

wait. Did Tim say why he killed the Pitchers?'

'Jewellery. Lee was working on several sets. Tim planted one on Larry, who he incidentally carried through the yard of the Angel and dumped in the outbuilding at the back of the Pitchers'. Pocketed the other sets and sold them.'

'Sold them where?'

'He wouldn't say.'

'I bet he wouldn't,' Trevor commented scathingly. 'Did he say why he needed the money?'

'No.'

'That's not surprising because there was no other jewellery. Let's try again.' Trevor suggested. 'Bring in Damian and Judy Howell and put them into an interview room.'

'Judy and Damian …'

'They'll need a solicitor as well. And put Tim Pryce in the viewing room. This is one interview I want him to see.'

Trevor and Peter sat down in front of Damian and Judy. Trevor's head was burning, he felt groggy and as though he were moving through a thick fog, but he'd primed Peter and Peter took control.

Peter held up a disc. 'Let me tell you a story, Constable and Mrs Howell. About a police inspector who retired from the force and bought a pub. But his dream was to retire not to a pub but to the South of France where he could enjoy fine wine and indulge his hobby of painting. He wanted to live his dream so much he told us that he killed all four members of the Pitcher family after robbing –'

'No.' White-faced, Judy looked Peter in the eye.

'That's not how it happened. I killed all the Pitchers.'

Damian stared down at the table and said nothing.

'Because of this.' Trevor switched on Sarah Merchant's computer. A photograph of Lee Pitcher and Damian Howell, naked and embracing, filled the screen.

'Lee Pitcher corrupted every man and woman who went near him. I wanted him to stop. I begged him to leave Damian alone. He laughed at me, told me I was imagining things,' Judy said. 'Then Dai Smith's wife came to see me. She had photographs of Lee and Dai and Damian, disgusting photographs. She told me she was leaving Dai and advised me to leave Damian. But Damian insisted they were old photographs. That he'd changed.' Her voice dropped to a whisper. 'That he loved me and I wanted to believe him. But I couldn't. That's why I waited in the outbuilding at the back of the Pitchers' that night. I told Damian that I'd be spending the night in the Angel after the Women in Business dinner. I had to find out if he'd go to Lee if he believed I wasn't coming home. My father didn't kill anyone. All he did was help us clean the scene afterwards ...'

Damian finally spoke 'She wasn't there. It wasn't her it was me. I killed the Pitchers. All of them.'

Trevor looked at both of them. 'Shall I ask Superintendent Moore to bring in your father, Mrs Howell, so we can get to the real truth of what happened that night? And this time, Constable Howell, I suggest you tell the truth.'

'You were right, Peter. It was a crime of passion.' Trevor, Reggie, Carol and Peter had congregated in

Reggie's office at the end of the working shift. They'd finished watching the filmed interviews that had finally wrapped the case and were sitting over a cup of coffee.

'A messy crime of passion,' Peter agreed.

'It doesn't bear thinking about. Judy bursting into Lee's attic, beating Lee to death. Damian killing James who walked in and saw Lee's body. Damian killing Alun with the Dying Gaul, while Judy killed Gillian. No motive other than to save their own skins.'

'And Tim was next door – the perfect cleaner with the knowledge required to neutralise the scene and prepared to do anything to protect his daughter. Even walk through town in his old uniform to get Judy and Damian fresh clothes.'

'And he carried on cleaning up after them when Damian visited him this morning with the news that Trevor had taken disks and USB pens from Dai Smith's house. Remind me to arrange to have all drugs destroyed when confiscated,' Reggie said to Carol. 'If Damian hadn't given Tim the date rape drug to use on Trevor we might never have noticed it had gone missing.'

'Can't destroy them if they're needed as evidence in a court case,' Peter observed. 'The one I feel sorry for and I'm kicking myself over is Ken.'

'You weren't to know Tim would kill him,' Reggie said.

'I'm not sure he meant to. Pushing someone down stone steps isn't a sure fire way to kill anyone,' Carol commented.

'And the will Ken found?' Peter asked Reggie.

'I sent it over to the Harvilles' solicitor to look at. They've e-mailed me. Their initial thoughts are that it's genuine. Normally you'd expect someone to file a copy of their will with their solicitor, but they said that even before she was diagnosed with dementia Mrs Harville was renowned in town for her absent-mindedness.'

'I'm sure there wasn't a sinister reason behind it not being found. If Mrs Harville didn't know what she doing for the last few years of her life she probably just pushed it in with a pile of papers and it was lost,' Carol remarked. 'Pamela George and her mother will be pleased, Llwynon Rectory and the entire Harville Estate. I wonder if she'll buy the pub. She's worked there long enough and Tim should be going down for a good few years.'

'Aiding and abetting after the fact of the Pitchers' murders. Helping to conceal a crime. I wish I could be sure he'd be convicted of Ken's murder and Ken's wife's manslaughter.'

'Given the way Ken died in a fall, we'll be lucky to get manslaughter on one charge,' Reggie said. 'And, on the will, I don't envy Pamela George and her mother the paperwork. Trying to prove what was lost in the Pitchers' fire …'

'It was all itemised,' Trevor interrupted. 'The only losers will be the state. Tell me, Reggie, senior officers only present,' he said when she lifted her eyebrows at his use of her Christian name. 'Did you suspect one of your own was involved in the Pitcher murders?'

'Playing it safe when I discovered a professional had cleaned the crime scene,' she admitted.

'They almost got away with it,' Carol observed.

'No they didn't. It was all down to legwork in the end. Mine,' Peter reminded her. 'In tracking down the brown paper. And Tim was stupid to drug Trevor and take the disks and Dai Smith's death ...'

'Unconnected,' Reggie interrupted. 'They scanned and e-mailed me his suicide note. He didn't want to live without his daughters.'

'But it was the gay porn on his computer that set us on the right track.' Trevor rose slowly from his chair. 'I'll clear my things from the office.'

'Mine are already in the boot of the car. Goodbye, Reggie. Thanks for the warm welcome.' Peter followed Trevor and Carol out of the door. When Trevor went into his office, she lingered in the corridor.

'You and Trevor leaving now?' Carol asked.

'First thing in the morning. Trevor wanted to make it tonight but Patrick wants to keep an eye on him.'

'Ready, Peter.' Trevor was in the doorway of the office they'd shared.

'Here, I'll give you a hand with the box.' Peter took the cardboard box Trevor was holding from him.

'I take it there'll be no celebration on this one,' Peter said to Reggie when she left her office.

'Not with Damian being involved. I've told Frank to take a couple of weeks off.'

'You think he knew?'

She shook her head. 'No I don't. If I did I'd retire him permanently. It was a pleasure working with you, Inspector Joseph.' She shook Trevor's hand. 'And you, Sergeant Collins.'

Peter ignored her hand and kissed her cheek. 'And you too, Super.'

The end of case "booze-up", if it could be called that, was the most subdued Peter and Trevor had ever attended. Apart from them, there were no police officers, only members of the forensic and pathologist teams.

Patrick raised his glass. 'To Pamela George and her fellow workers without whom we would have all been put out on the street.'

'Before you drink that toast, look at your bills. The prices have doubled under the management,' Jen joked.

'Send them to the local constabulary, darling,' Patrick suggested.

Carol March appeared in the doorway. Jen moved her chair back. 'We can fit another one in here, Inspector.'

'No thanks, Jen. I can't stay. I just wanted a word with Sergeant Collins.'

Trevor gave Peter a hard look.

'Back in a minute.' Peter filled a clean water glass with wine and took his glass with him. 'Want to sit outside?' he asked Carol.

'Just for a minute.' She took the glass he handed her and sat on the "smoker's bench" in the courtyard. 'I just wanted to say I'm sorry.'

'For what?' Peter asked.

'For messing up our marriage. I was a fool.'

'We both were. But then it was a long time ago.'

'Another lifetime.' She kissed Peter's cheek.

Trevor walked out of the pub. 'Excuse me.'

'There's no need for me to excuse you, Inspector Joseph. I know when I'm beaten. My divorce from Peter was finalised a long time ago …'

'Your divorce?' Trevor repeated.

'I take it Peter never showed you our wedding photographs?'

'No, just said a lot about you.'

'Probably some of it was true,' Carol smiled. 'I never worked out what attracted me to him. But whatever it is, I wanted more of it than he was prepared to give.'

'Just keep looking you'll find the right one.' Peter winked at Trevor. 'We did and I can't wait to get back to her. I'm about to become a father'

'The idea of little Peters is a strange one.' She abandoned her wine glass on the bench.

Trevor held out his hand. 'Good luck, Inspector March.'

'And to you, Inspector Joseph.'

'Just take note of our methods,' Peter teased. 'And don't take this the wrong way. But we'd rather stay on our home turf from now on if you Welsh can do without us.'

'We'll try, Sergeant Collins.' Reggie appeared behind Carol. 'We'll try,' she repeated, looking at Trevor.